Elle(s)

VOLUME 1

THE NEW GIRL

Elle(s)

writer
KID TOUSSAINT

artist
AVELINE STOKART

Thank you to Aveline for her trust and her incredible work.
A fantastic first comic book!

Thank you to Benoît, Mathias, Camille, Gauthier, Christel, Gregor,
Kévin, Sophie V., Éric, and the rest of the Lombard team.

Thanks to Nounette for telling me, "Hey! Check out her awesome drawings!"

And thanks to Emilia for introducing me to "Nounette" ;-p.

KID

Thank you to Kid for his trust and for this fascinating project.
Thanks for always being able to find the right words to
push me onward and upward in this new adventure!

Thank you to the entire Lombard team for their warm
welcome and for making this project possible!

Thanks to Mathias and Camille for their good humor, their
unfailing kindness, and their willingness to listen.

Thanks to my family for believing in me, and for always
supporting me and encouraging me to follow my passions.
I shower you all with hearts, glitter, and confetti!

AVELINE

---

art director: **ÉRIC LAURIN**

graphic designer : **SOPHIE VETS**

special thanks to **CONSTANCE MALBOIS & TEAM AT MEDIATOON**

in memory of **SOPHIE CASTILLE**

---

for ablaze

managing editor **RICH YOUNG**

editor **KEVIN KETNER**

designers **RODOLFO MURAGUCHI & CINTHIA TAKEDA**

Publisher's Cataloging-in-Publication data

Names: Toussaint, Kid, author . | Stokart, Aveline, artist.
Title: Elle(s) vol 1 : The New Girl / written by Kid Toussaint; art by Aveline Stokart.
Description: Portland, OR: Ablaze Publications, 2022.
Identifiers: ISBN: 978-1-68497-093-3
Subjects: LCSH Friendship—Comic books, strips, etc. | High school students—Comic books, strips, etc. | Teenagers—
Comic books, strips, etc.| Science fiction. | Graphic novels. | BISAC YOUNG ADULT FICTION / Comics & Graphic
Novels / General | YOUNG ADULT FICTION / Comics & Graphic Novels / Science Fiction
Classification: LCC PN6727.T68 E55 2022 | DDC 741.5—dc23

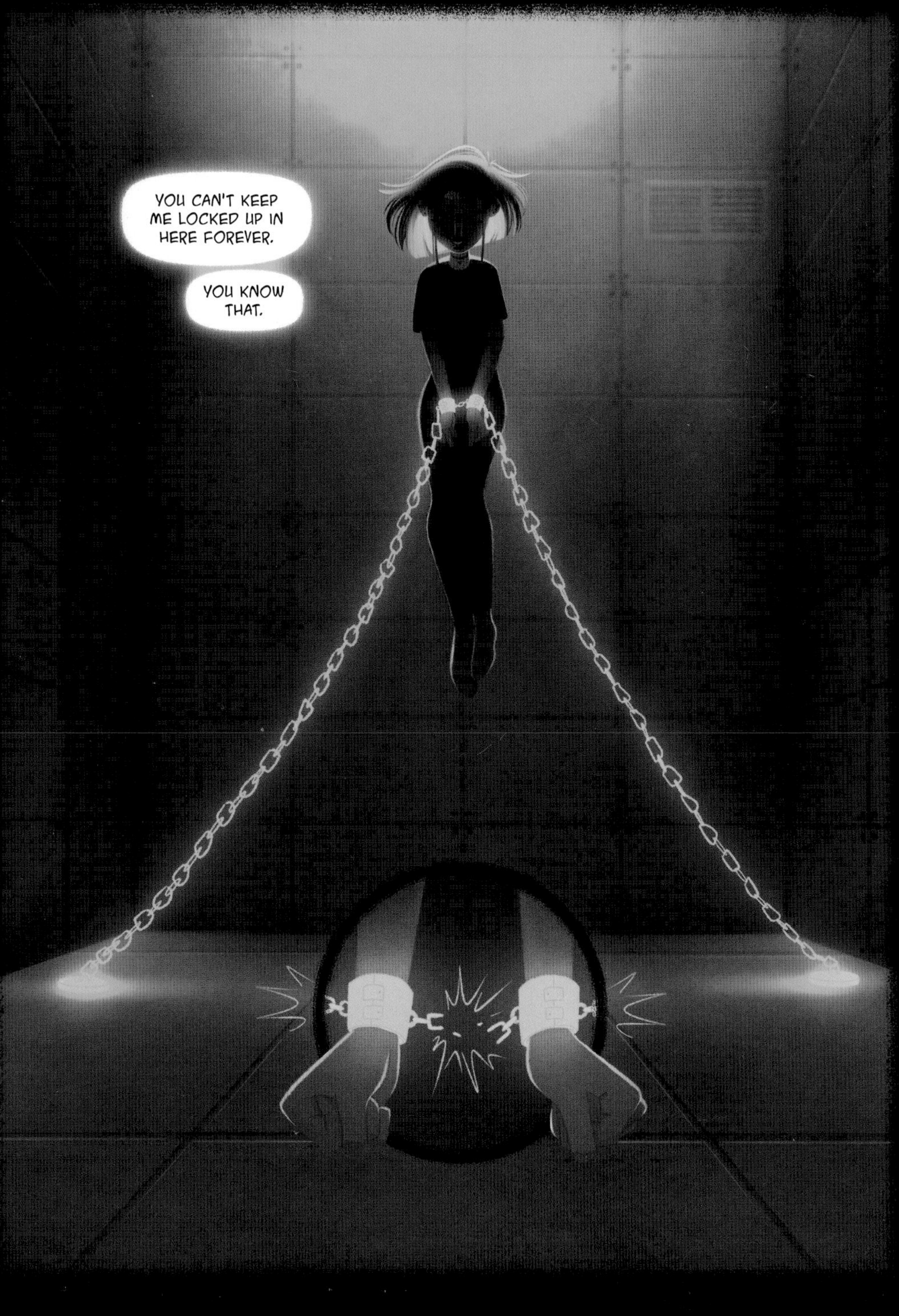
YOU CAN'T KEEP ME LOCKED UP IN HERE FOREVER.
YOU KNOW THAT.

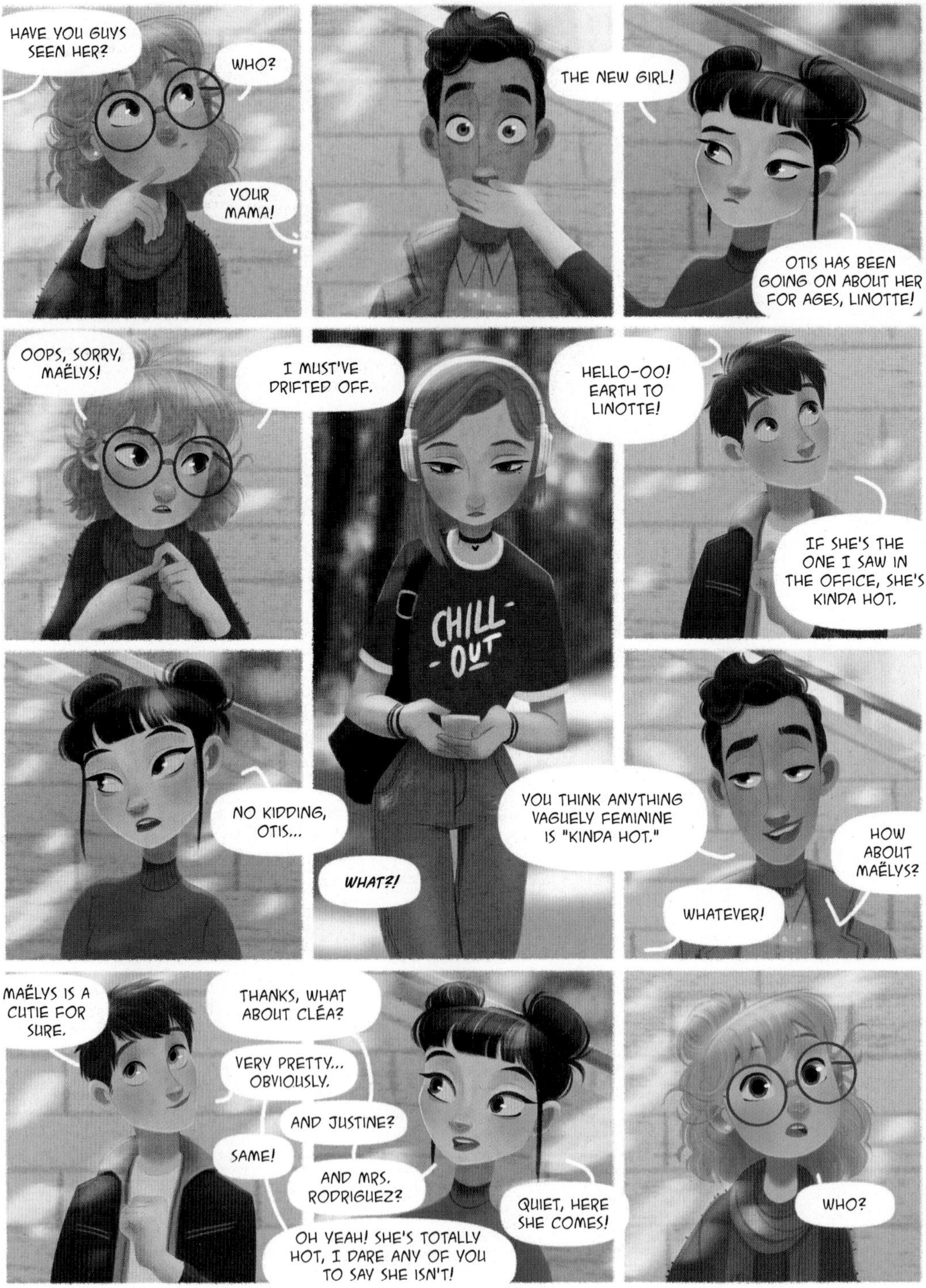
HAVE YOU GUYS SEEN HER?
WHO?
YOUR MAMA!
THE NEW GIRL!
OTIS HAS BEEN GOING ON ABOUT HER FOR AGES, LINOTTE!
OOPS, SORRY, MAËLYS!
I MUST'VE DRIFTED OFF.
CHILL OUT
HELLO-OO! EARTH TO LINOTTE!
IF SHE'S THE ONE I SAW IN THE OFFICE, SHE'S KINDA HOT.
NO KIDDING, OTIS...
WHAT?!
YOU THINK ANYTHING VAGUELY FEMININE IS "KINDA HOT."
HOW ABOUT MAËLYS?
WHATEVER!
MAËLYS IS A CUTIE FOR SURE.
THANKS, WHAT ABOUT CLÉA?
VERY PRETTY... OBVIOUSLY.
AND JUSTINE?
SAME!
AND MRS. RODRIGUEZ?
OH YEAH! SHE'S TOTALLY HOT, I DARE ANY OF YOU TO SAY SHE ISN'T!
QUIET, HERE SHE COMES!
WHO?

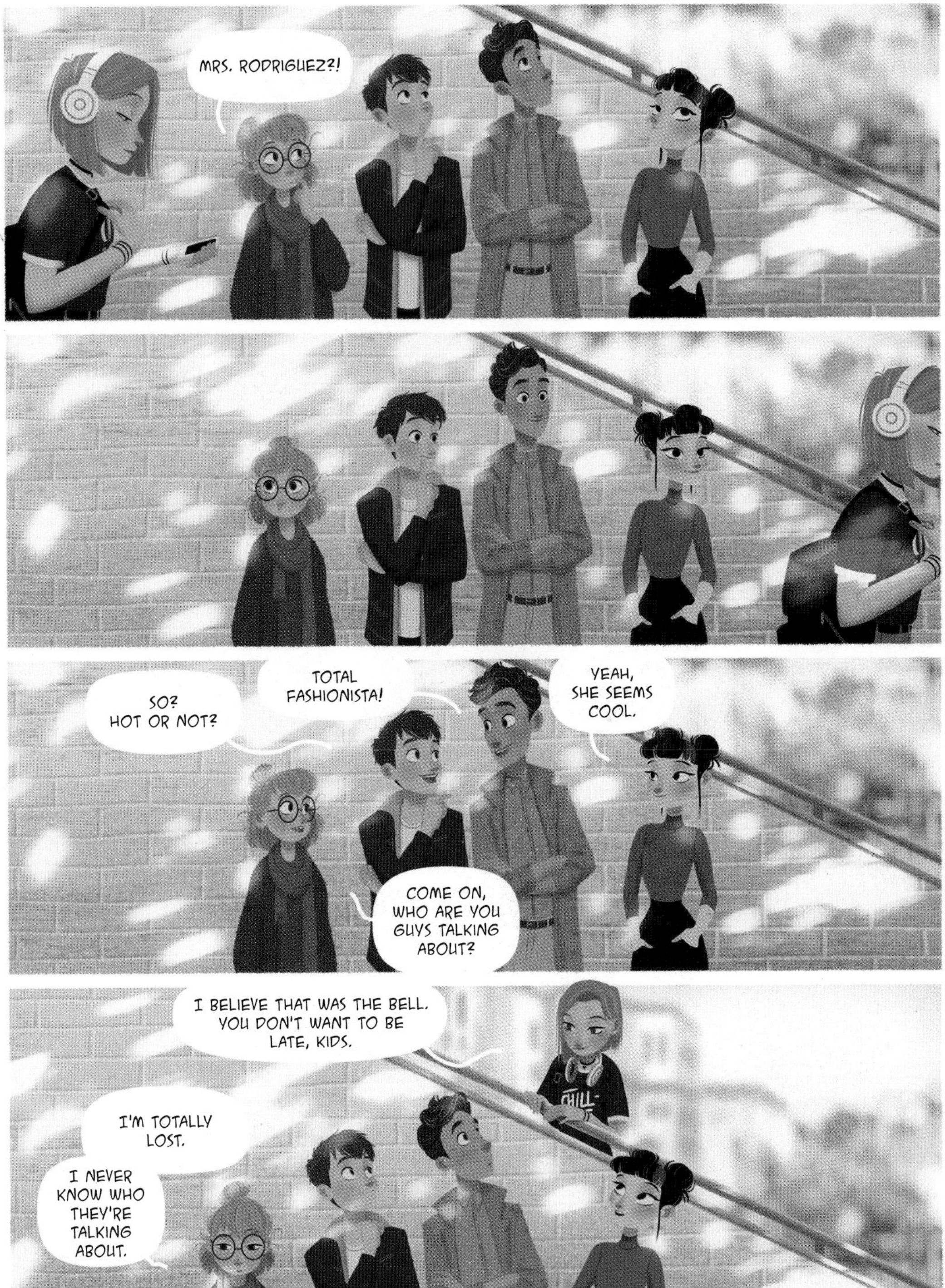
MRS. RODRIGUEZ?!
SO? HOT OR NOT?
TOTAL FASHIONISTA!
YEAH, SHE SEEMS COOL.
COME ON, WHO ARE YOU GUYS TALKING ABOUT?
I BELIEVE THAT WAS THE BELL. YOU DON'T WANT TO BE LATE, KIDS.
CHILL
I'M TOTALLY LOST.
I NEVER KNOW WHO THEY'RE TALKING ABOUT.

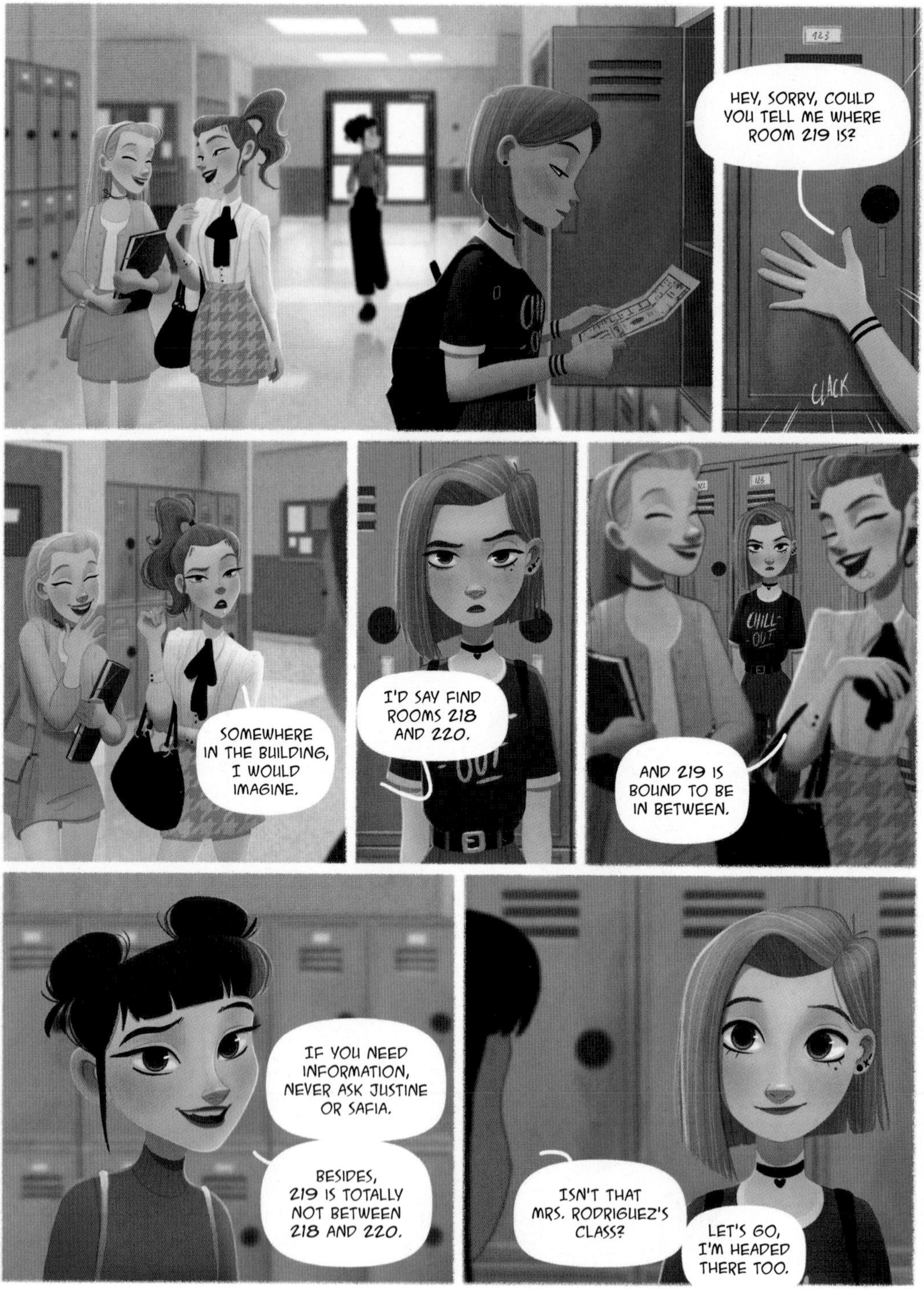
HEY, SORRY, COULD YOU TELL ME WHERE ROOM 219 IS?
CLACK
SOMEWHERE IN THE BUILDING, I WOULD IMAGINE.
I'D SAY FIND ROOMS 218 AND 220.
AND 219 IS BOUND TO BE IN BETWEEN.
IF YOU NEED INFORMATION, NEVER ASK JUSTINE OR SAFIA.
BESIDES, 219 IS TOTALLY NOT BETWEEN 218 AND 220.
ISN'T THAT MRS. RODRIGUEZ'S CLASS?
LET'S GO, I'M HEADED THERE TOO.

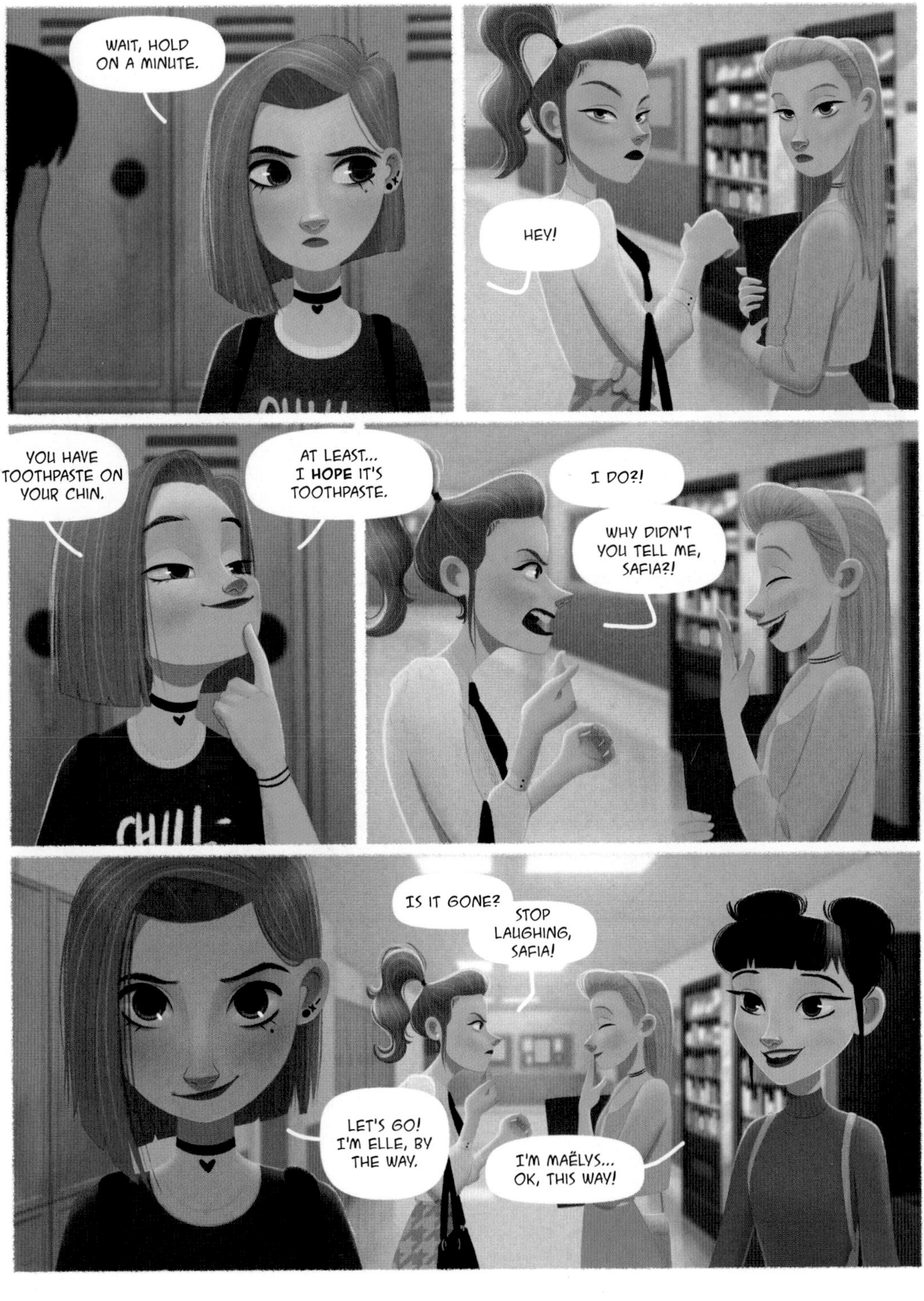
WAIT, HOLD ON A MINUTE.
HEY!
YOU HAVE TOOTHPASTE ON YOUR CHIN.
AT LEAST... I **HOPE** IT'S TOOTHPASTE.
I DO?!
WHY DIDN'T YOU TELL ME, SAFIA?!
IS IT GONE?
STOP LAUGHING, SAFIA!
LET'S GO! I'M ELLE, BY THE WAY.
I'M MAËLYS... OK, THIS WAY!

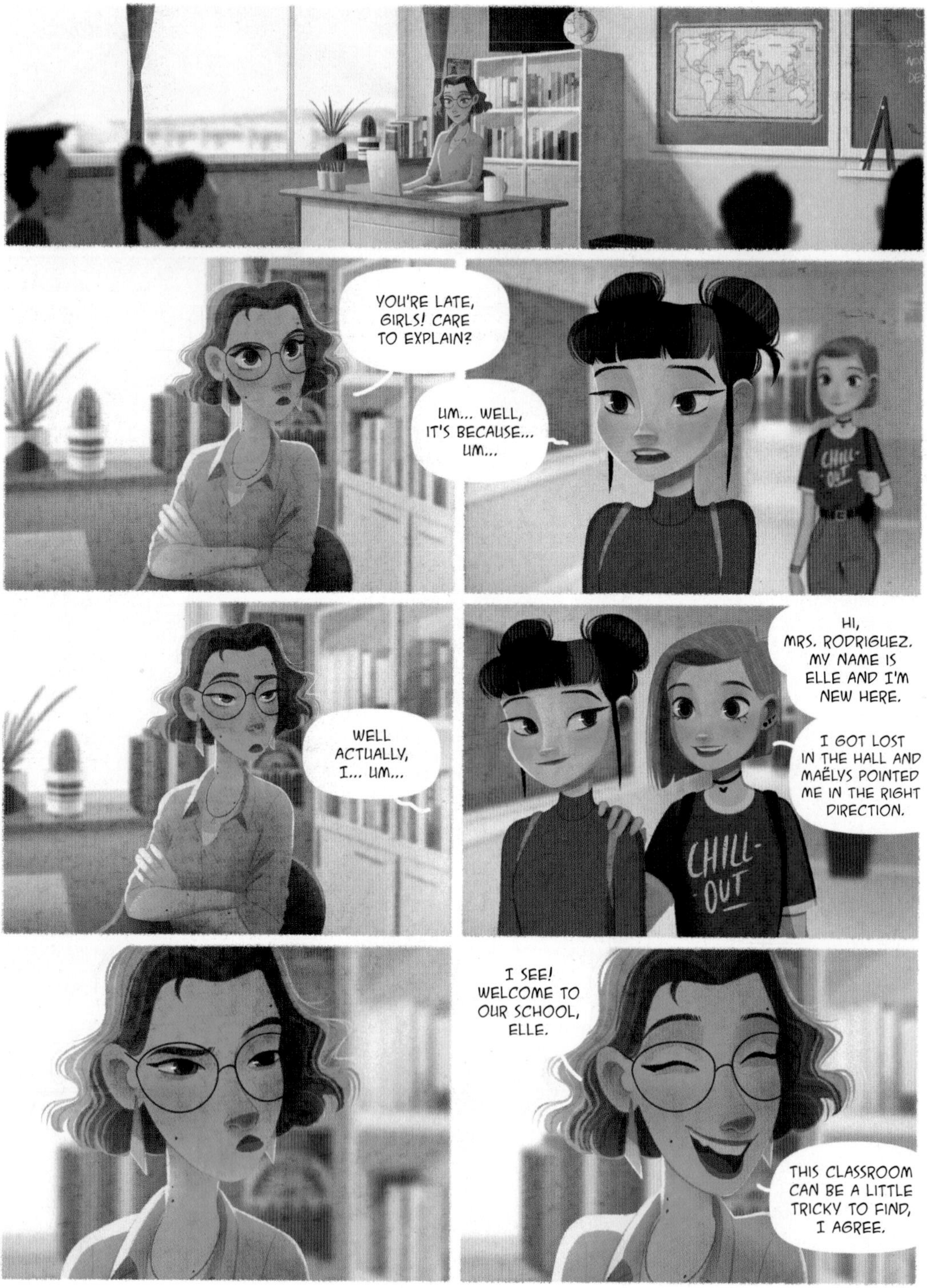
YOU'RE LATE, GIRLS! CARE TO EXPLAIN?
UM... WELL, IT'S BECAUSE... UM...
WELL ACTUALLY, I... UM...
HI, MRS. RODRIGUEZ. MY NAME IS ELLE AND I'M NEW HERE.
I GOT LOST IN THE HALL AND MAËLYS POINTED ME IN THE RIGHT DIRECTION.
I SEE! WELCOME TO OUR SCHOOL, ELLE.
THIS CLASSROOM CAN BE A LITTLE TRICKY TO FIND, I AGREE.

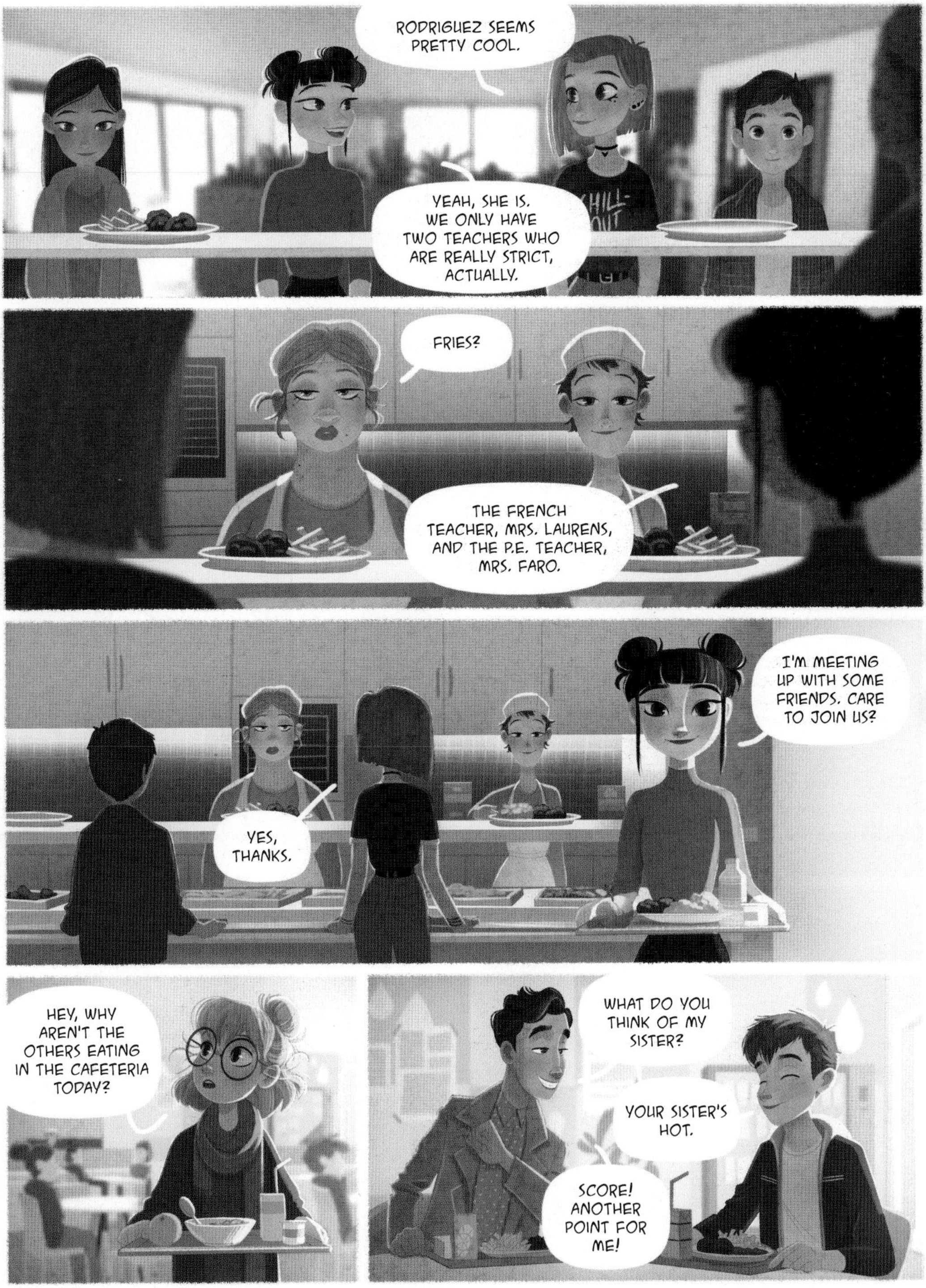
RODRIGUEZ SEEMS PRETTY COOL.
YEAH, SHE IS. WE ONLY HAVE TWO TEACHERS WHO ARE REALLY STRICT, ACTUALLY.
FRIES?
THE FRENCH TEACHER, MRS. LAURENS, AND THE P.E. TEACHER, MRS. FARO.
I'M MEETING UP WITH SOME FRIENDS. CARE TO JOIN US?
YES, THANKS.
HEY, WHY AREN'T THE OTHERS EATING IN THE CAFETERIA TODAY?
WHAT DO YOU THINK OF MY SISTER?
YOUR SISTER'S HOT.
SCORE! ANOTHER POINT FOR ME!

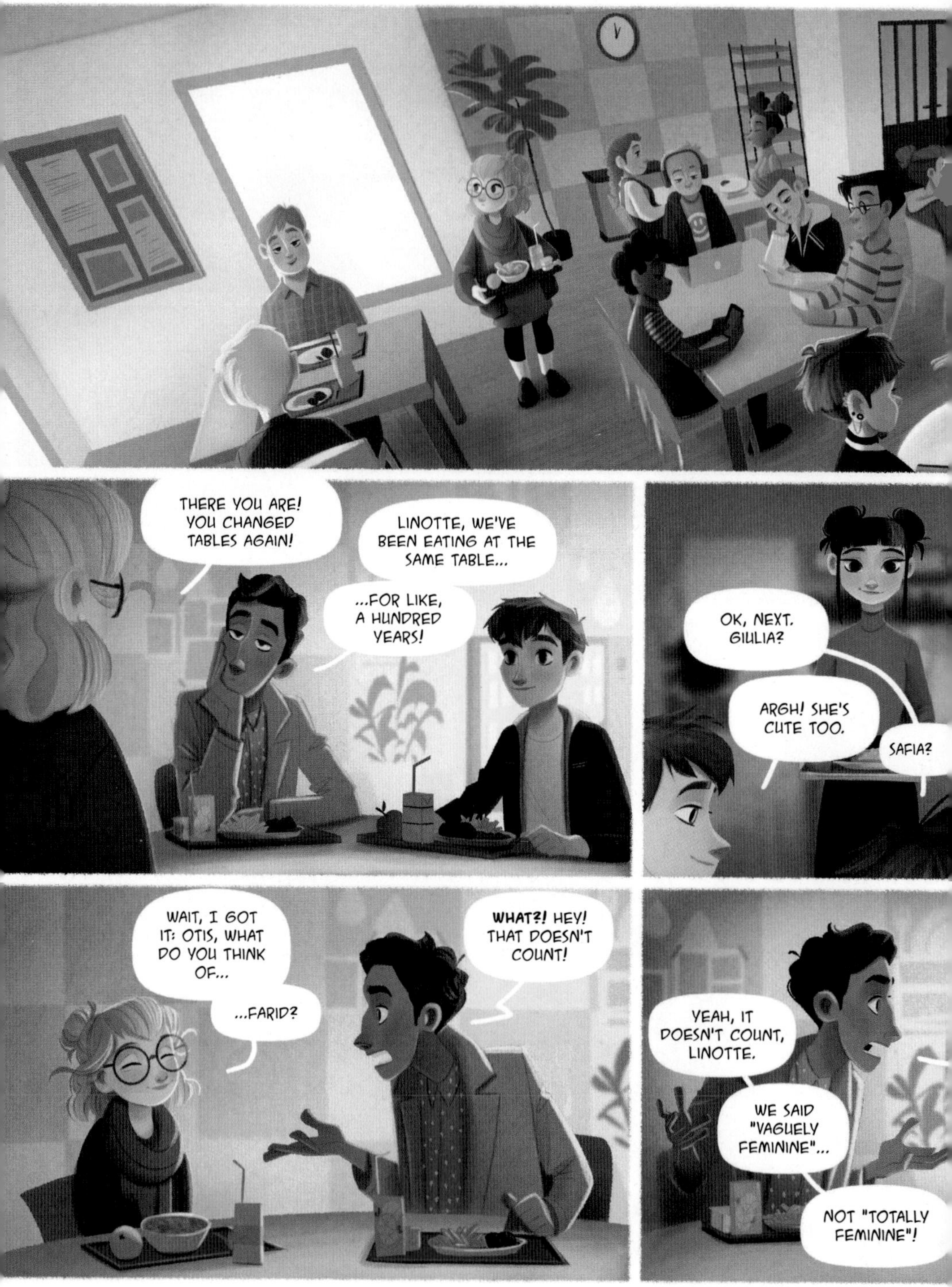
THERE YOU ARE! YOU CHANGED TABLES AGAIN!
LINOTTE, WE'VE BEEN EATING AT THE SAME TABLE...
...FOR LIKE, A HUNDRED YEARS!
OK, NEXT. GIULIA?
ARGH! SHE'S CUTE TOO.
SAFIA?
WAIT, I GOT IT: OTIS, WHAT DO YOU THINK OF...
...FARID?
WHAT?! HEY! THAT DOESN'T COUNT!
YEAH, IT DOESN'T COUNT, LINOTTE.
WE SAID "VAGUELY FEMININE"...
NOT "TOTALLY FEMININE"!

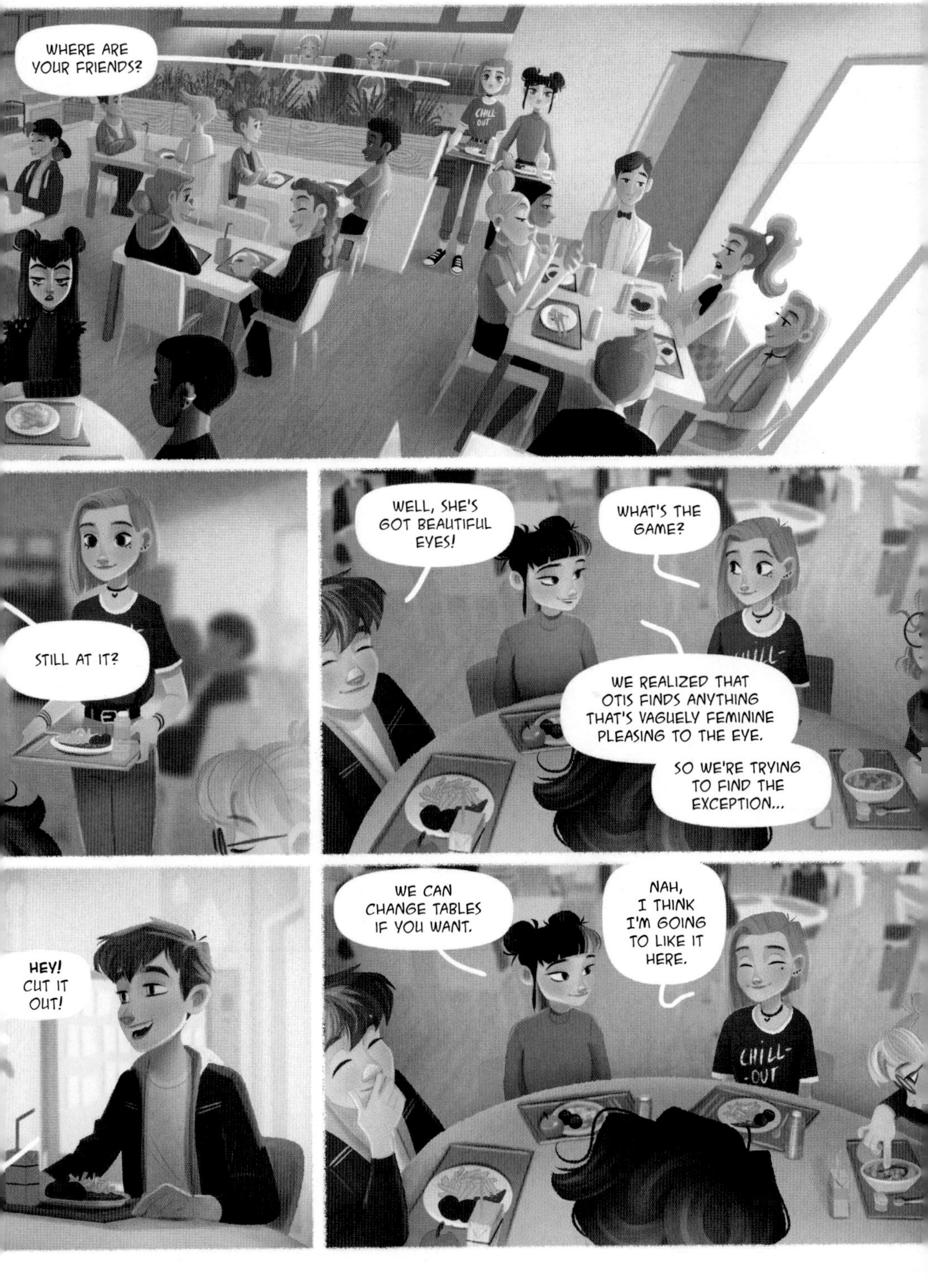
WHERE ARE YOUR FRIENDS?
CHILL OUT
STILL AT IT?
WELL, SHE'S GOT BEAUTIFUL EYES!
WHAT'S THE GAME?
WE REALIZED THAT OTIS FINDS ANYTHING THAT'S VAGUELY FEMININE PLEASING TO THE EYE.
SO WE'RE TRYING TO FIND THE EXCEPTION...
HEY! CUT IT OUT!
WE CAN CHANGE TABLES IF YOU WANT.
NAH, I THINK I'M GOING TO LIKE IT HERE.
CHILL-OUT

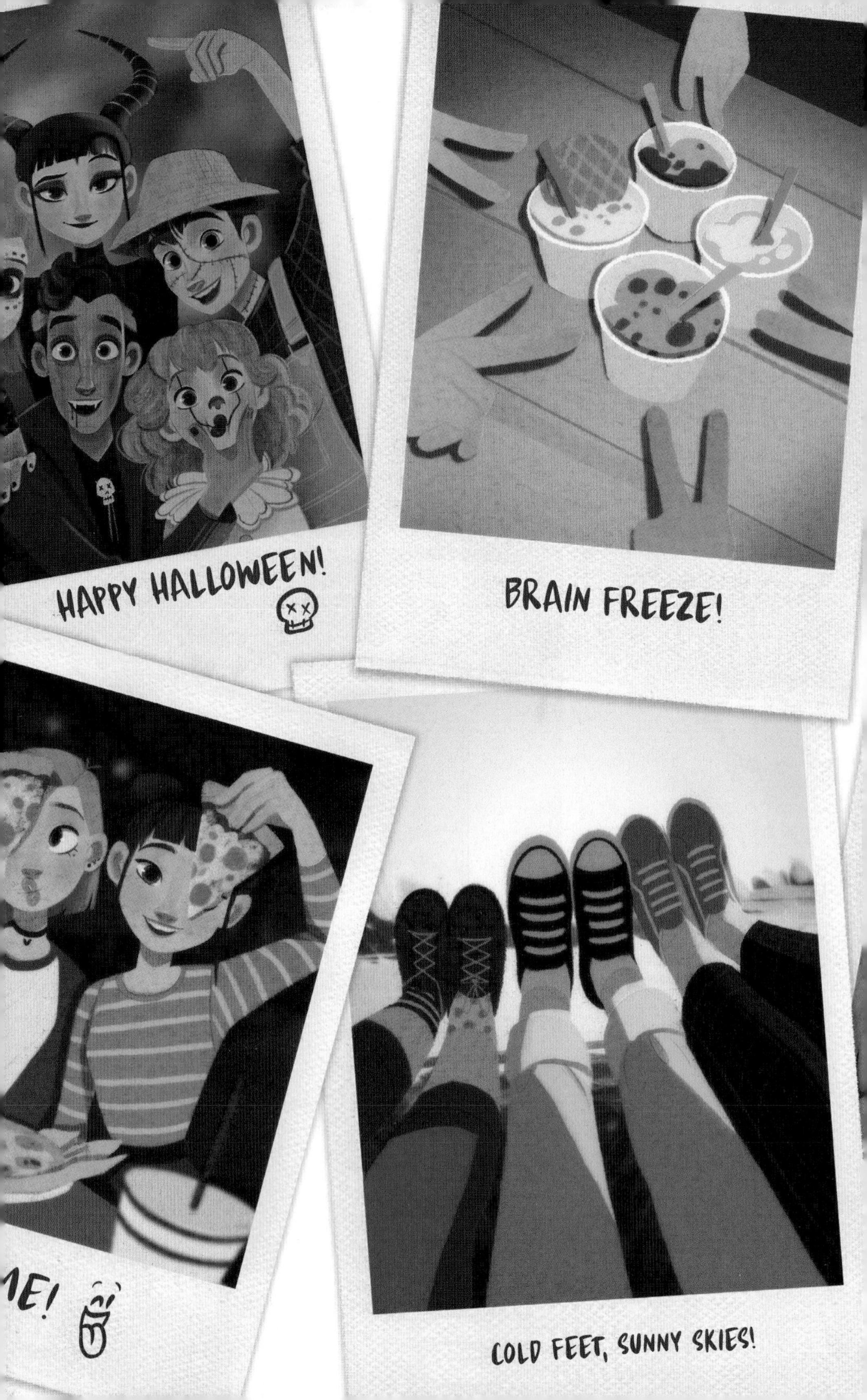
HAPPY HALLOWEEN!
BRAIN FREEZE!
COLD FEET, SUNNY SKIES!

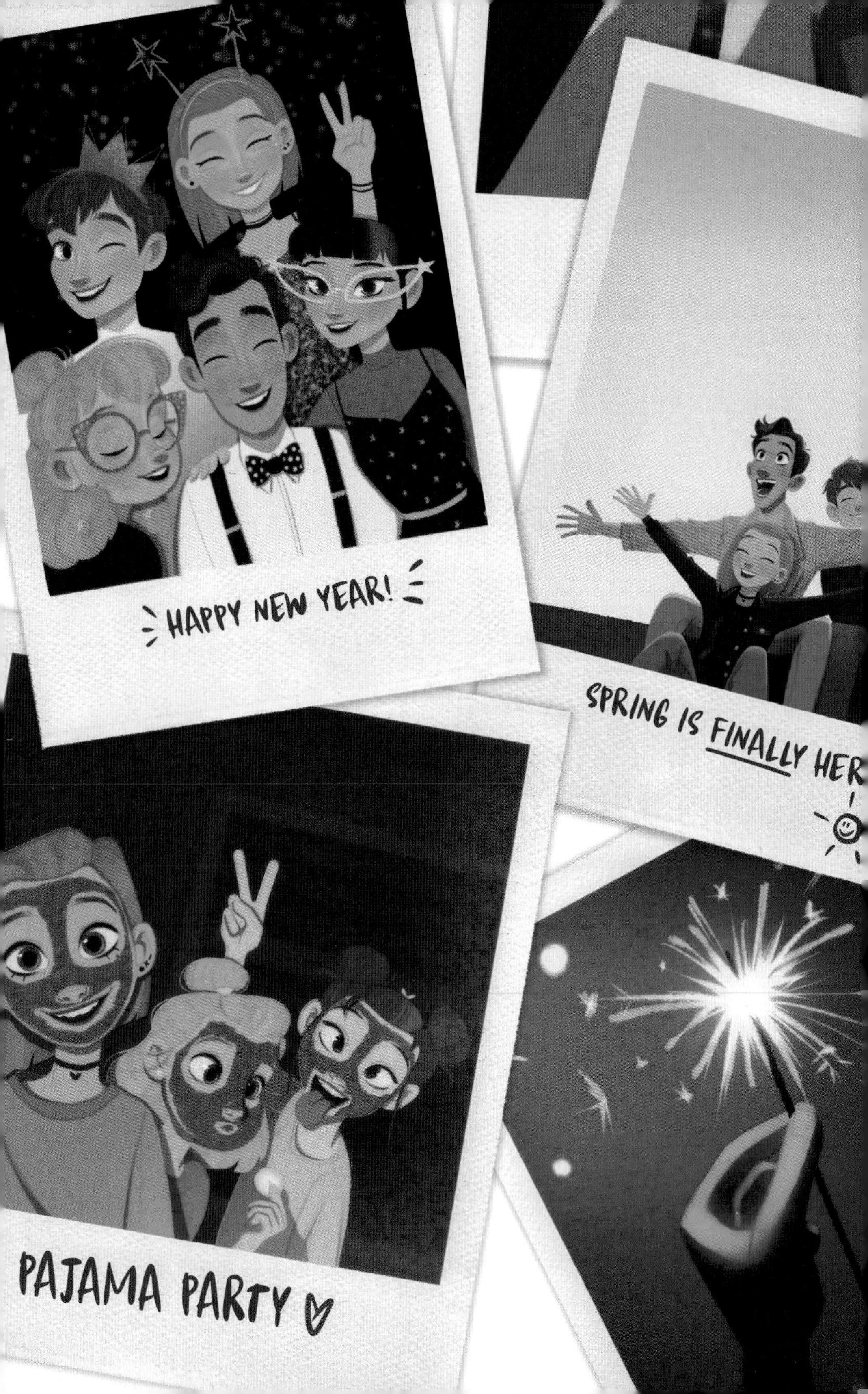
HAPPY NEW YEAR!
SPRING IS FINALLY HER
PAJAMA PARTY

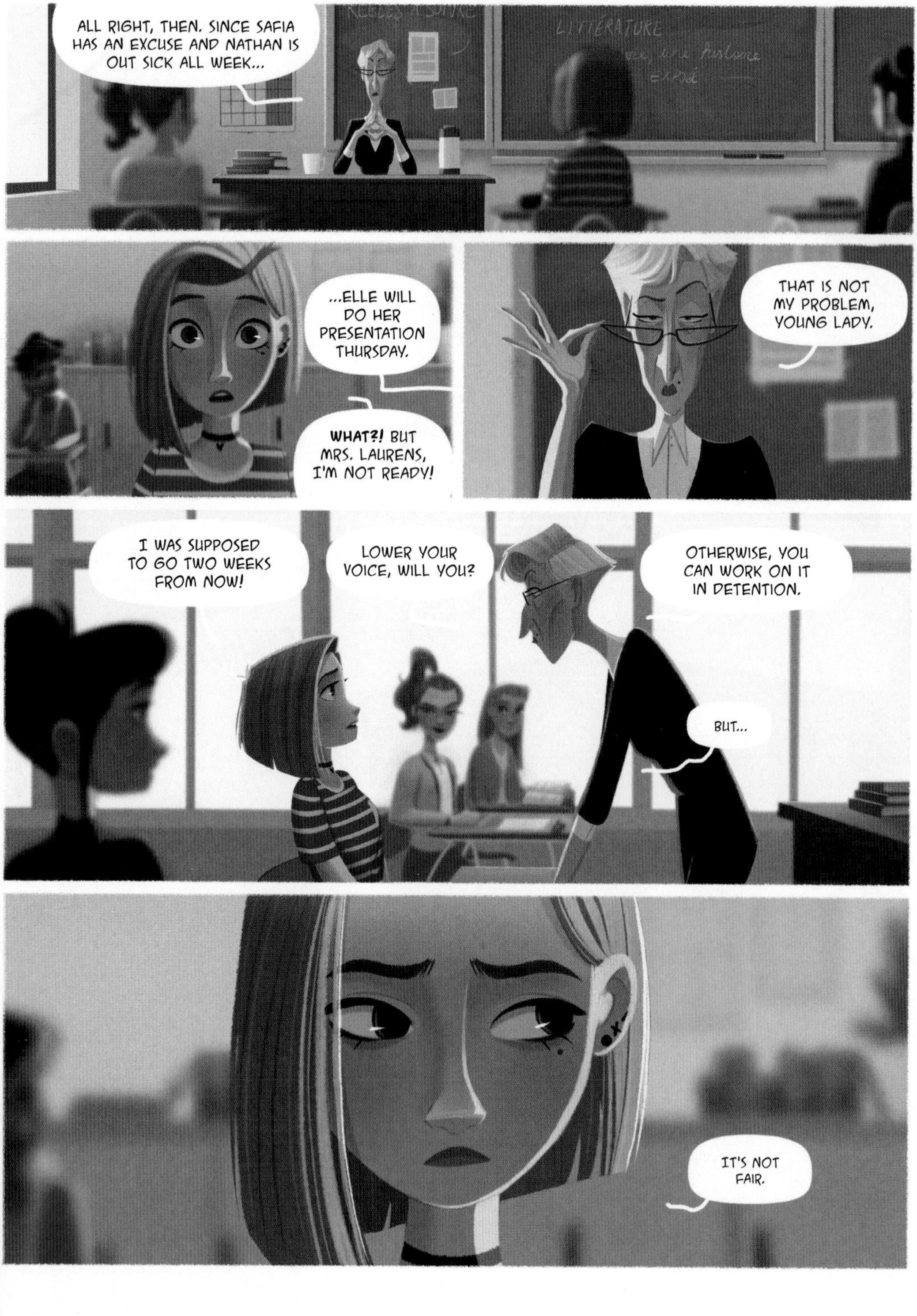
ALL RIGHT, THEN. SINCE SAFIA HAS AN EXCUSE AND NATHAN IS OUT SICK ALL WEEK...
...ELLE WILL DO HER PRESENTATION THURSDAY.
WHAT?! BUT MRS. LAURENS, I'M NOT READY!
THAT IS NOT MY PROBLEM, YOUNG LADY.
I WAS SUPPOSED TO GO TWO WEEKS FROM NOW!
LOWER YOUR VOICE, WILL YOU?
OTHERWISE, YOU CAN WORK ON IT IN DETENTION.
BUT...
IT'S NOT FAIR.

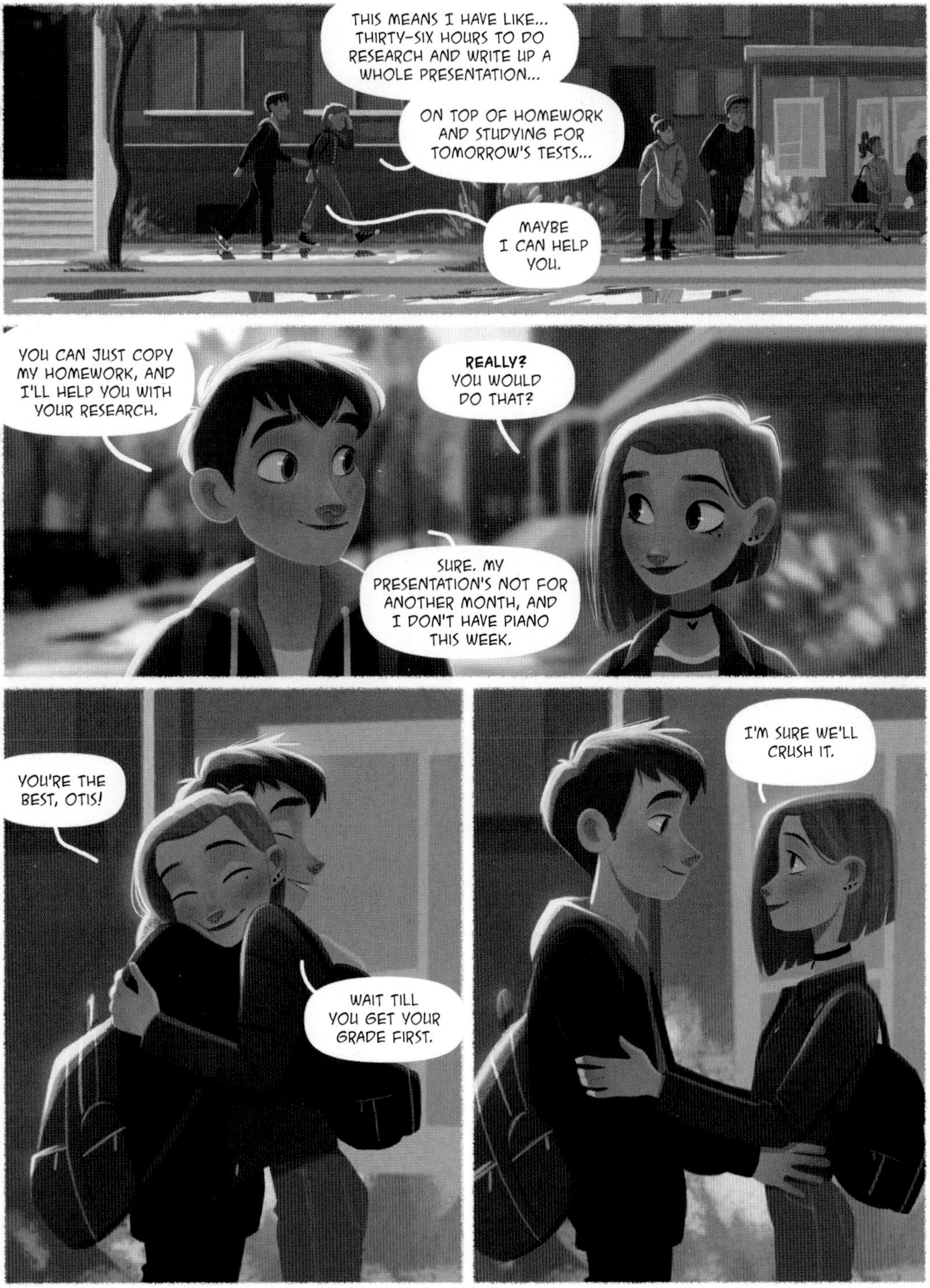
THIS MEANS I HAVE LIKE... THIRTY-SIX HOURS TO DO RESEARCH AND WRITE UP A WHOLE PRESENTATION...
ON TOP OF HOMEWORK AND STUDYING FOR TOMORROW'S TESTS...
MAYBE I CAN HELP YOU.
YOU CAN JUST COPY MY HOMEWORK, AND I'LL HELP YOU WITH YOUR RESEARCH.
REALLY? YOU WOULD DO THAT?
SURE. MY PRESENTATION'S NOT FOR ANOTHER MONTH, AND I DON'T HAVE PIANO THIS WEEK.
YOU'RE THE BEST, OTIS!
WAIT TILL YOU GET YOUR GRADE FIRST.
I'M SURE WE'LL CRUSH IT.

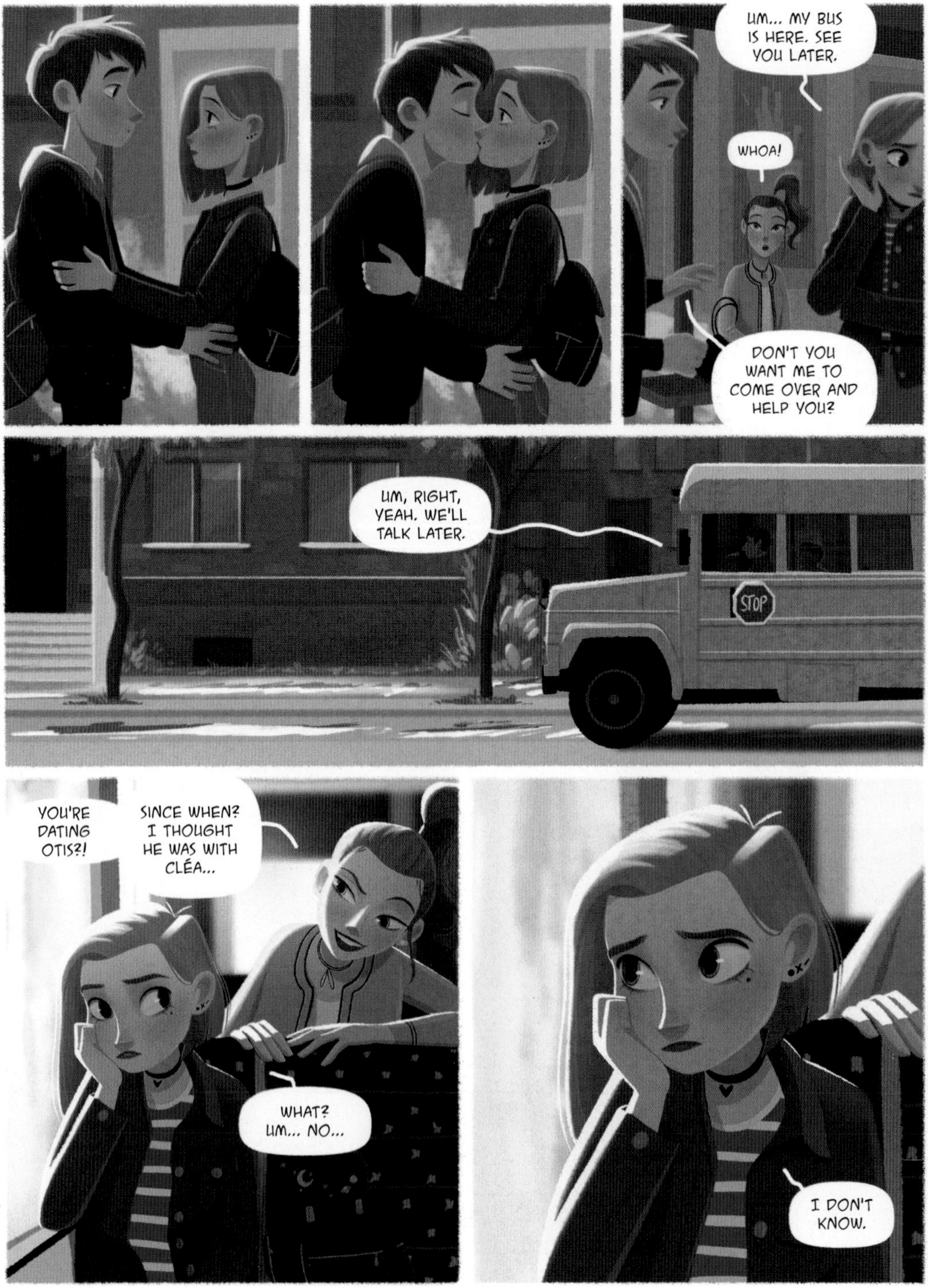
UM... MY BUS IS HERE. SEE YOU LATER.
WHOA!
DON'T YOU WANT ME TO COME OVER AND HELP YOU?
UM, RIGHT, YEAH. WE'LL TALK LATER.
STOP
YOU'RE DATING OTIS?!
SINCE WHEN? I THOUGHT HE WAS WITH CLÉA...
WHAT? UM... NO...
I DON'T KNOW.

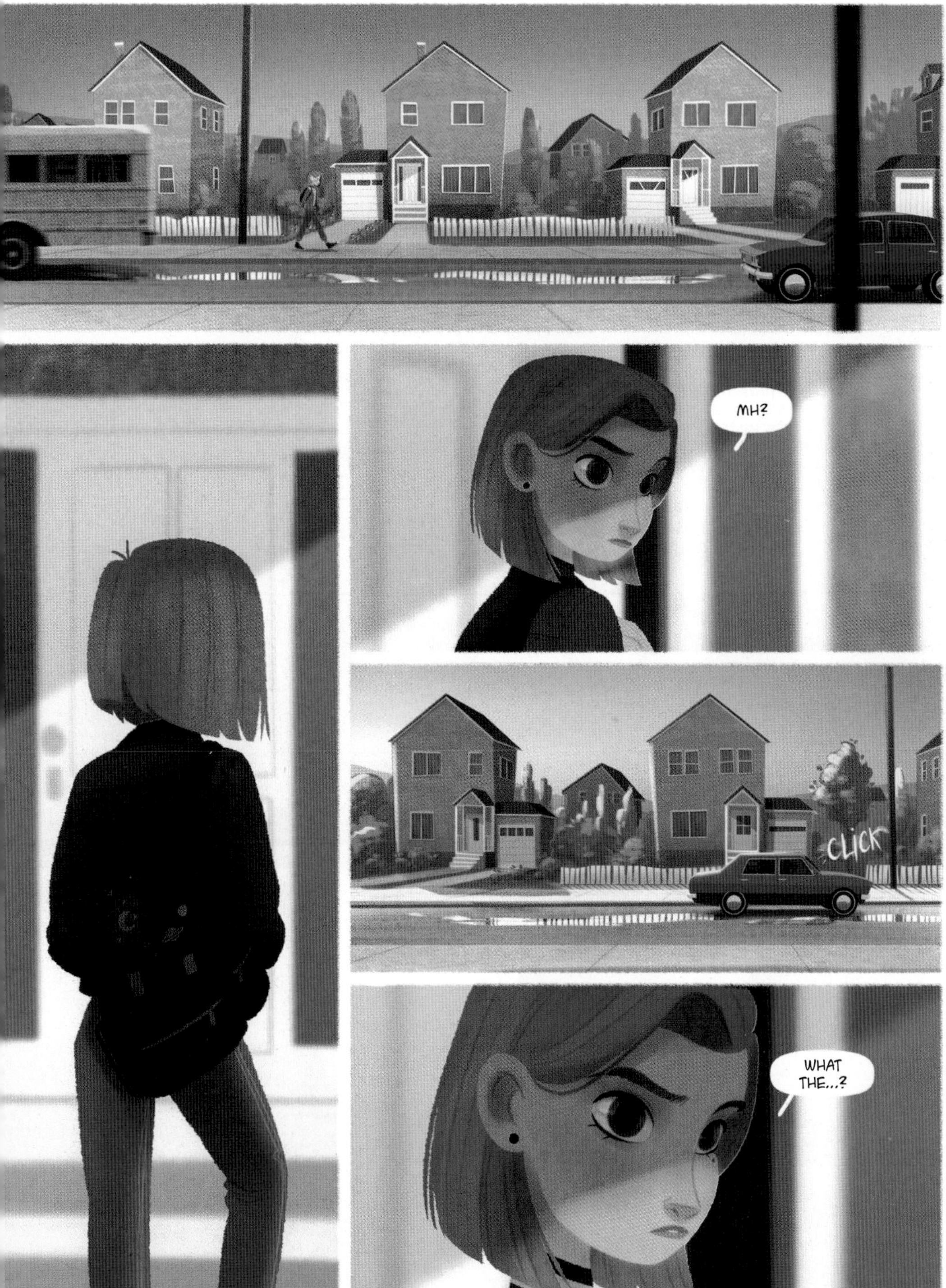
MH?
CLICK
WHAT THE...?

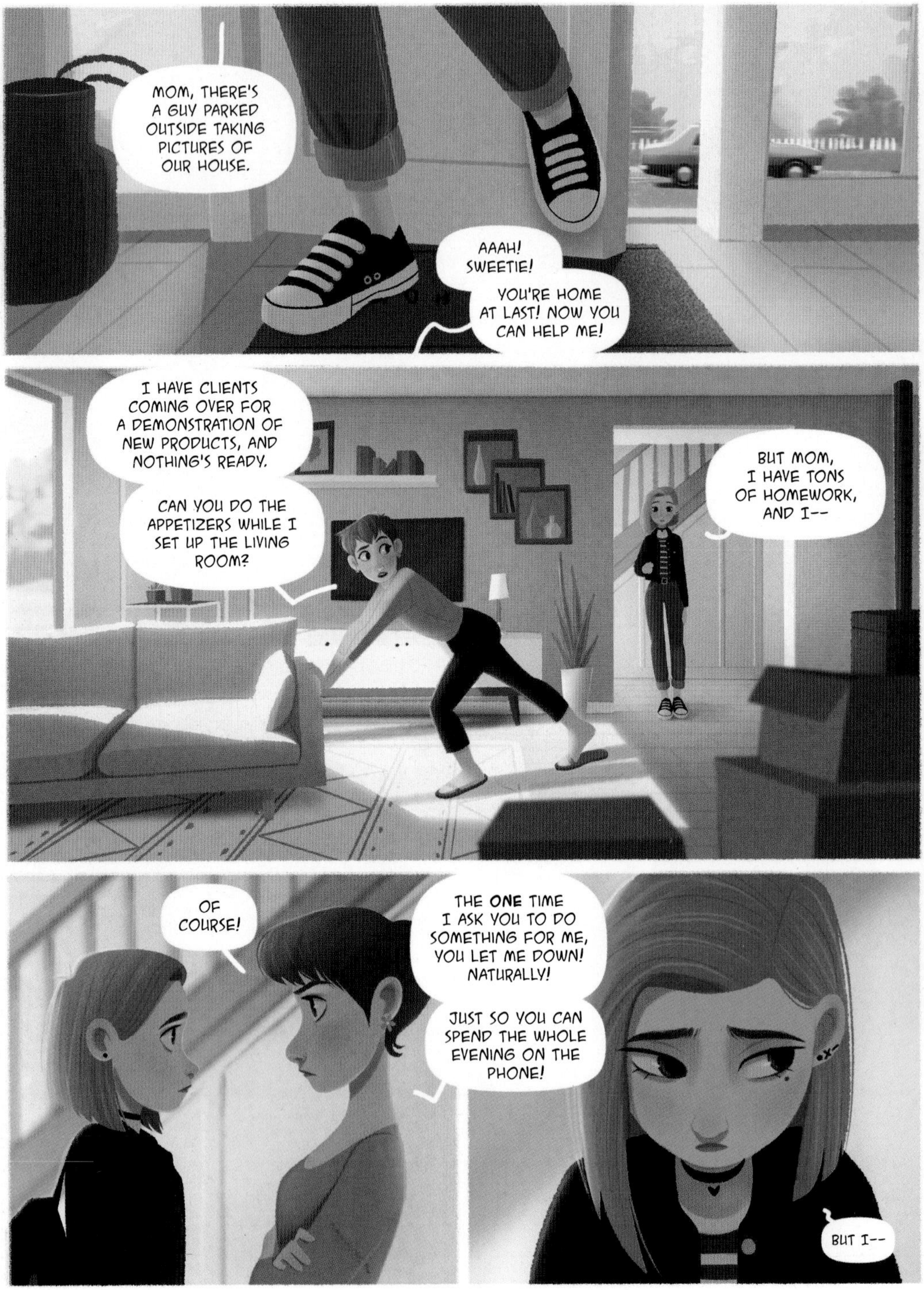
MOM, THERE'S A GUY PARKED OUTSIDE TAKING PICTURES OF OUR HOUSE.
AAAH! SWEETIE!
YOU'RE HOME AT LAST! NOW YOU CAN HELP ME!
I HAVE CLIENTS COMING OVER FOR A DEMONSTRATION OF NEW PRODUCTS, AND NOTHING'S READY.
CAN YOU DO THE APPETIZERS WHILE I SET UP THE LIVING ROOM?
BUT MOM, I HAVE TONS OF HOMEWORK, AND I--
OF COURSE!
THE **ONE** TIME I ASK YOU TO DO SOMETHING FOR ME, YOU LET ME DOWN! NATURALLY!
JUST SO YOU CAN SPEND THE WHOLE EVENING ON THE PHONE!
BUT I--

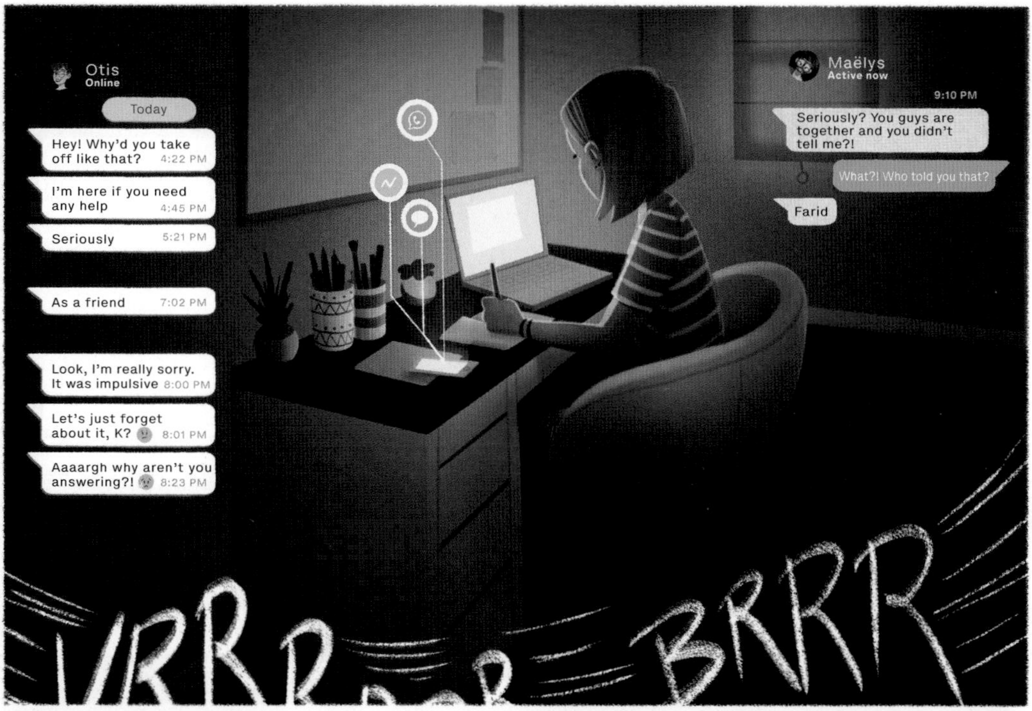
Otis
Online
Today
Hey! Why'd you take off like that? 4:22 PM
I'm here if you need any help 4:45 PM
Seriously 5:21 PM
As a friend 7:02 PM
Look, I'm really sorry. It was impulsive 8:00 PM
Let's just forget about it, K? 8:01 PM
Aaaargh why aren't you answering?! 8:23 PM
Maëlys
Active now
9:10 PM
Seriously? You guys are together and you didn't tell me?!
What?! Who told you that?
Farid
VRRRRRR
BRRR

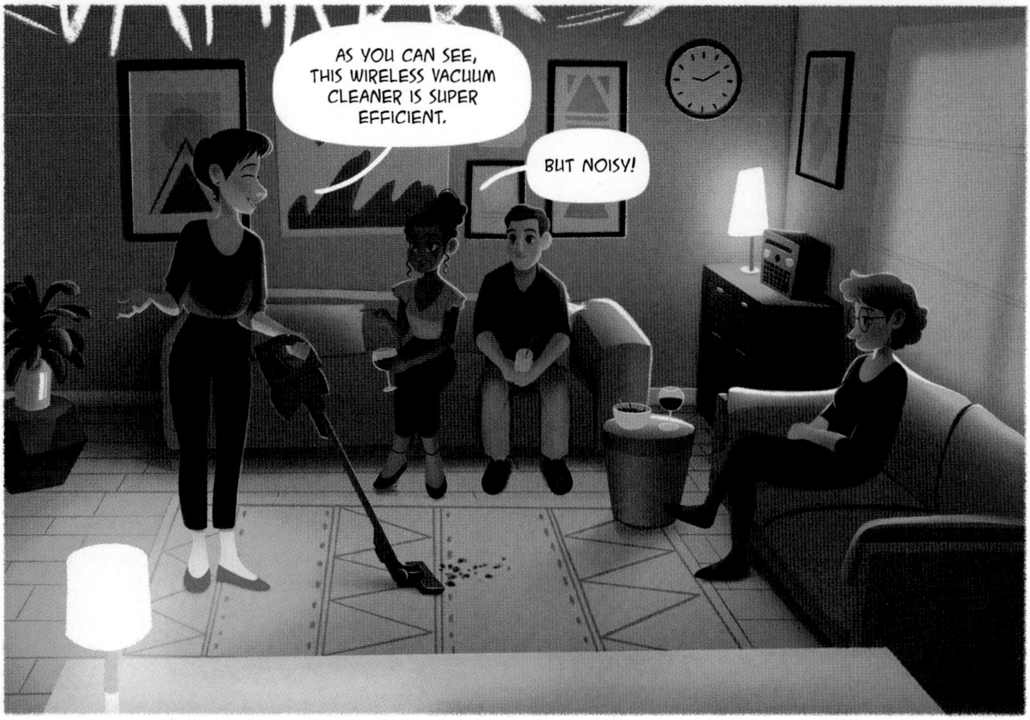
AS YOU CAN SEE, THIS WIRELESS VACUUM CLEANER IS SUPER EFFICIENT.
BUT NOISY!

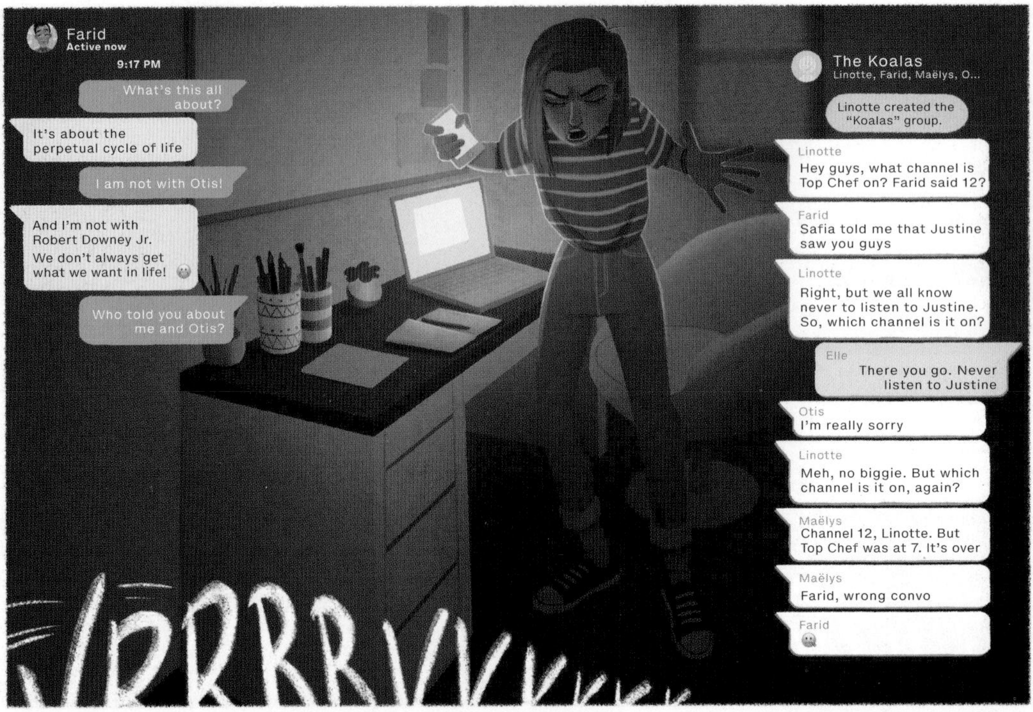
Farid
Active now
9:17 PM
What's this all about?
It's about the perpetual cycle of life
I am not with Otis!
And I'm not with Robert Downey Jr.
We don't always get what we want in life!
Who told you about me and Otis?
The Koalas
Linotte, Farid, Maëlys, O...
Linotte created the "Koalas" group.
Linotte
Hey guys, what channel is Top Chef on? Farid said 12?
Farid
Safia told me that Justine saw you guys
Linotte
Right, but we all know never to listen to Justine. So, which channel is it on?
Elle
There you go. Never listen to Justine
Otis
I'm really sorry
Linotte
Meh, no biggie. But which channel is it on, again?
Maëlys
Channel 12, Linotte. But Top Chef was at 7. It's over
Maëlys
Farid, wrong convo
Farid
VRRRRVVVVVV

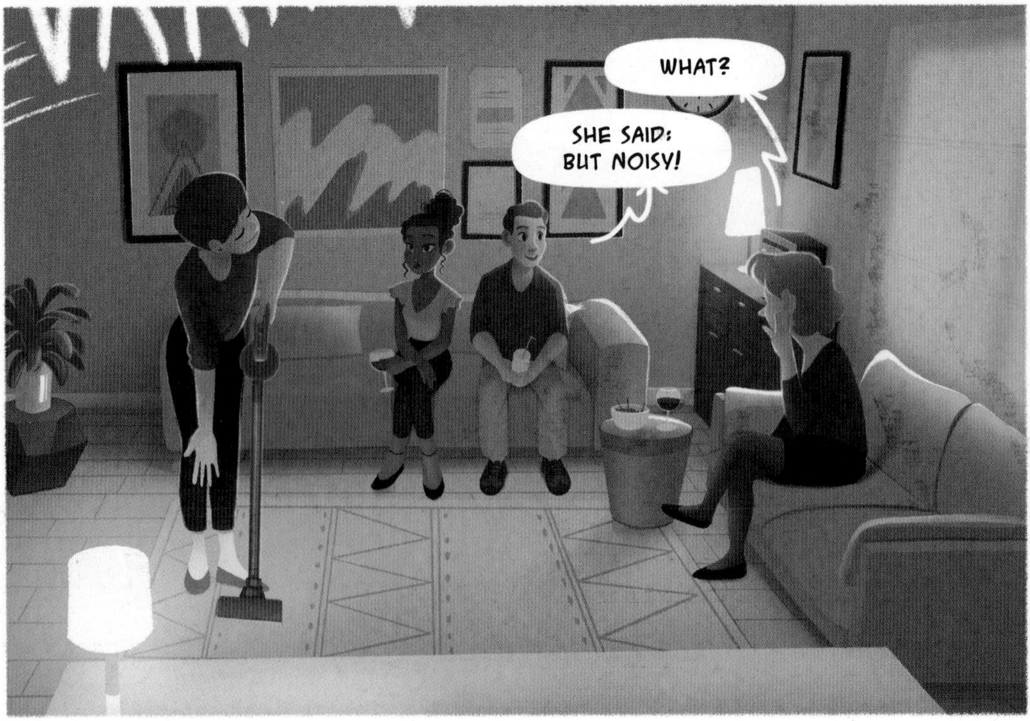
WHAT?
SHE SAID: BUT NOISY!

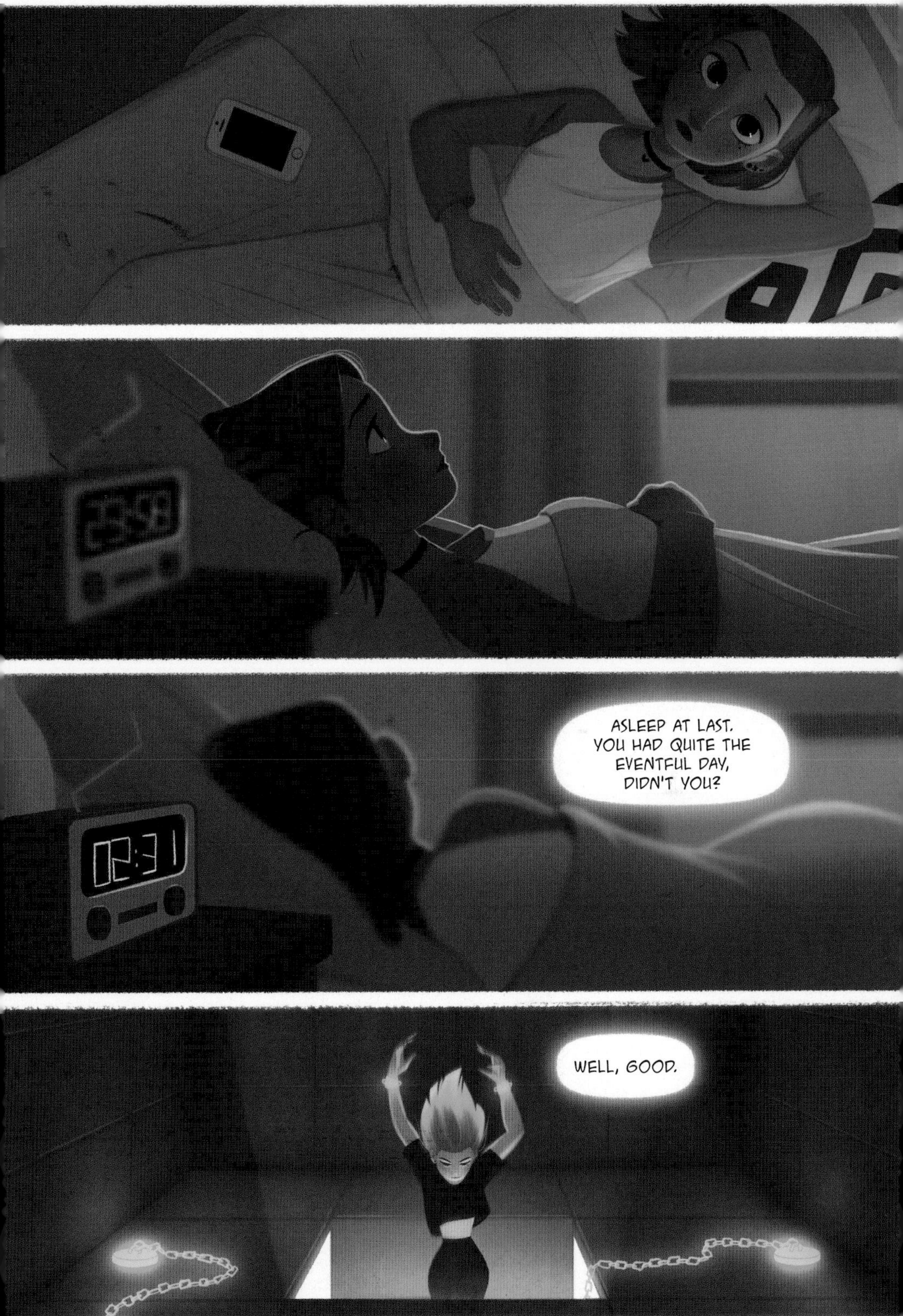
ASLEEP AT LAST. YOU HAD QUITE THE EVENTFUL DAY, DIDN'T YOU?
WELL, GOOD.

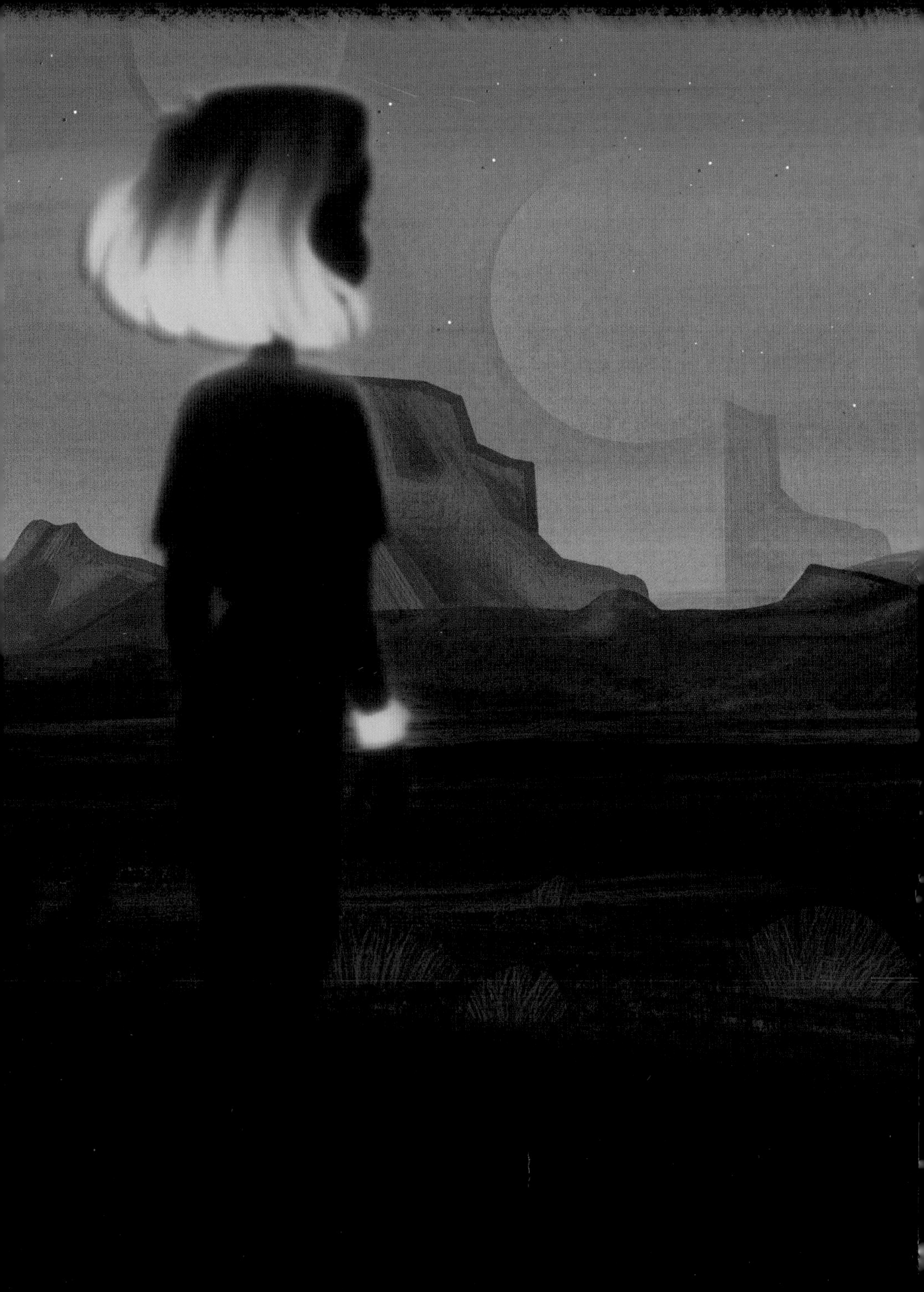

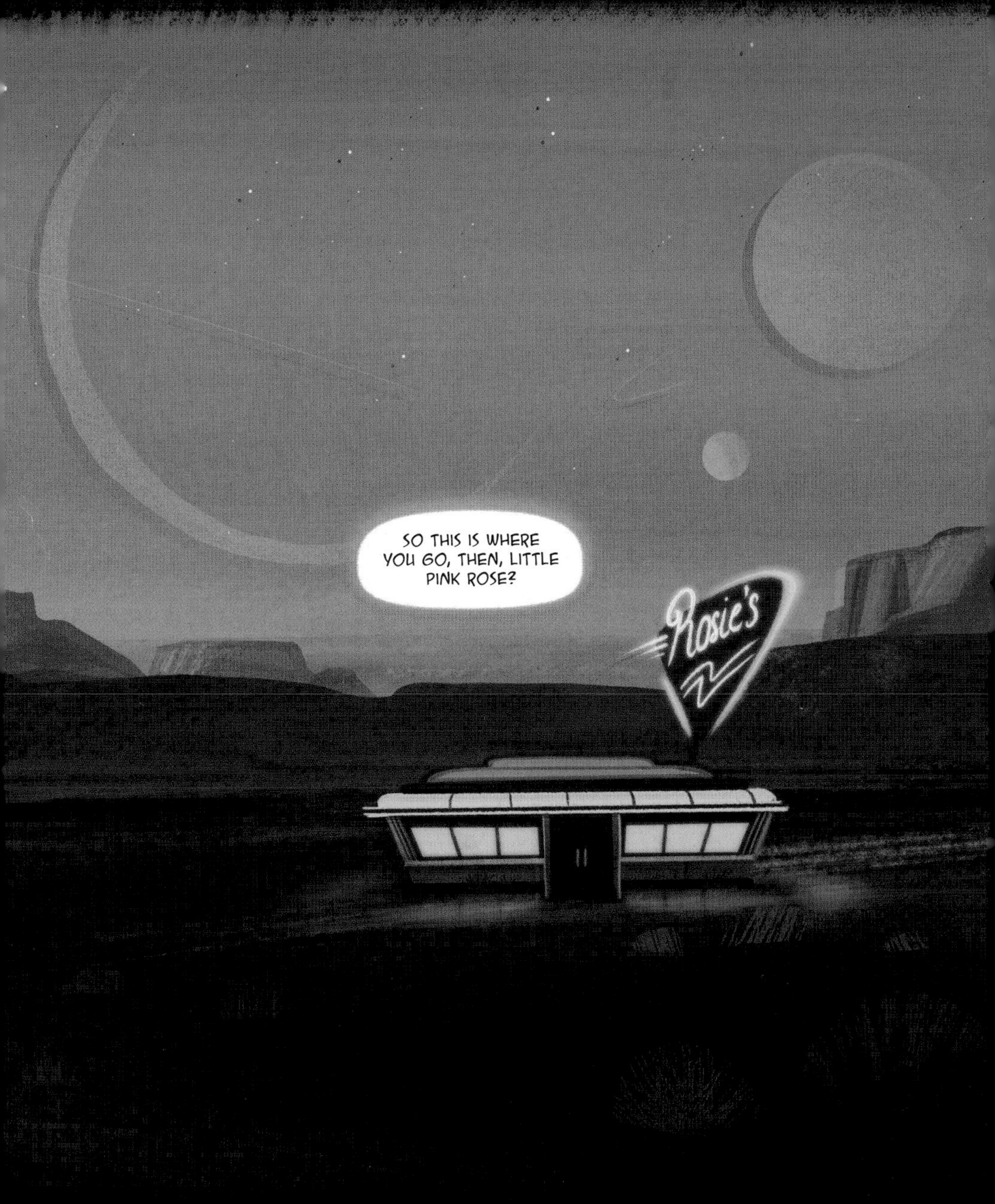
SO THIS IS WHERE YOU GO, THEN, LITTLE PINK ROSE?
Rosie's

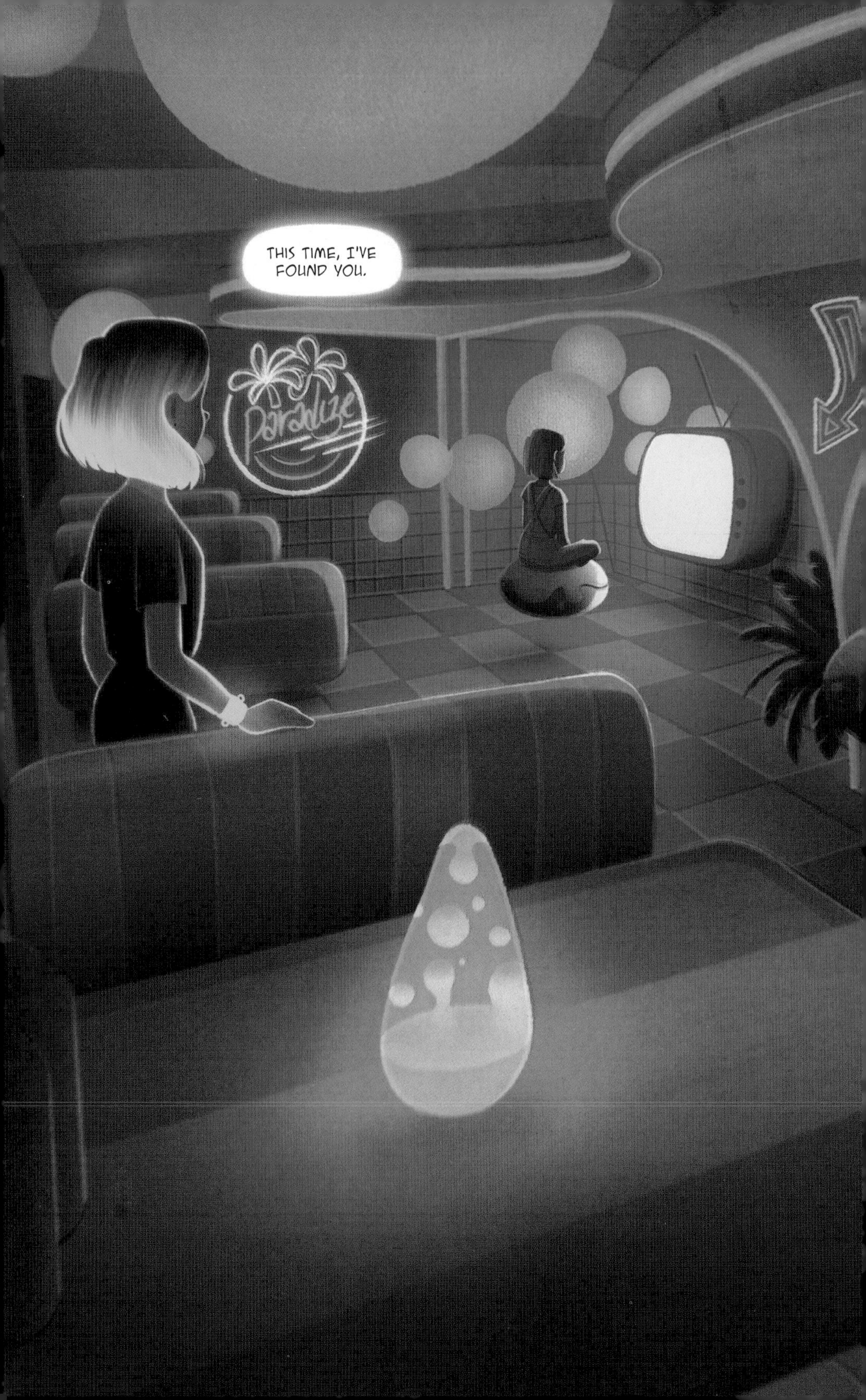
THIS TIME, I'VE FOUND YOU.
Paradize

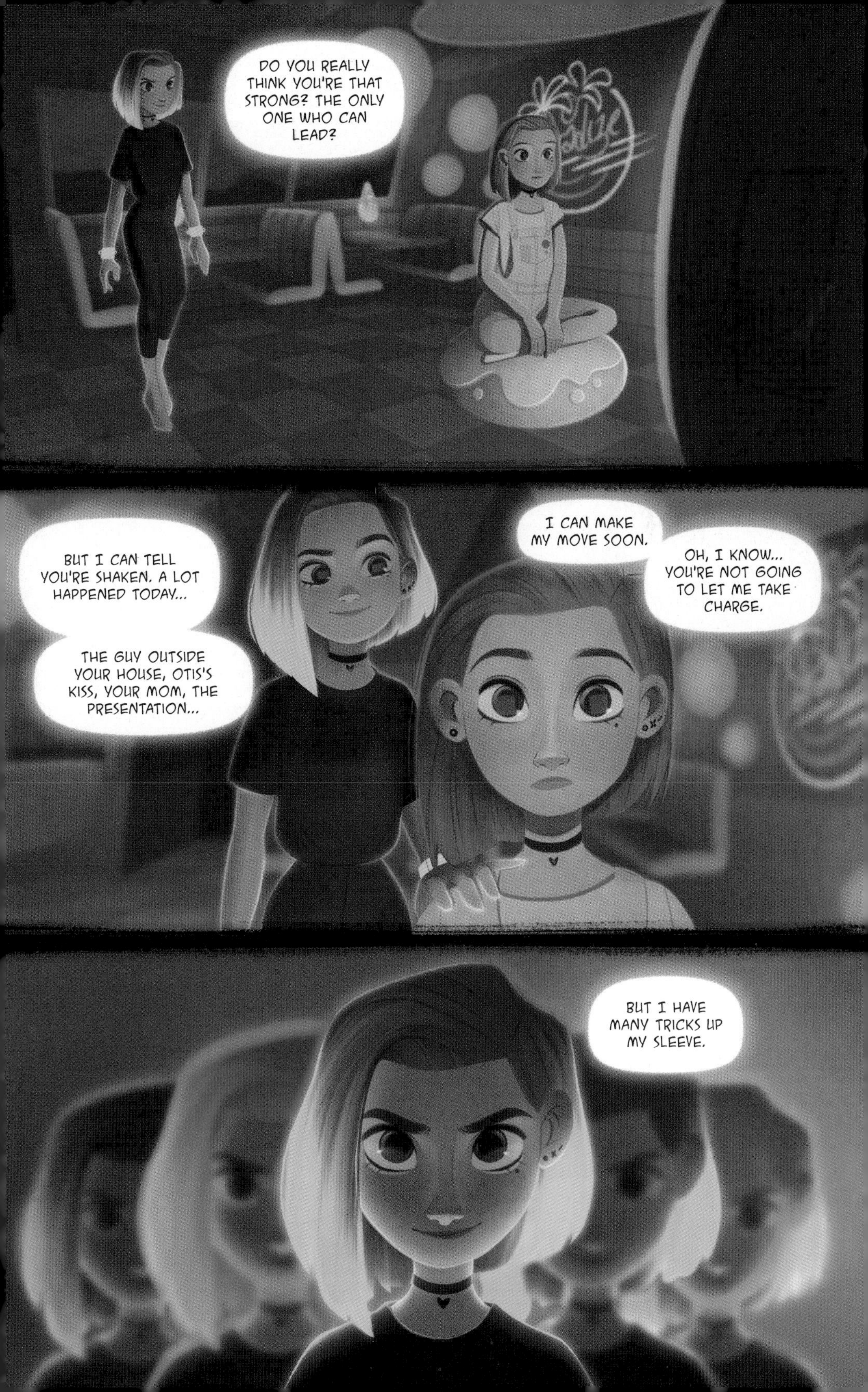
DO YOU REALLY THINK YOU'RE THAT STRONG? THE ONLY ONE WHO CAN LEAD?
BUT I CAN TELL YOU'RE SHAKEN. A LOT HAPPENED TODAY...
THE GUY OUTSIDE YOUR HOUSE, OTIS'S KISS, YOUR MOM, THE PRESENTATION...
I CAN MAKE MY MOVE SOON.
OH, I KNOW... YOU'RE NOT GOING TO LET ME TAKE CHARGE.
BUT I HAVE MANY TRICKS UP MY SLEEVE.

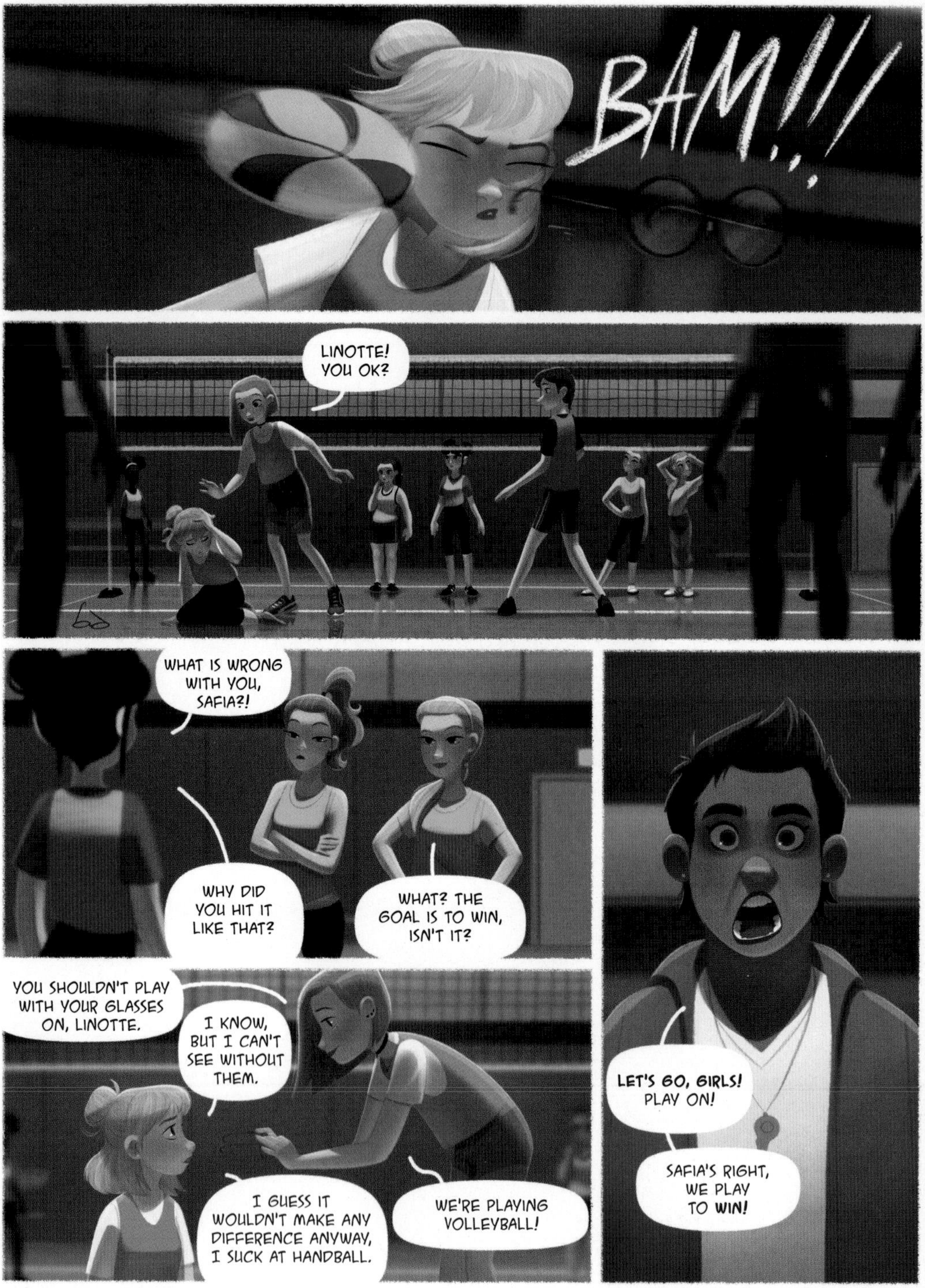
BAM!!!
LINOTTE! YOU OK?
WHAT IS WRONG WITH YOU, SAFIA?!
WHY DID YOU HIT IT LIKE THAT?
WHAT? THE GOAL IS TO WIN, ISN'T IT?
LET'S GO, GIRLS! PLAY ON!
SAFIA'S RIGHT, WE PLAY TO WIN!
YOU SHOULDN'T PLAY WITH YOUR GLASSES ON, LINOTTE.
I KNOW, BUT I CAN'T SEE WITHOUT THEM.
I GUESS IT WOULDN'T MAKE ANY DIFFERENCE ANYWAY, I SUCK AT HANDBALL.
WE'RE PLAYING VOLLEYBALL!

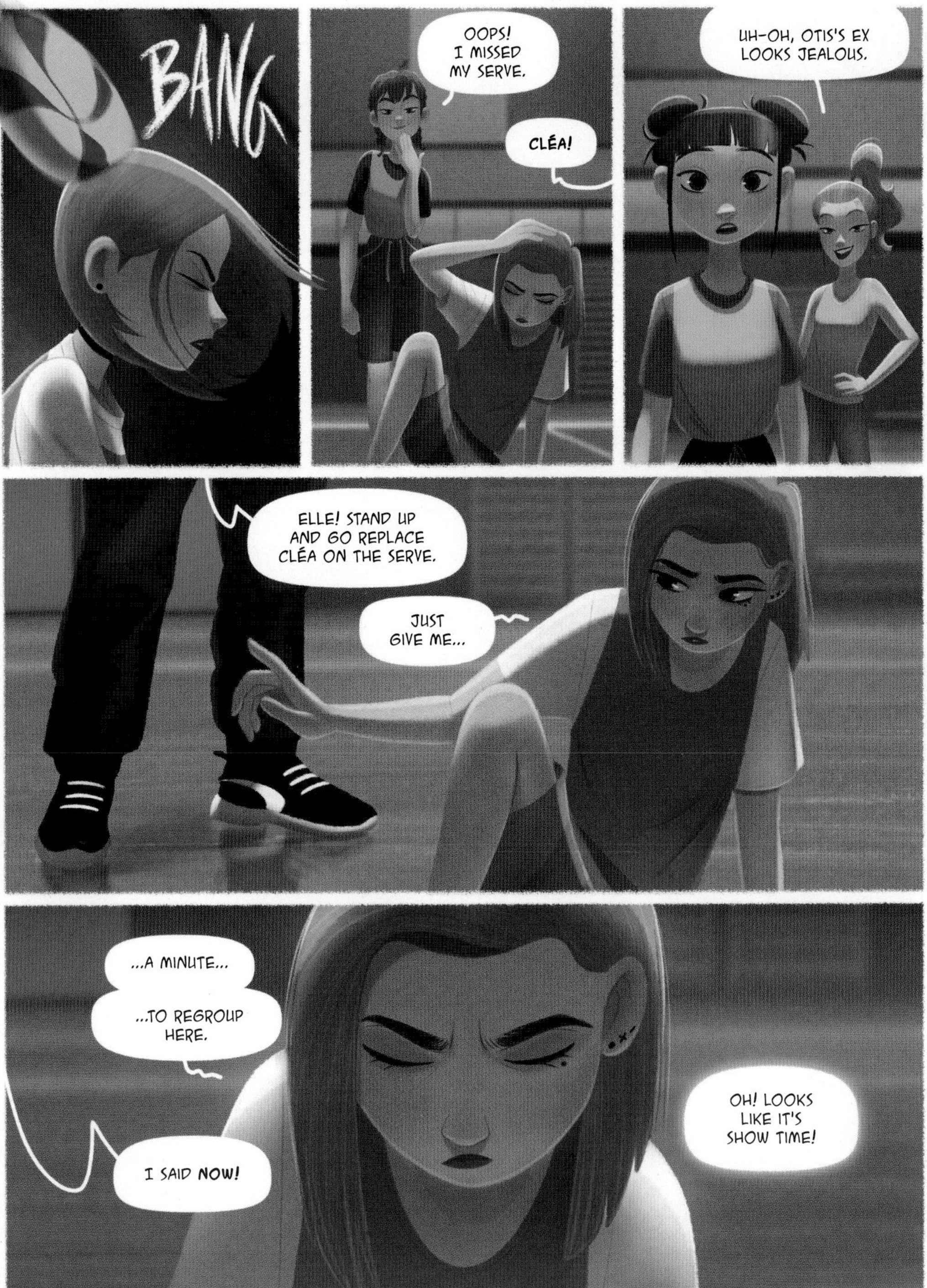
BANG
OOPS! I MISSED MY SERVE.
CLÉA!
UH-OH, OTIS'S EX LOOKS JEALOUS.
ELLE! STAND UP AND GO REPLACE CLÉA ON THE SERVE.
JUST GIVE ME...
...A MINUTE...
...TO REGROUP HERE.
I SAID **NOW!**
OH! LOOKS LIKE IT'S SHOW TIME!

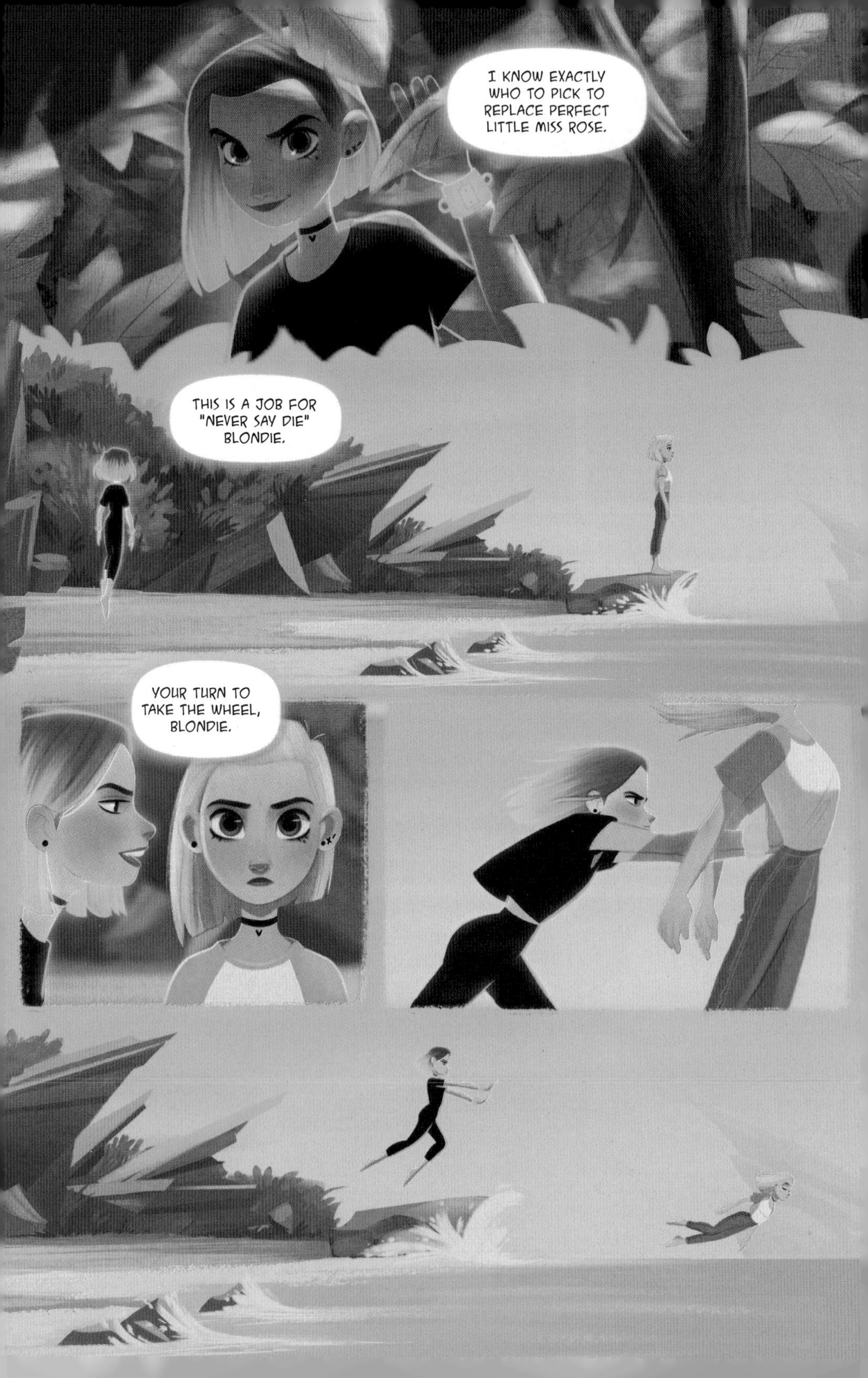
I KNOW EXACTLY WHO TO PICK TO REPLACE PERFECT LITTLE MISS ROSE.
THIS IS A JOB FOR "NEVER SAY DIE" BLONDIE.
YOUR TURN TO TAKE THE WHEEL, BLONDIE.

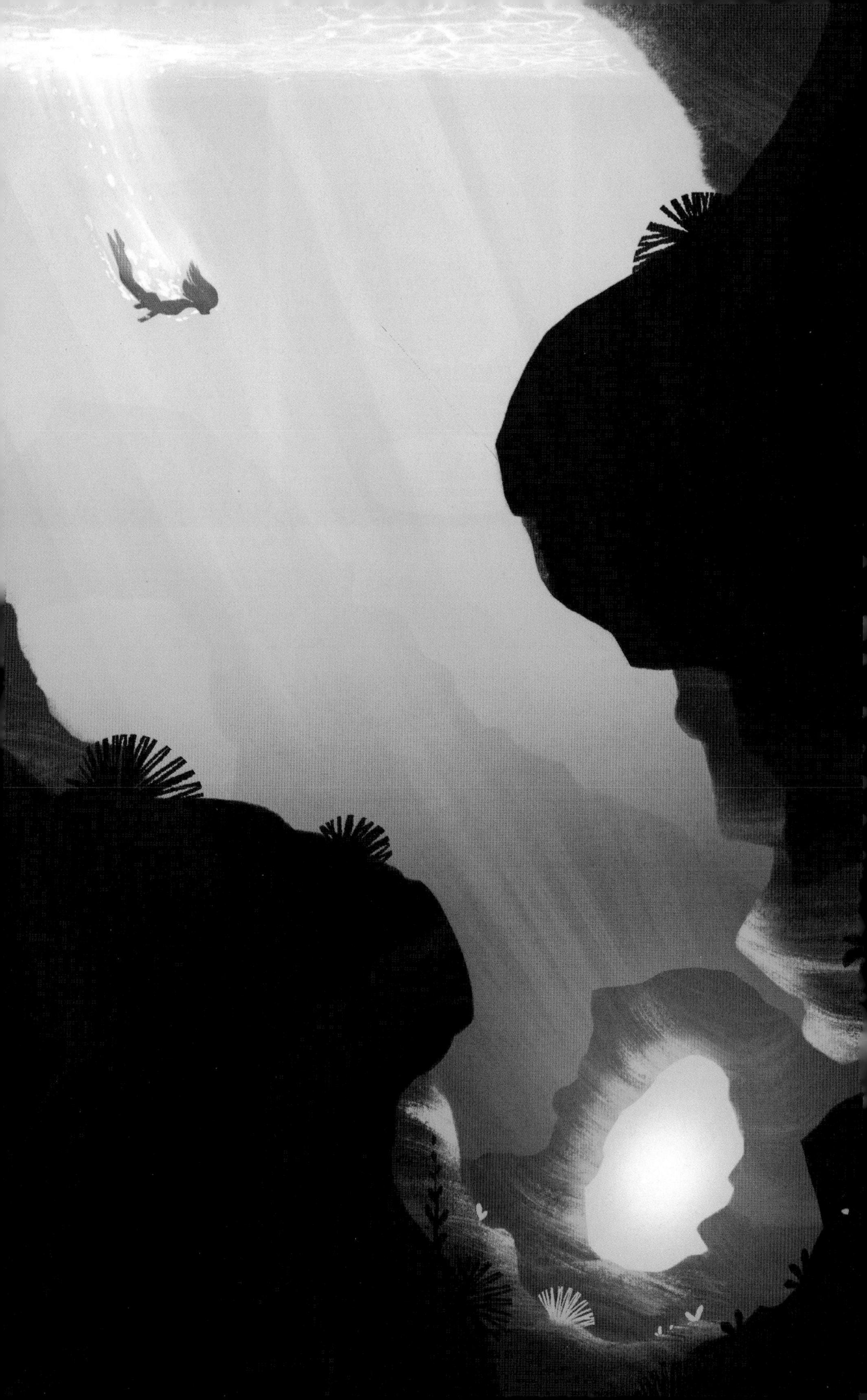

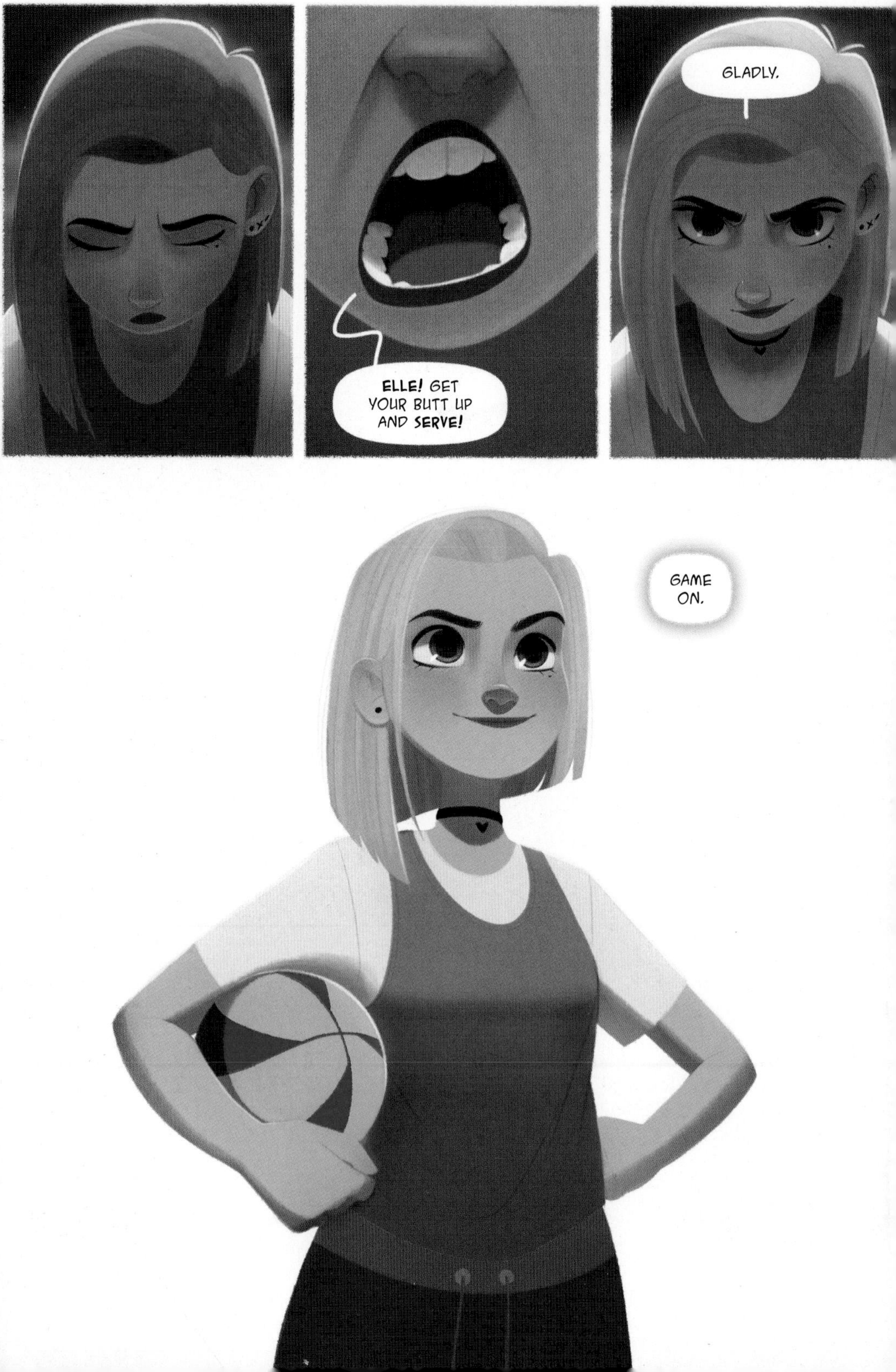
ELLE! GET YOUR BUTT UP AND SERVE!
GLADLY.
GAME ON.

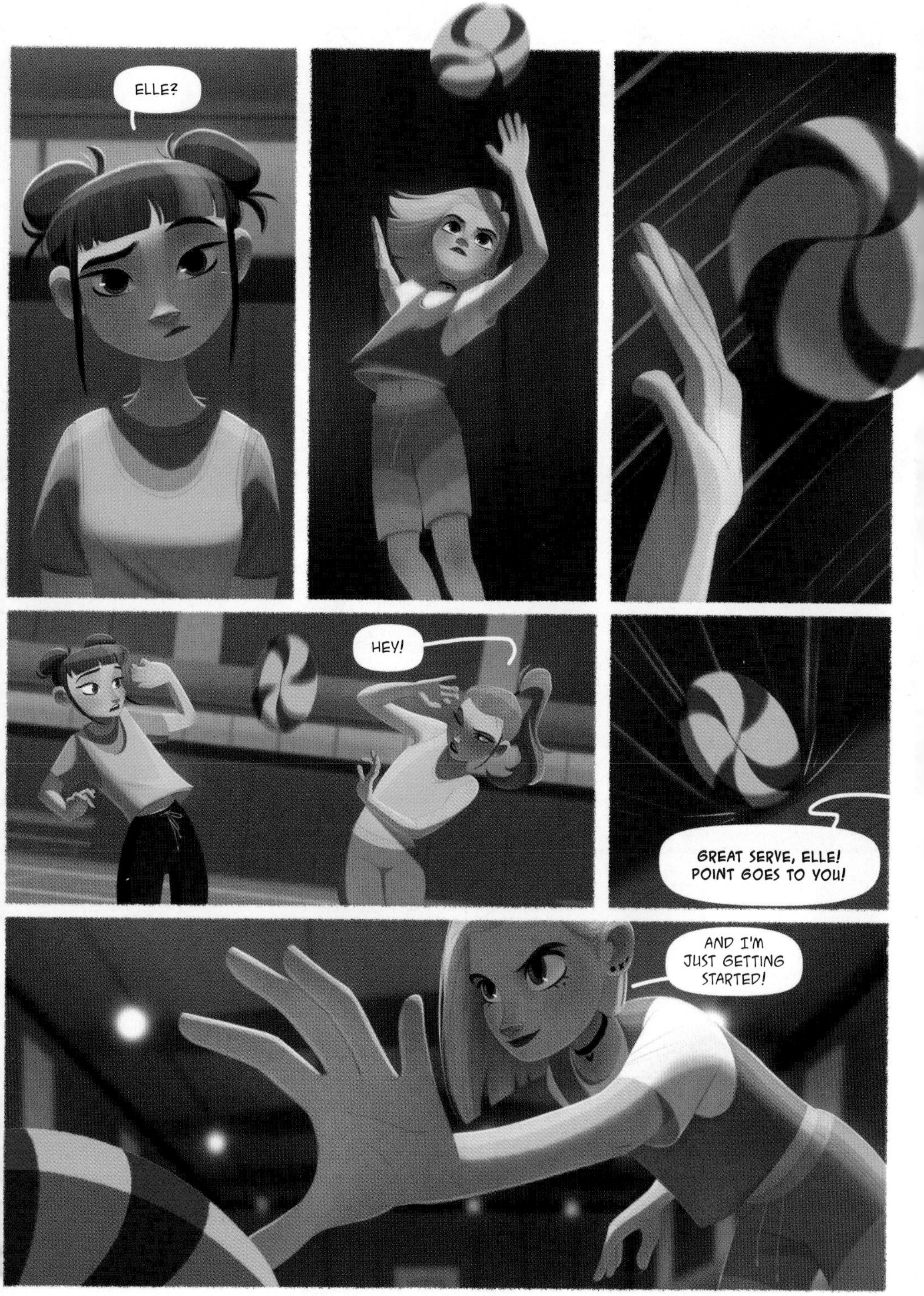
ELLE?
HEY!
GREAT SERVE, ELLE! POINT GOES TO YOU!
AND I'M JUST GETTING STARTED!

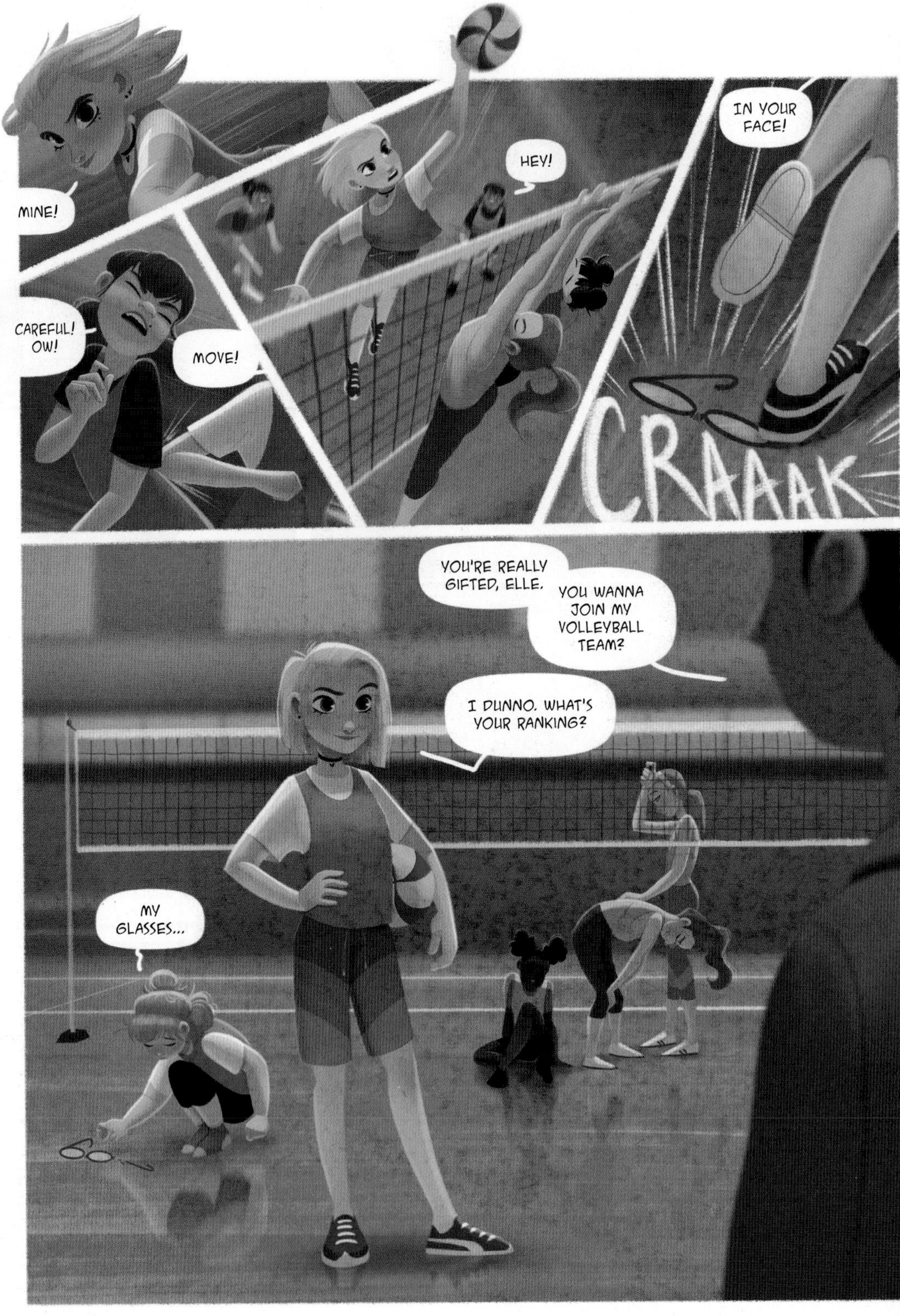
MINE!
HEY!
IN YOUR FACE!
CAREFUL! OW!
MOVE!
CRAAAK
YOU'RE REALLY GIFTED, ELLE.
YOU WANNA JOIN MY VOLLEYBALL TEAM?
I DUNNO. WHAT'S YOUR RANKING?
MY GLASSES...

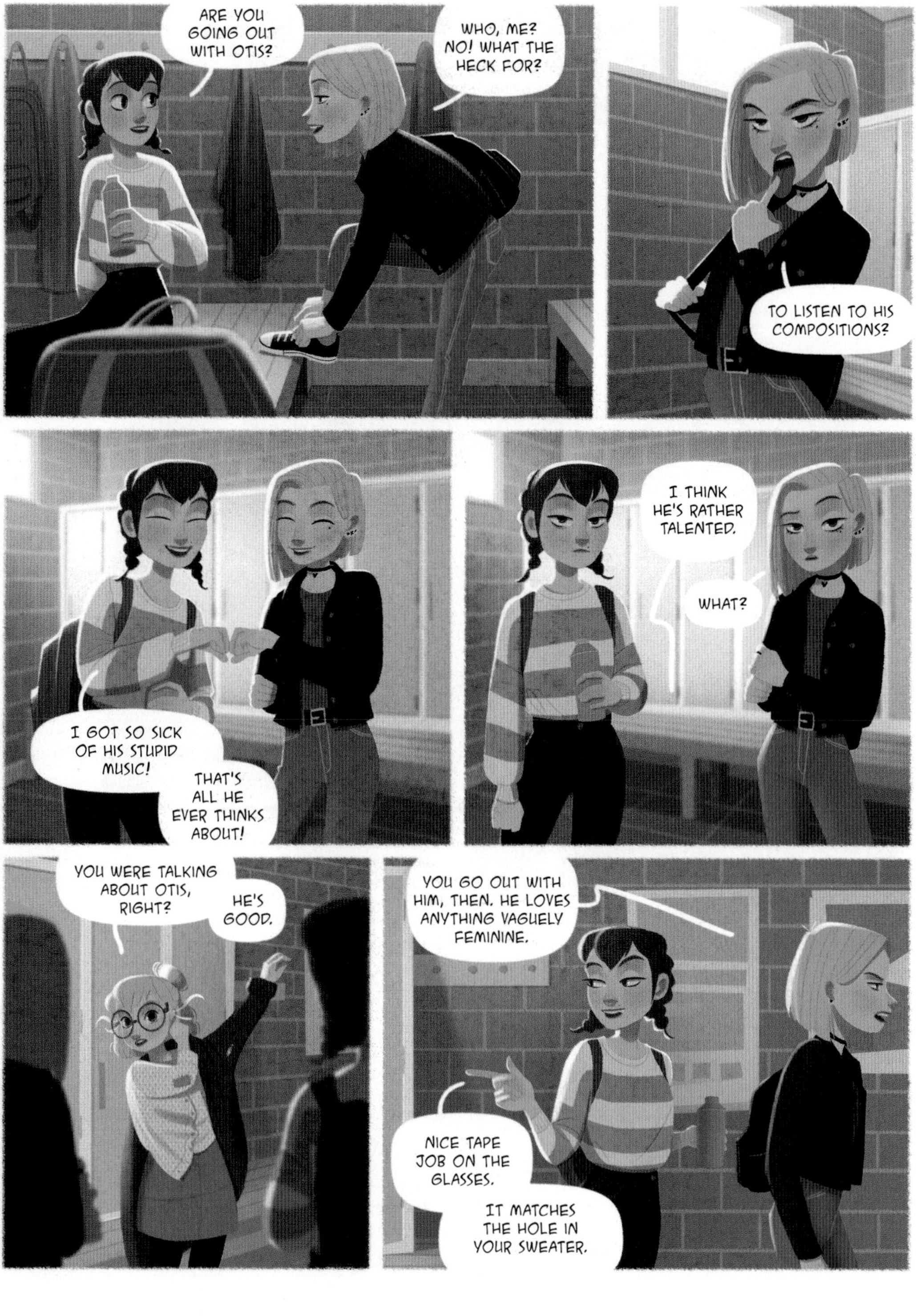
ARE YOU GOING OUT WITH OTIS?
WHO, ME? NO! WHAT THE HECK FOR?
TO LISTEN TO HIS COMPOSITIONS?
I GOT SO SICK OF HIS STUPID MUSIC!
THAT'S ALL HE EVER THINKS ABOUT!
I THINK HE'S RATHER TALENTED.
WHAT?
YOU WERE TALKING ABOUT OTIS, RIGHT?
HE'S GOOD.
YOU GO OUT WITH HIM, THEN. HE LOVES ANYTHING VAGUELY FEMININE.
NICE TAPE JOB ON THE GLASSES.
IT MATCHES THE HOLE IN YOUR SWEATER.

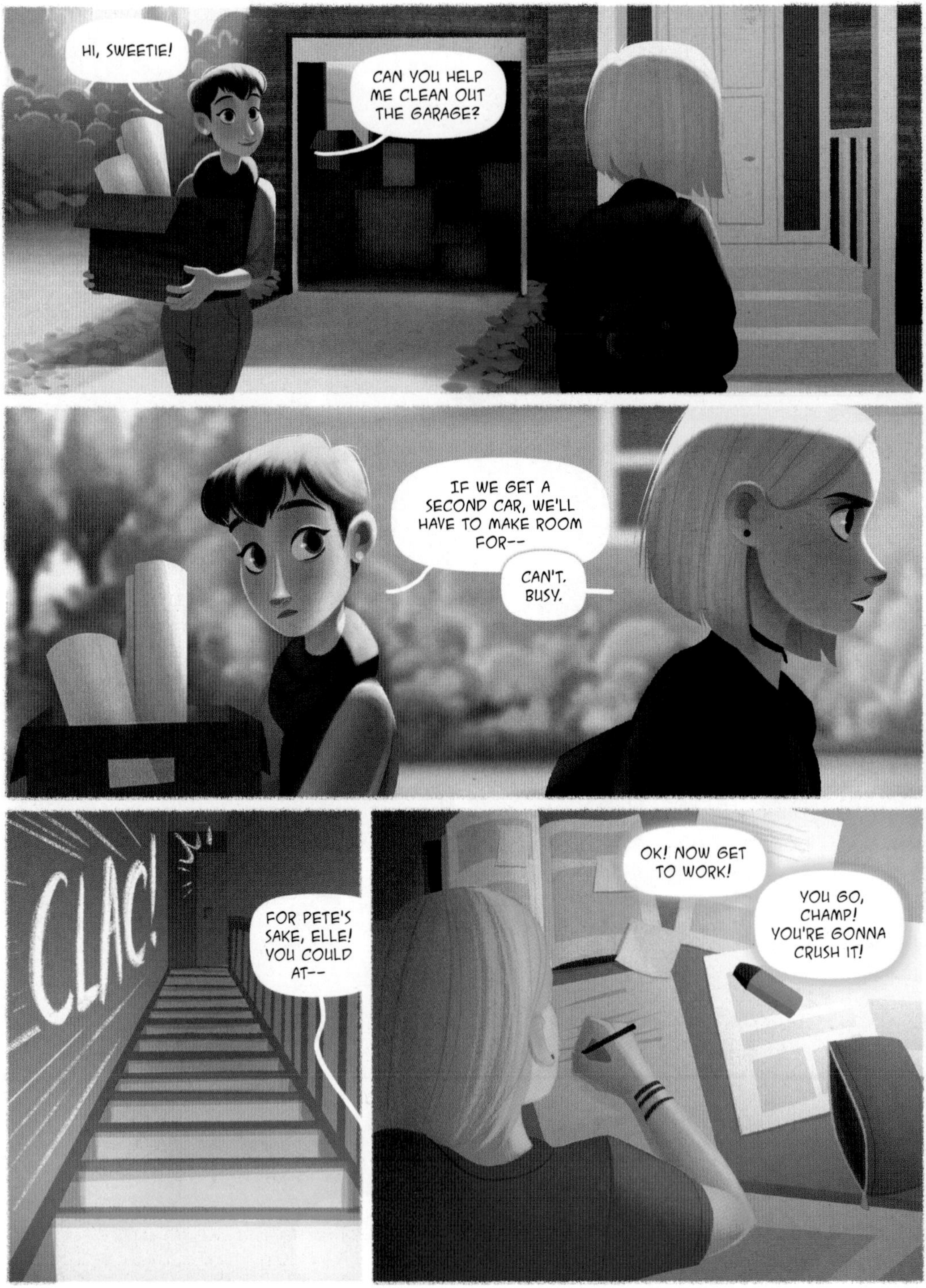
HI, SWEETIE!
CAN YOU HELP ME CLEAN OUT THE GARAGE?
IF WE GET A SECOND CAR, WE'LL HAVE TO MAKE ROOM FOR--
CAN'T. BUSY.
CLAC!
FOR PETE'S SAKE, ELLE! YOU COULD AT--
OK! NOW GET TO WORK!
YOU GO, CHAMP! YOU'RE GONNA CRUSH IT!

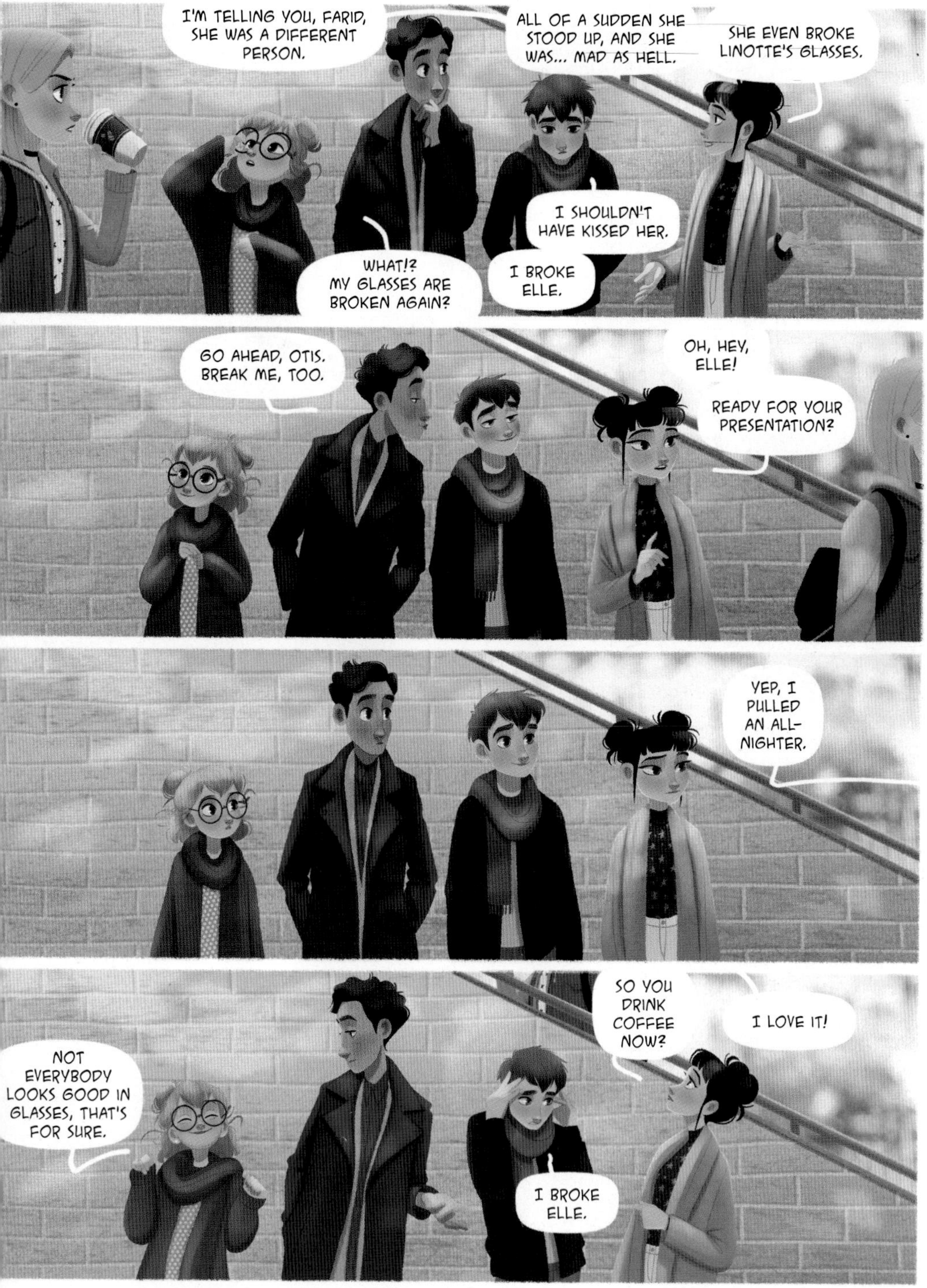
I'M TELLING YOU, FARID, SHE WAS A DIFFERENT PERSON.
ALL OF A SUDDEN SHE STOOD UP, AND SHE WAS... MAD AS HELL.
SHE EVEN BROKE LINOTTE'S GLASSES.
WHAT!? MY GLASSES ARE BROKEN AGAIN?
I SHOULDN'T HAVE KISSED HER.
I BROKE ELLE.
GO AHEAD, OTIS. BREAK ME, TOO.
OH, HEY, ELLE!
READY FOR YOUR PRESENTATION?
YEP, I PULLED AN ALL-NIGHTER.
NOT EVERYBODY LOOKS GOOD IN GLASSES, THAT'S FOR SURE.
SO YOU DRINK COFFEE NOW?
I LOVE IT!
I BROKE ELLE.

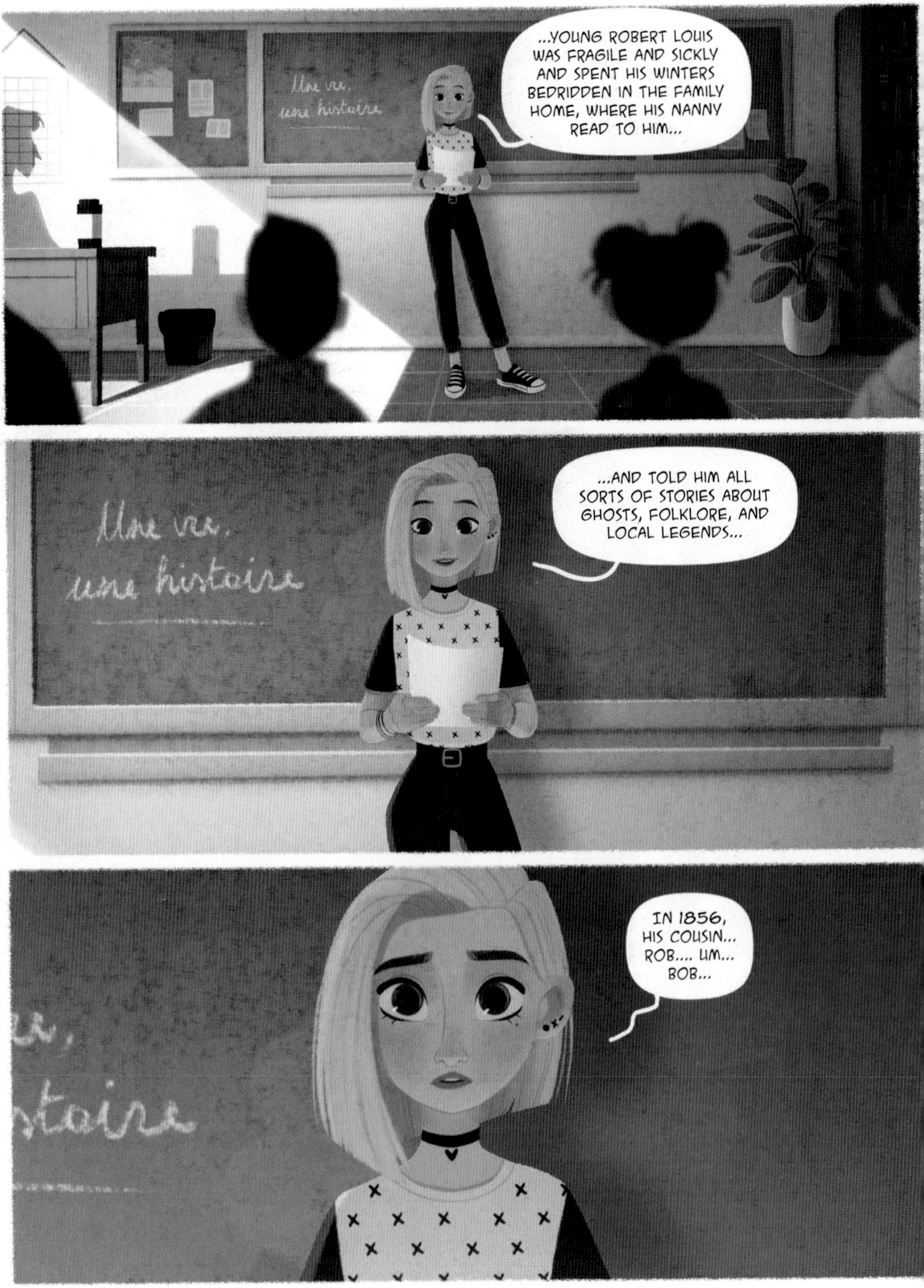
Une vie, une histoire
...YOUNG ROBERT LOUIS WAS FRAGILE AND SICKLY AND SPENT HIS WINTERS BEDRIDDEN IN THE FAMILY HOME, WHERE HIS NANNY READ TO HIM...
...AND TOLD HIM ALL SORTS OF STORIES ABOUT GHOSTS, FOLKLORE, AND LOCAL LEGENDS...
IN 1856, HIS COUSIN... ROB.... UM... BOB...

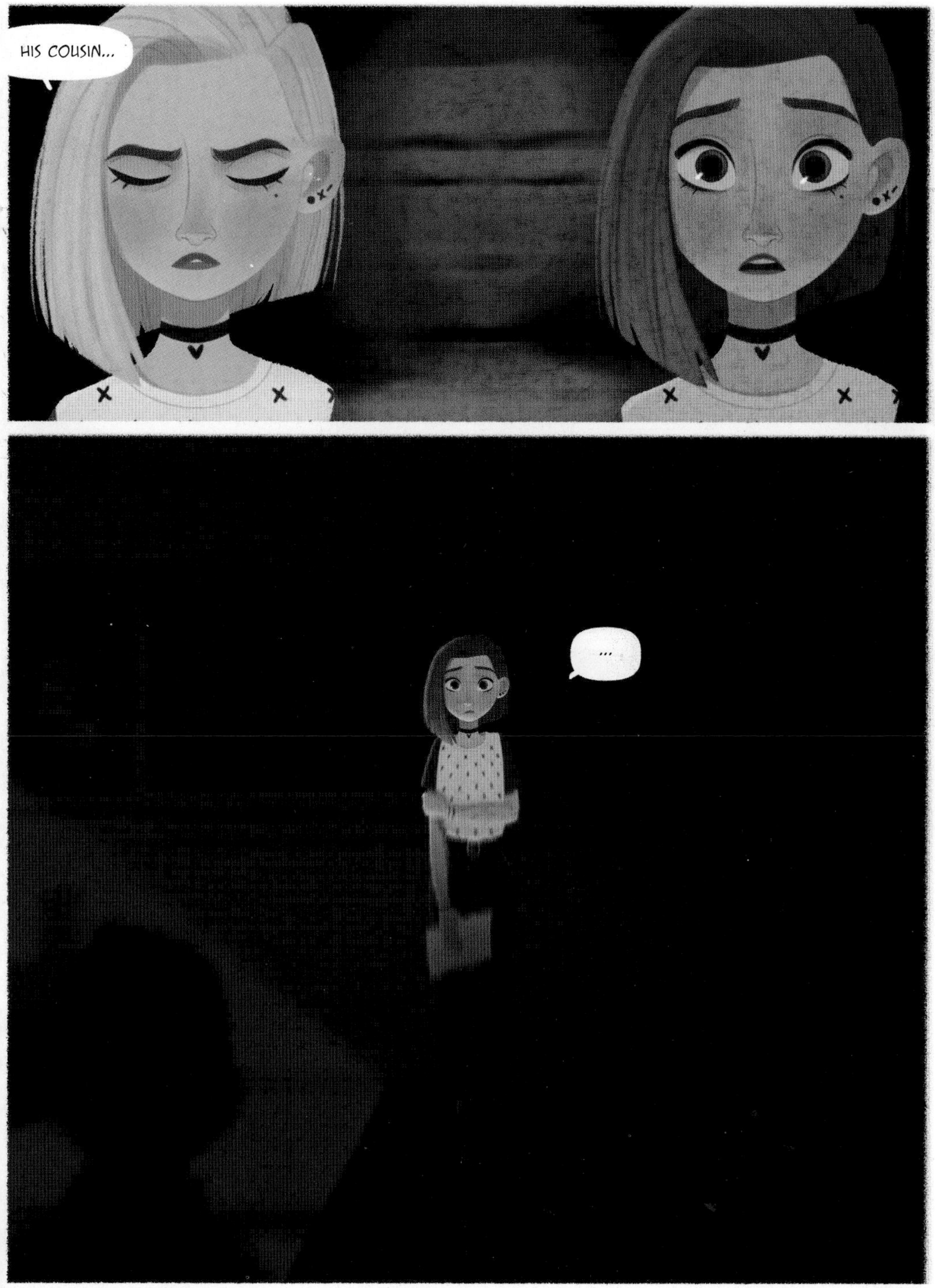
HIS COUSIN...
...

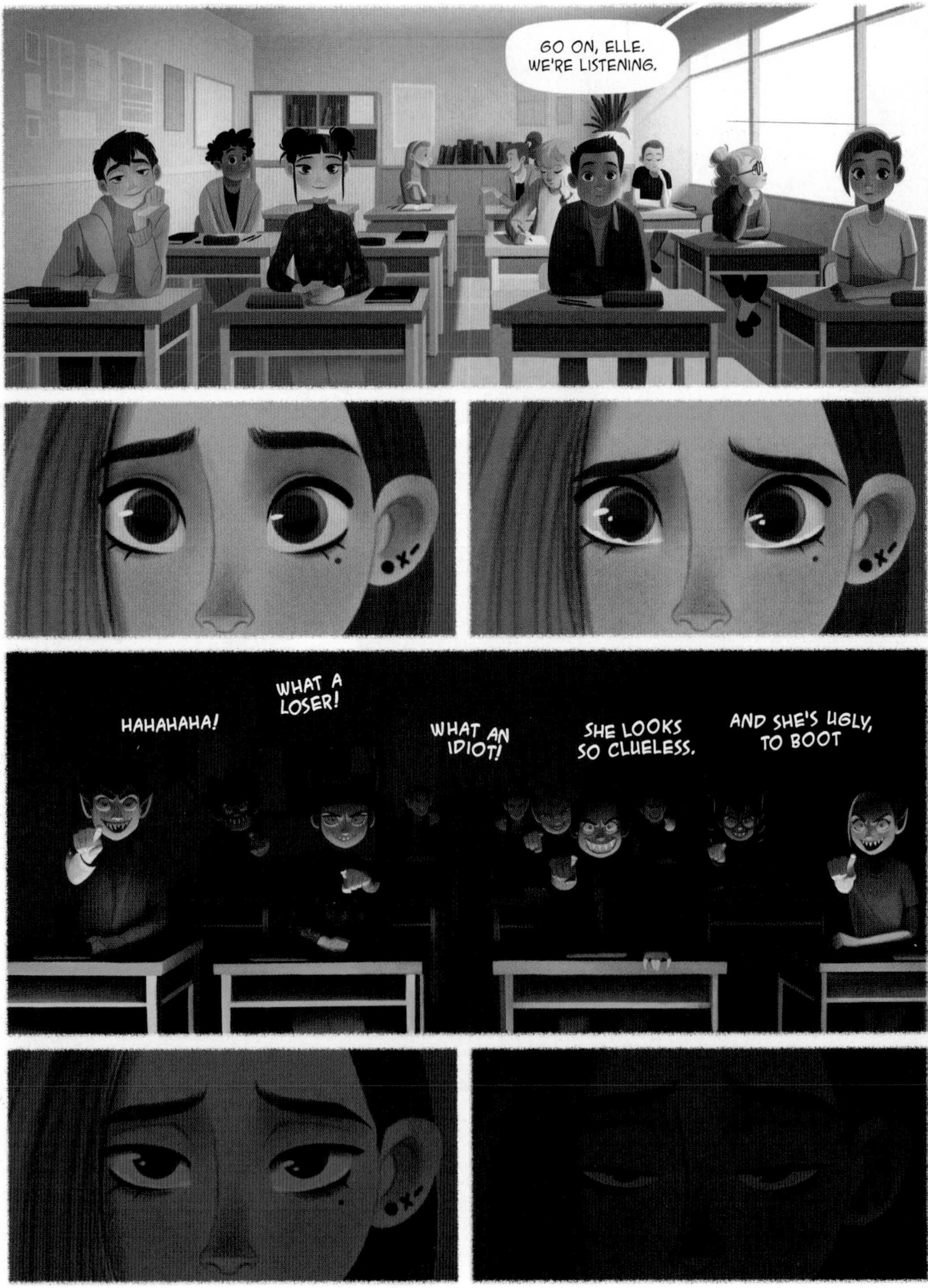
GO ON, ELLE.
WE'RE LISTENING.
HAHAHAHA!
WHAT A
LOSER!
WHAT AN
IDIOT!
SHE LOOKS
SO CLUELESS.
AND SHE'S UGLY,
TO BOOT

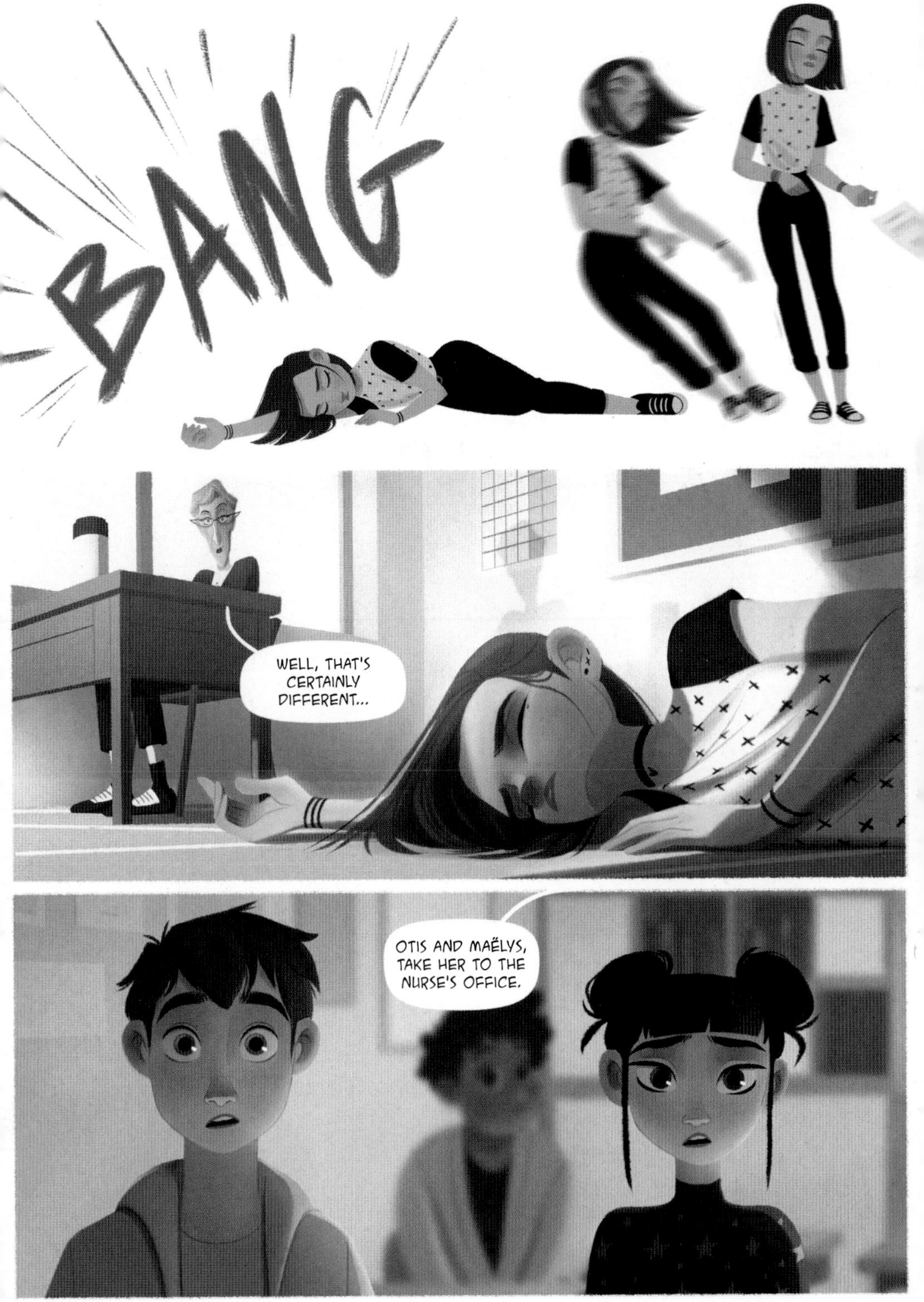
BANG
WELL, THAT'S CERTAINLY DIFFERENT...
OTIS AND MAËLYS, TAKE HER TO THE NURSE'S OFFICE.

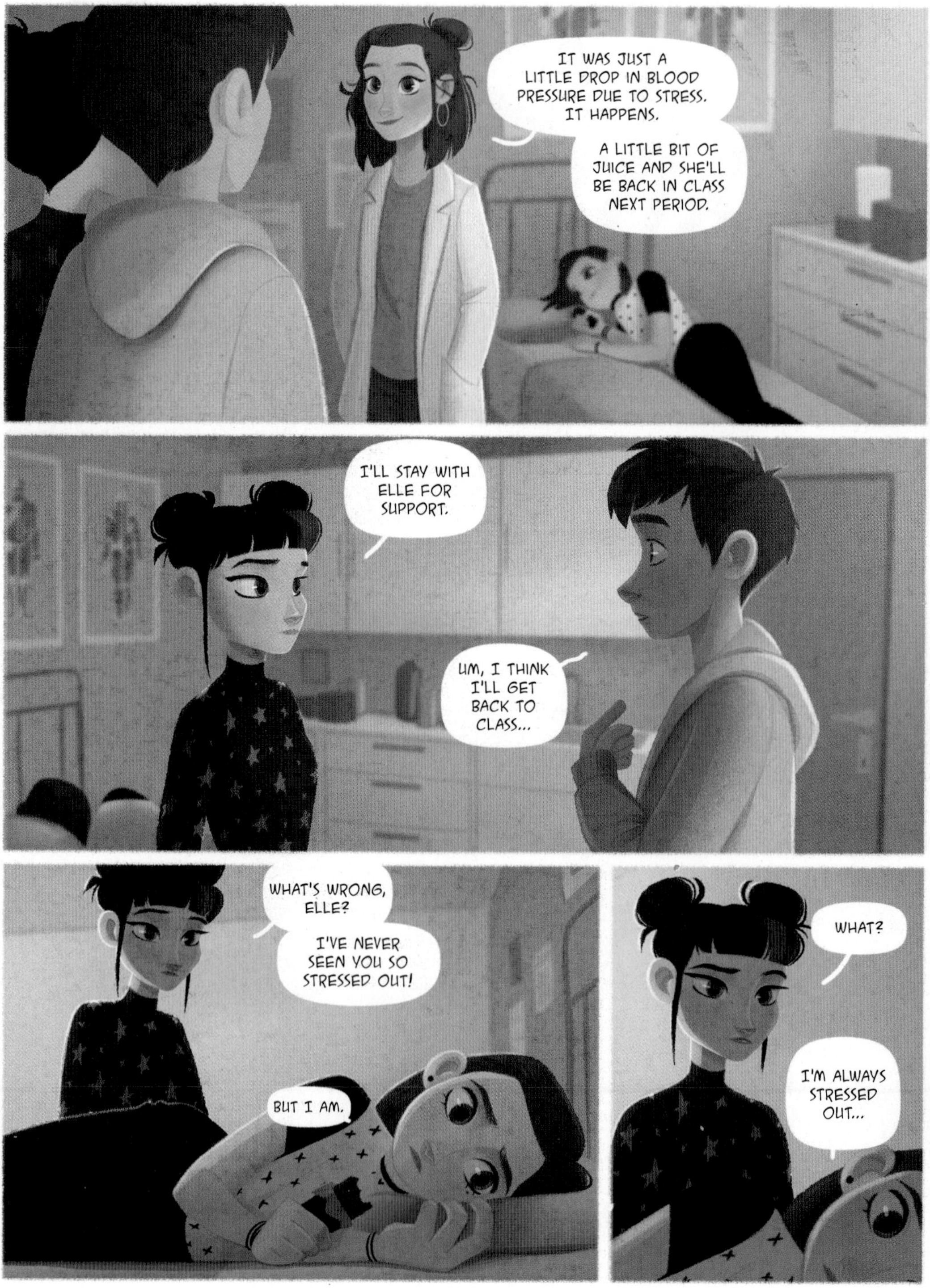
IT WAS JUST A LITTLE DROP IN BLOOD PRESSURE DUE TO STRESS. IT HAPPENS.
A LITTLE BIT OF JUICE AND SHE'LL BE BACK IN CLASS NEXT PERIOD.
I'LL STAY WITH ELLE FOR SUPPORT.
UM, I THINK I'LL GET BACK TO CLASS...
WHAT'S WRONG, ELLE?
I'VE NEVER SEEN YOU SO STRESSED OUT!
BUT I AM.
WHAT?
I'M ALWAYS STRESSED OUT...

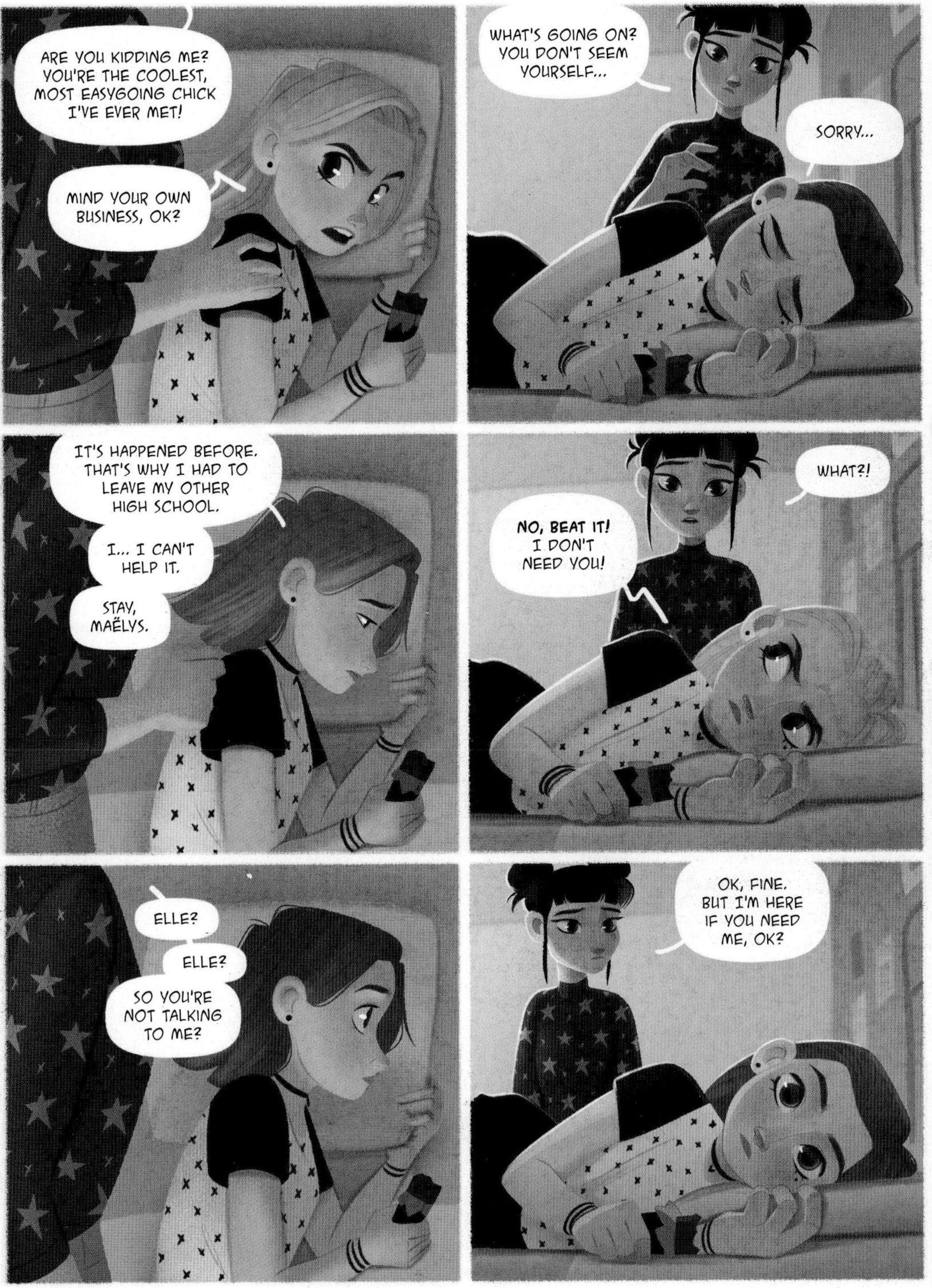
ARE YOU KIDDING ME? YOU'RE THE COOLEST, MOST EASYGOING CHICK I'VE EVER MET!
MIND YOUR OWN BUSINESS, OK?
WHAT'S GOING ON? YOU DON'T SEEM YOURSELF...
SORRY...
IT'S HAPPENED BEFORE. THAT'S WHY I HAD TO LEAVE MY OTHER HIGH SCHOOL.
I... I CAN'T HELP IT.
STAY, MAËLYS.
WHAT?!
NO, BEAT IT! I DON'T NEED YOU!
ELLE?
ELLE?
SO YOU'RE NOT TALKING TO ME?
OK, FINE. BUT I'M HERE IF YOU NEED ME, OK?

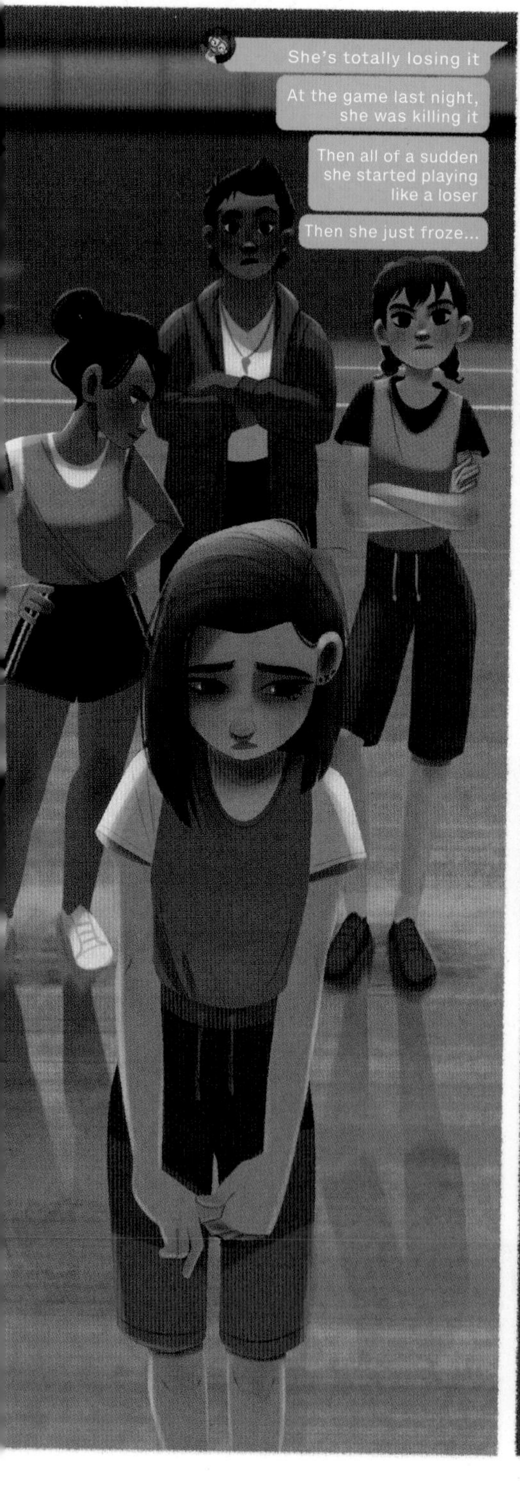
She's totally losing it
At the game last night, she was killing it
Then all of a sudden she started playing like a loser
Then she just froze...

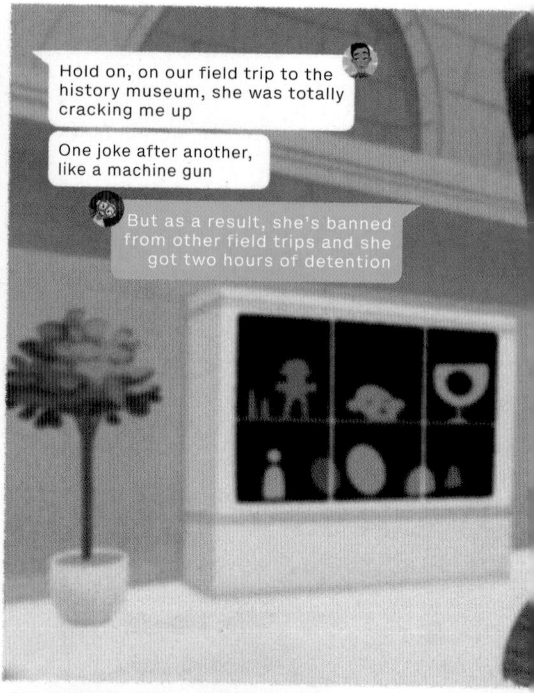
Hold on, on our field trip to the history museum, she was totally cracking me up
One joke after another, like a machine gun
But as a result, she's banned from other field trips and she got two hours of detention

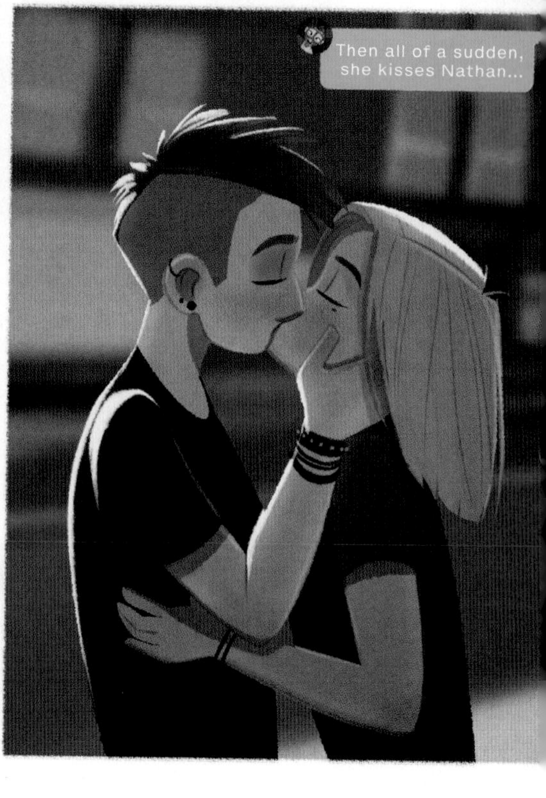
Then all of a sudden, she kisses Nathan...

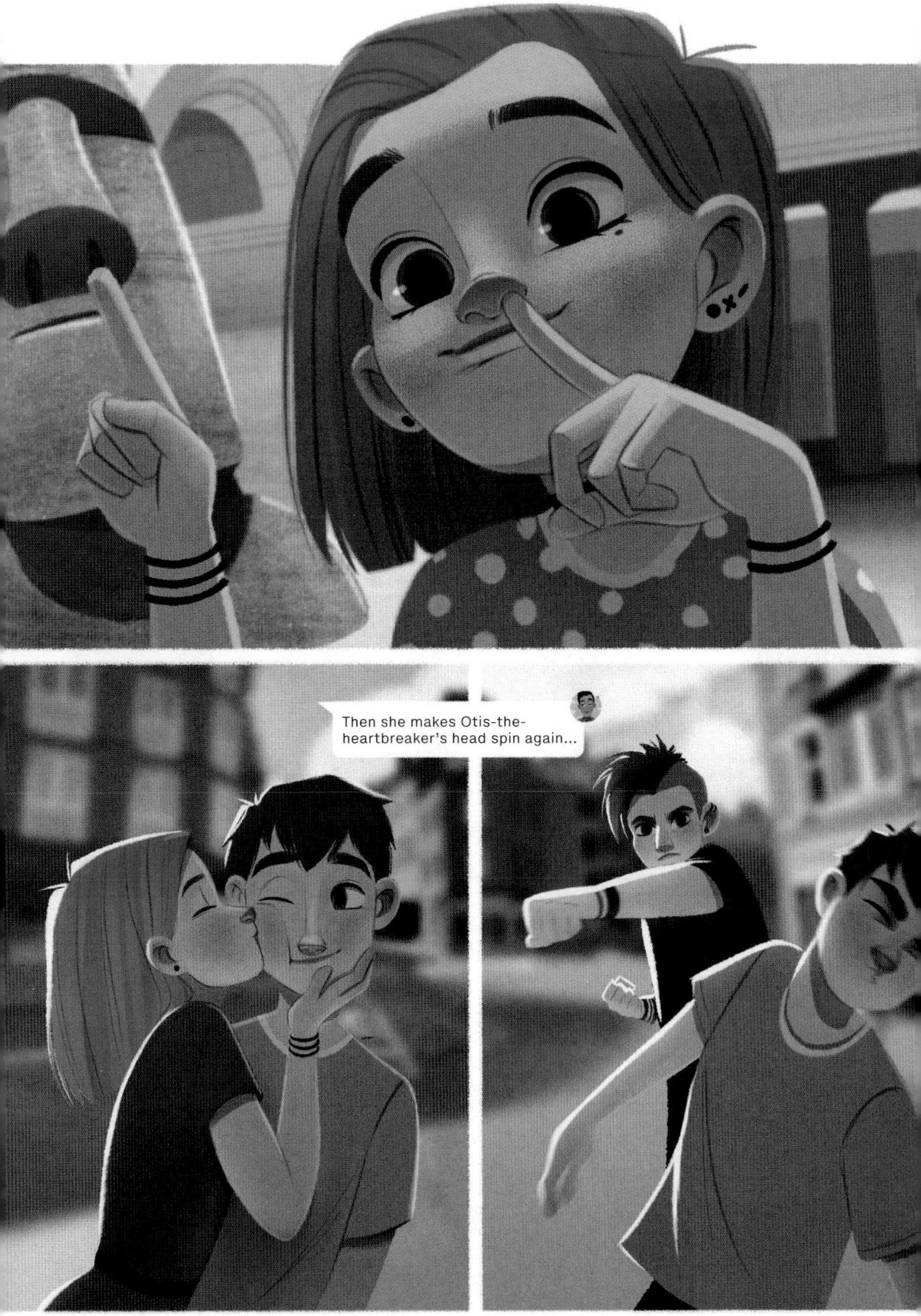
Then she makes Otis-the-heartbreaker's head spin again...

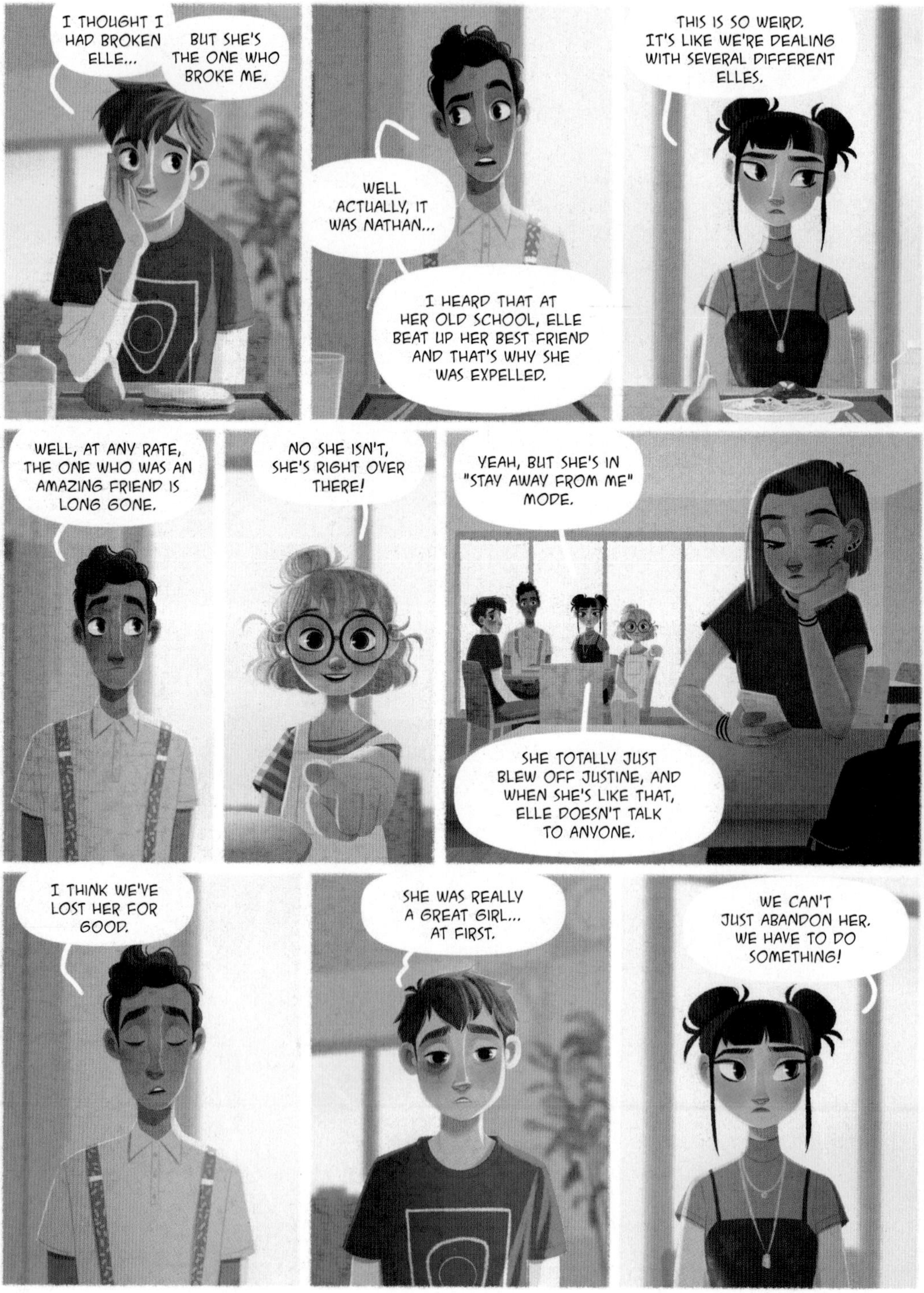
I THOUGHT I HAD BROKEN ELLE...
BUT SHE'S THE ONE WHO BROKE ME.
WELL ACTUALLY, IT WAS NATHAN...
I HEARD THAT AT HER OLD SCHOOL, ELLE BEAT UP HER BEST FRIEND AND THAT'S WHY SHE WAS EXPELLED.
THIS IS SO WEIRD. IT'S LIKE WE'RE DEALING WITH SEVERAL DIFFERENT ELLES.
WELL, AT ANY RATE, THE ONE WHO WAS AN AMAZING FRIEND IS LONG GONE.
NO SHE ISN'T, SHE'S RIGHT OVER THERE!
YEAH, BUT SHE'S IN "STAY AWAY FROM ME" MODE.
SHE TOTALLY JUST BLEW OFF JUSTINE, AND WHEN SHE'S LIKE THAT, ELLE DOESN'T TALK TO ANYONE.
I THINK WE'VE LOST HER FOR GOOD.
SHE WAS REALLY A GREAT GIRL... AT FIRST.
WE CAN'T JUST ABANDON HER. WE HAVE TO DO SOMETHING!

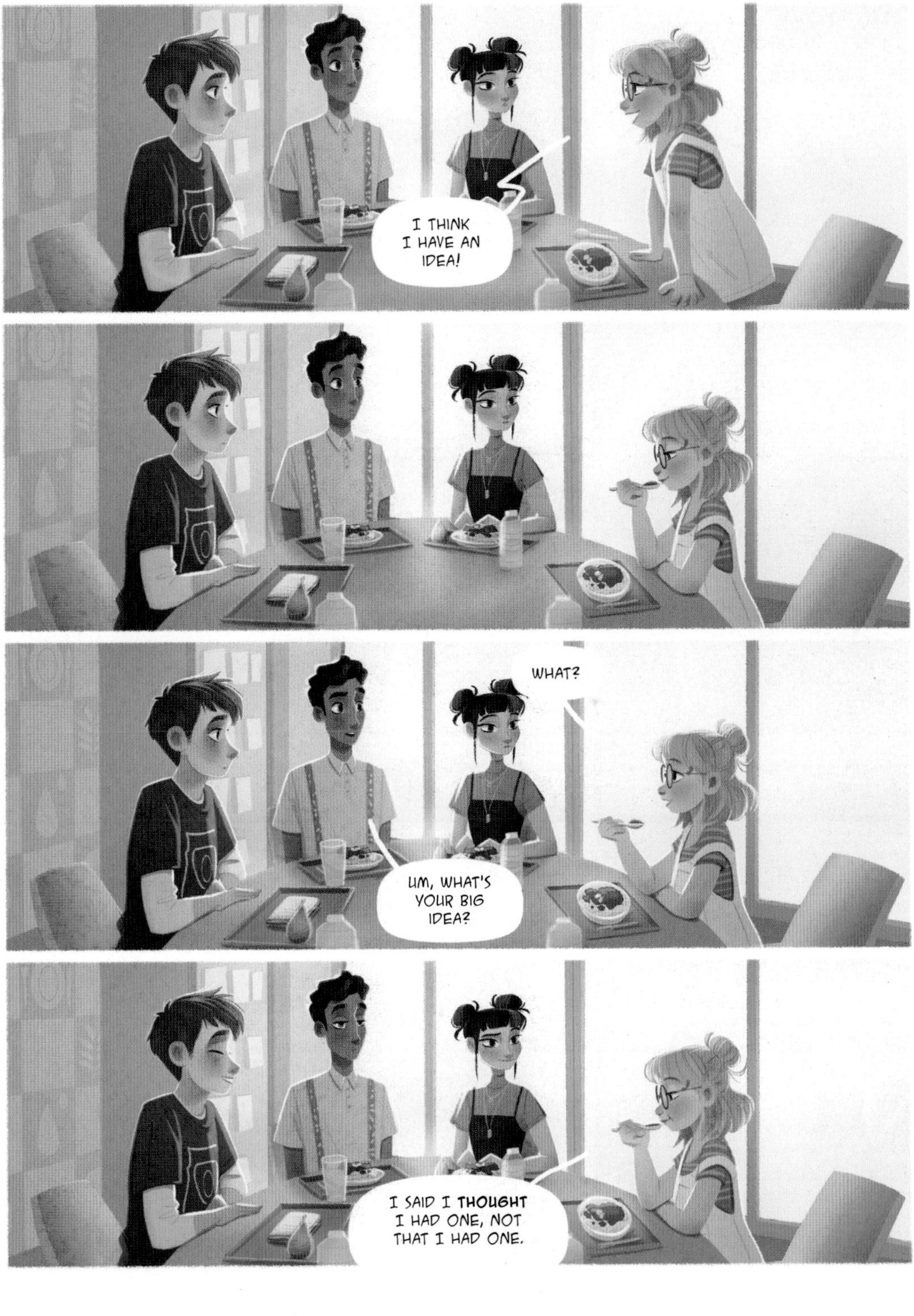
I THINK I HAVE AN IDEA!
WHAT?
UM, WHAT'S YOUR BIG IDEA?
I SAID I **THOUGHT** I HAD ONE, NOT THAT I HAD ONE.

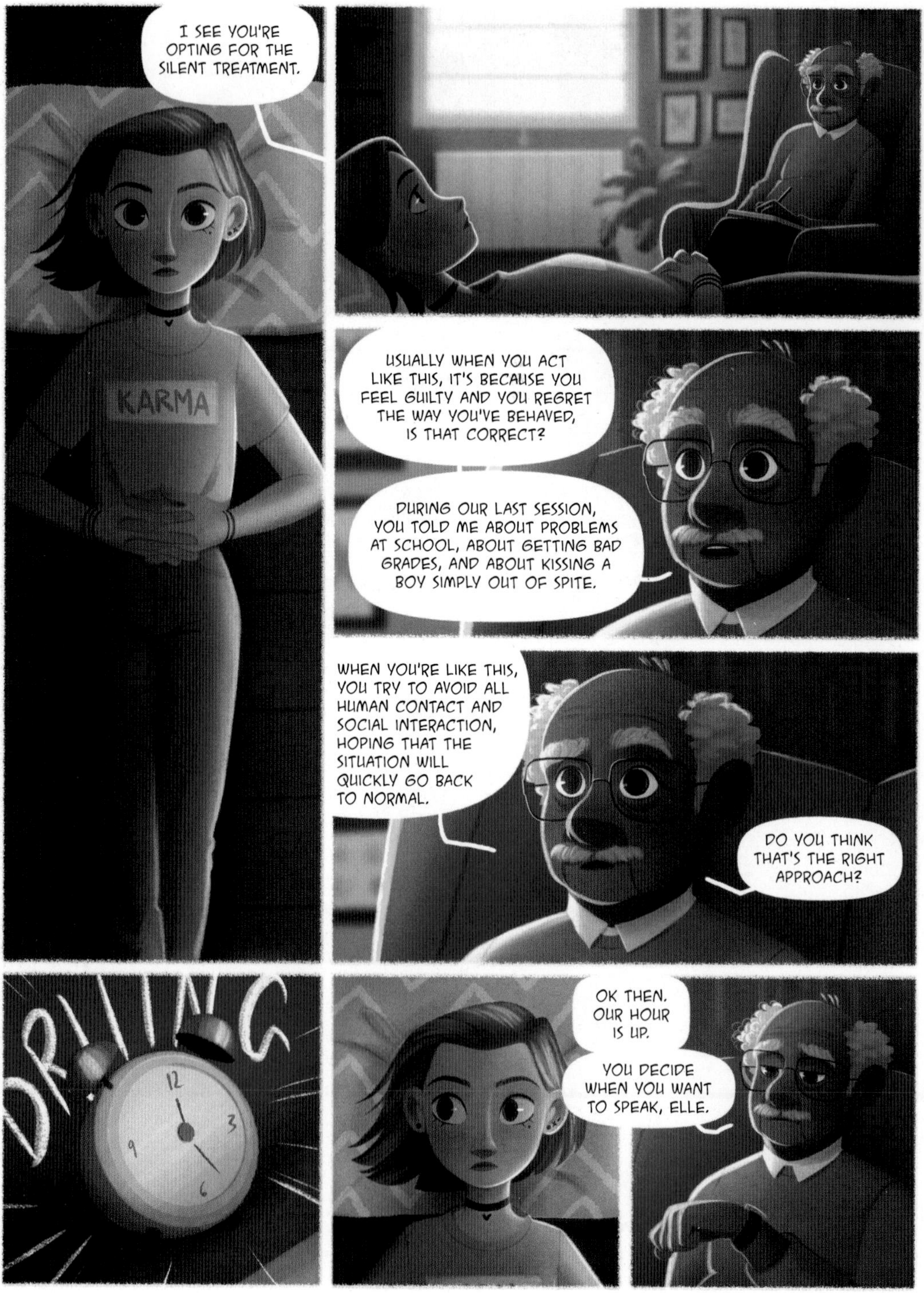
I SEE YOU'RE OPTING FOR THE SILENT TREATMENT.
KARMA
USUALLY WHEN YOU ACT LIKE THIS, IT'S BECAUSE YOU FEEL GUILTY AND YOU REGRET THE WAY YOU'VE BEHAVED, IS THAT CORRECT?
DURING OUR LAST SESSION, YOU TOLD ME ABOUT PROBLEMS AT SCHOOL, ABOUT GETTING BAD GRADES, AND ABOUT KISSING A BOY SIMPLY OUT OF SPITE.
WHEN YOU'RE LIKE THIS, YOU TRY TO AVOID ALL HUMAN CONTACT AND SOCIAL INTERACTION, HOPING THAT THE SITUATION WILL QUICKLY GO BACK TO NORMAL.
DO YOU THINK THAT'S THE RIGHT APPROACH?
DRIIING
OK THEN. OUR HOUR IS UP.
YOU DECIDE WHEN YOU WANT TO SPEAK, ELLE.

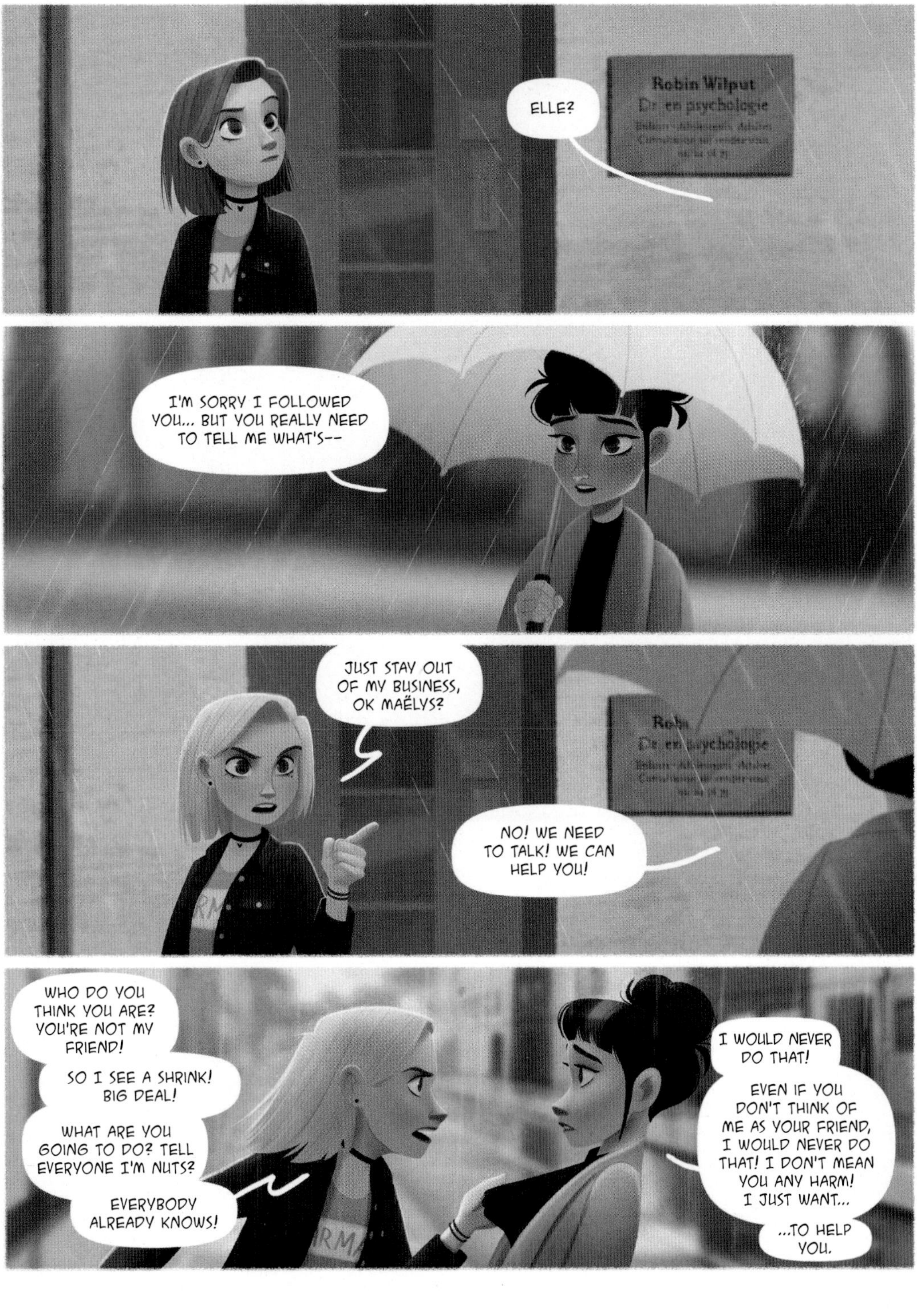
Robin Wilput
Dr. en psychologie
ELLE?
I'M SORRY I FOLLOWED YOU... BUT YOU REALLY NEED TO TELL ME WHAT'S--
JUST STAY OUT OF MY BUSINESS, OK MAËLYS?
NO! WE NEED TO TALK! WE CAN HELP YOU!
WHO DO YOU THINK YOU ARE? YOU'RE NOT MY FRIEND!
SO I SEE A SHRINK! BIG DEAL!
WHAT ARE YOU GOING TO DO? TELL EVERYONE I'M NUTS?
EVERYBODY ALREADY KNOWS!
I WOULD NEVER DO THAT!
EVEN IF YOU DON'T THINK OF ME AS YOUR FRIEND, I WOULD NEVER DO THAT! I DON'T MEAN YOU ANY HARM! I JUST WANT...
...TO HELP YOU.

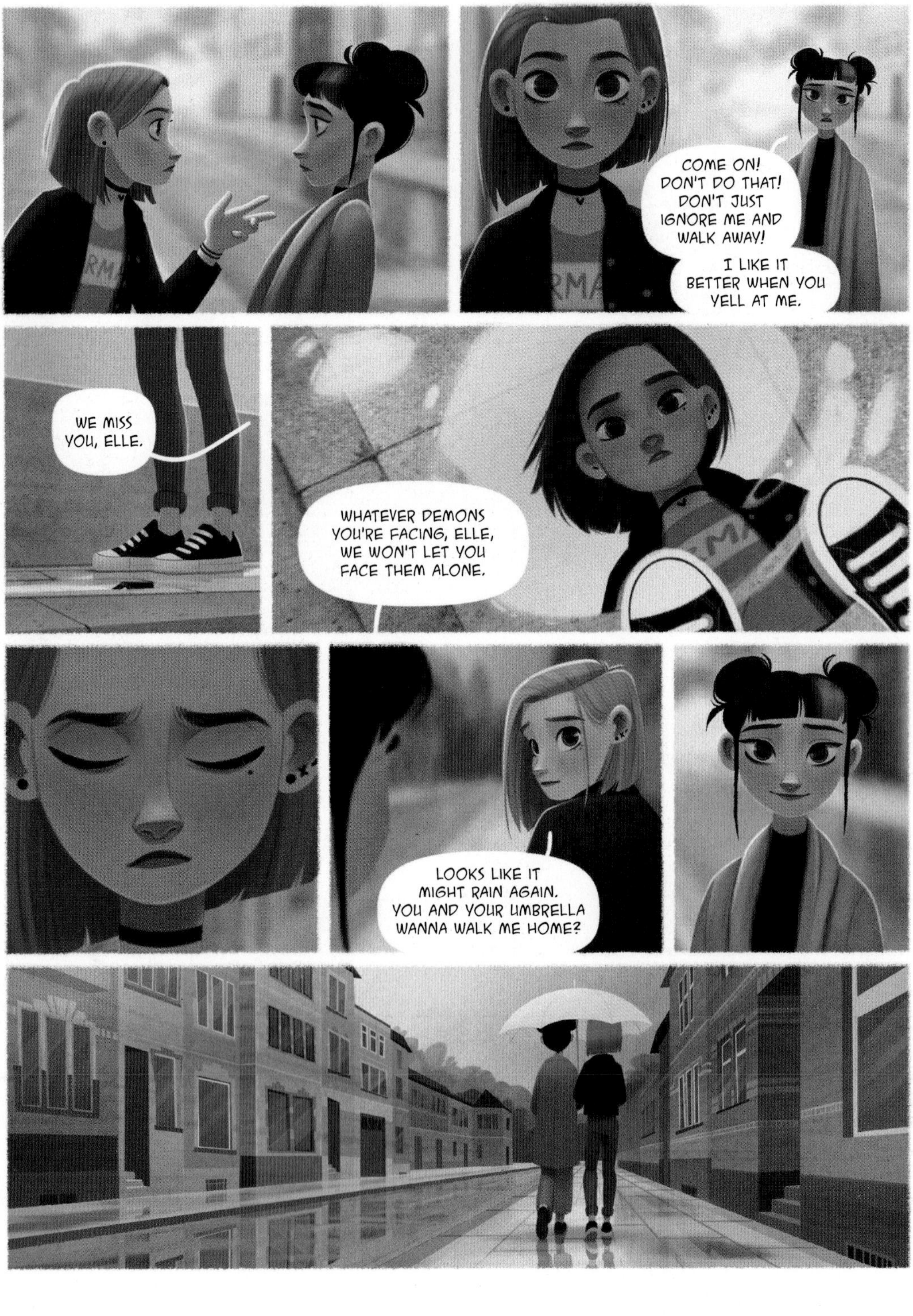
COME ON! DON'T DO THAT! DON'T JUST IGNORE ME AND WALK AWAY!
I LIKE IT BETTER WHEN YOU YELL AT ME.
WE MISS YOU, ELLE.
WHATEVER DEMONS YOU'RE FACING, ELLE, WE WON'T LET YOU FACE THEM ALONE.
LOOKS LIKE IT MIGHT RAIN AGAIN. YOU AND YOUR UMBRELLA WANNA WALK ME HOME?

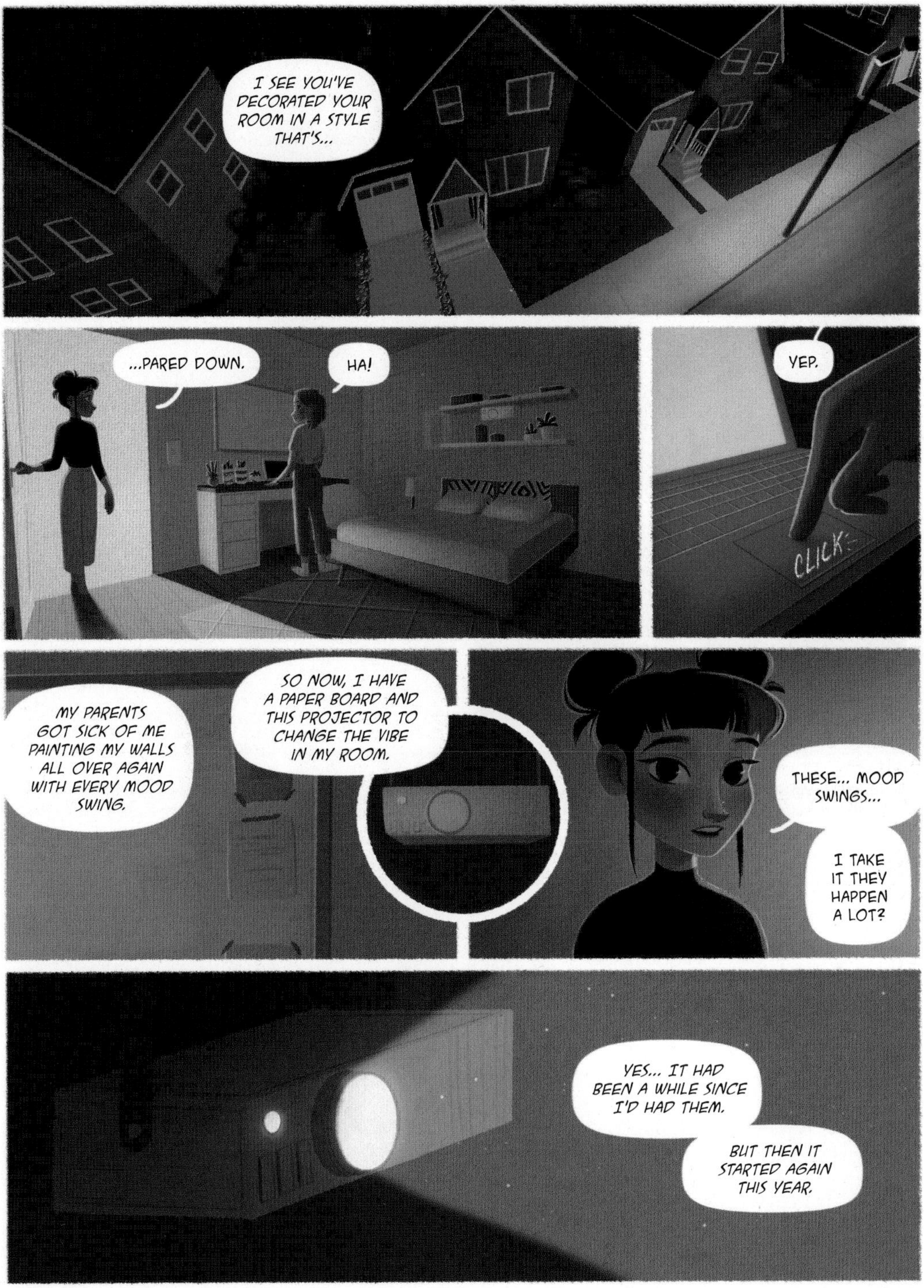

I SEE YOU'VE DECORATED YOUR ROOM IN A STYLE THAT'S...
...PARED DOWN.
HA!
YEP.
CLICK
MY PARENTS GOT SICK OF ME PAINTING MY WALLS ALL OVER AGAIN WITH EVERY MOOD SWING.
SO NOW, I HAVE A PAPER BOARD AND THIS PROJECTOR TO CHANGE THE VIBE IN MY ROOM.
THESE... MOOD SWINGS...
I TAKE IT THEY HAPPEN A LOT?
YES... IT HAD BEEN A WHILE SINCE I'D HAD THEM.
BUT THEN IT STARTED AGAIN THIS YEAR.

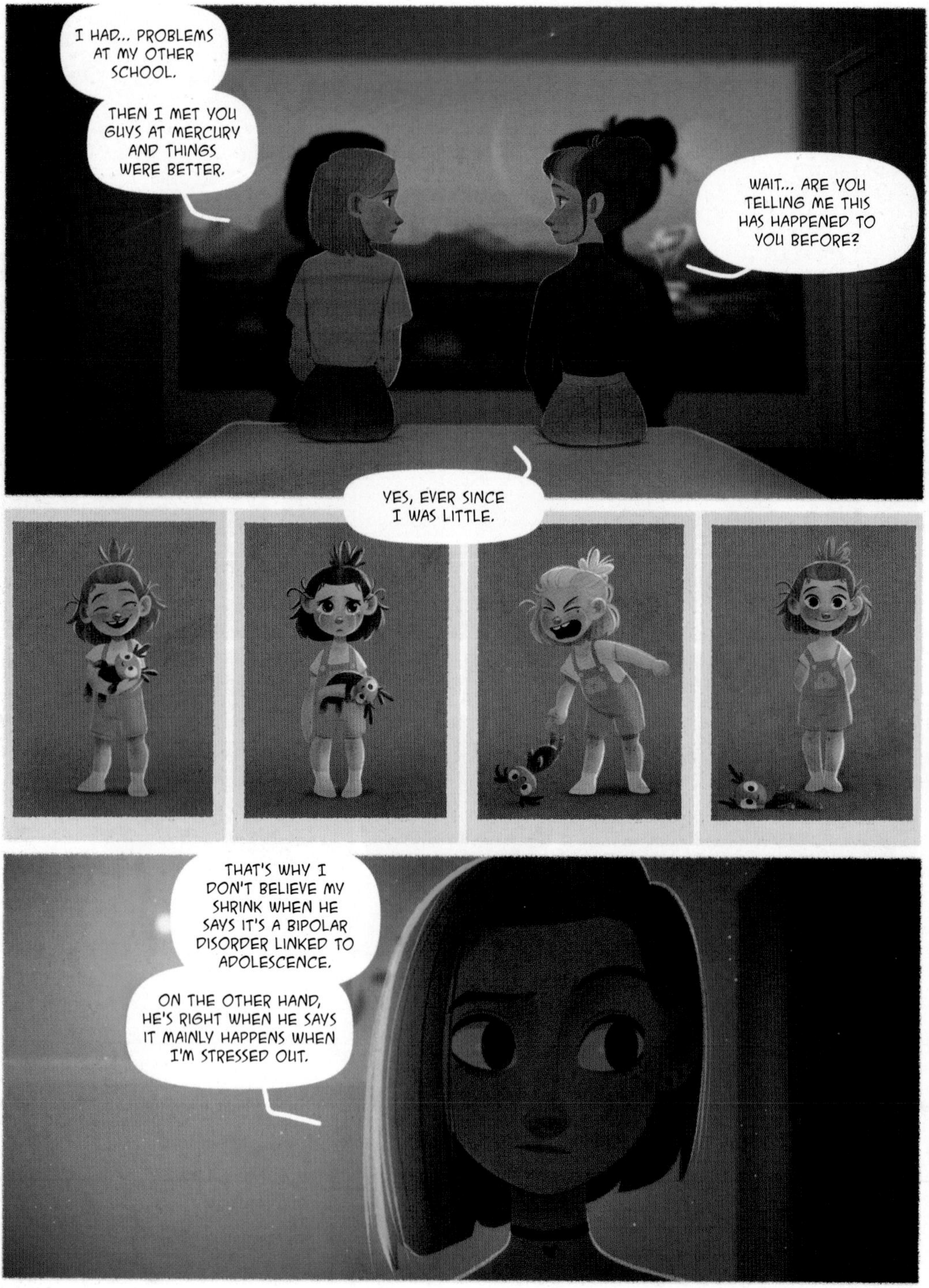
I HAD... PROBLEMS AT MY OTHER SCHOOL.
THEN I MET YOU GUYS AT MERCURY AND THINGS WERE BETTER.
WAIT... ARE YOU TELLING ME THIS HAS HAPPENED TO YOU BEFORE?
YES, EVER SINCE I WAS LITTLE.
THAT'S WHY I DON'T BELIEVE MY SHRINK WHEN HE SAYS IT'S A BIPOLAR DISORDER LINKED TO ADOLESCENCE.
ON THE OTHER HAND, HE'S RIGHT WHEN HE SAYS IT MAINLY HAPPENS WHEN I'M STRESSED OUT.

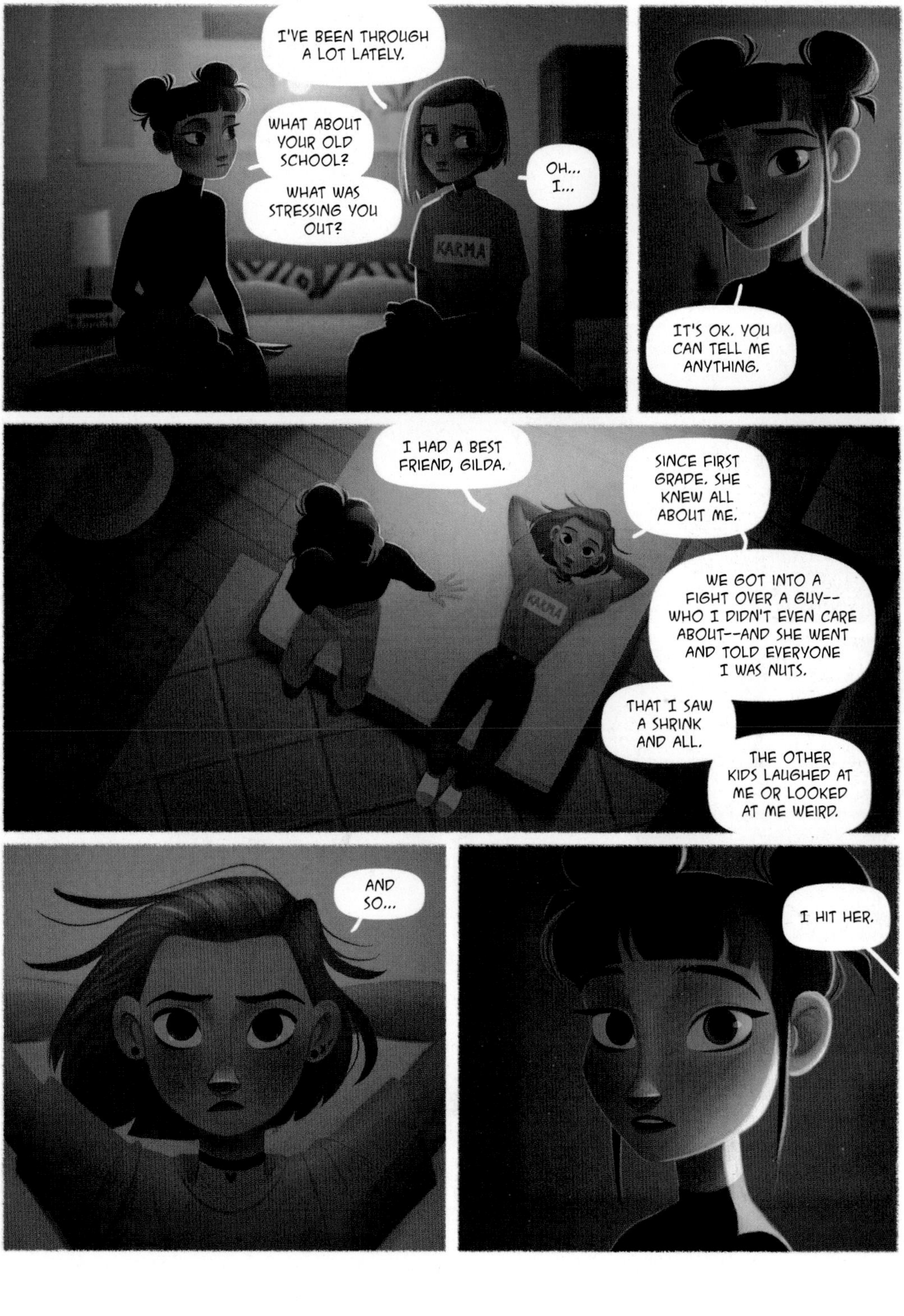

I'VE BEEN THROUGH A LOT LATELY.
WHAT ABOUT YOUR OLD SCHOOL?
WHAT WAS STRESSING YOU OUT?
OH... I...
IT'S OK. YOU CAN TELL ME ANYTHING.
I HAD A BEST FRIEND, GILDA.
SINCE FIRST GRADE. SHE KNEW ALL ABOUT ME.
WE GOT INTO A FIGHT OVER A GUY--WHO I DIDN'T EVEN CARE ABOUT--AND SHE WENT AND TOLD EVERYONE I WAS NUTS.
THAT I SAW A SHRINK AND ALL.
THE OTHER KIDS LAUGHED AT ME OR LOOKED AT ME WEIRD.
AND SO...
I HIT HER.

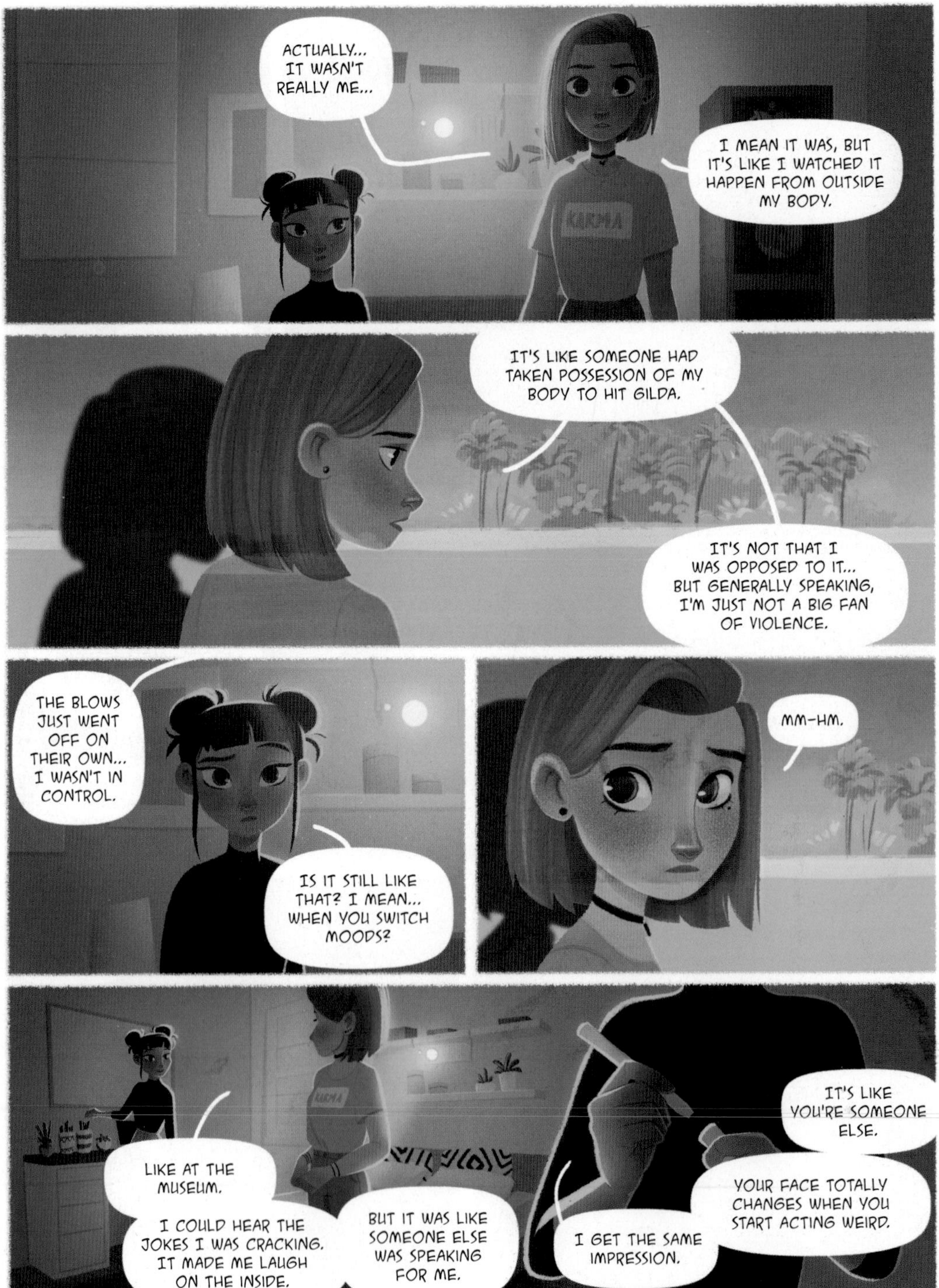
ACTUALLY... IT WASN'T REALLY ME...
I MEAN IT WAS, BUT IT'S LIKE I WATCHED IT HAPPEN FROM OUTSIDE MY BODY.
IT'S LIKE SOMEONE HAD TAKEN POSSESSION OF MY BODY TO HIT GILDA.
IT'S NOT THAT I WAS OPPOSED TO IT... BUT GENERALLY SPEAKING, I'M JUST NOT A BIG FAN OF VIOLENCE.
THE BLOWS JUST WENT OFF ON THEIR OWN... I WASN'T IN CONTROL.
IS IT STILL LIKE THAT? I MEAN... WHEN YOU SWITCH MOODS?
MM-HM.
LIKE AT THE MUSEUM.
I COULD HEAR THE JOKES I WAS CRACKING. IT MADE ME LAUGH ON THE INSIDE.
BUT IT WAS LIKE SOMEONE ELSE WAS SPEAKING FOR ME.
I GET THE SAME IMPRESSION.
IT'S LIKE YOU'RE SOMEONE ELSE.
YOUR FACE TOTALLY CHANGES WHEN YOU START ACTING WEIRD.

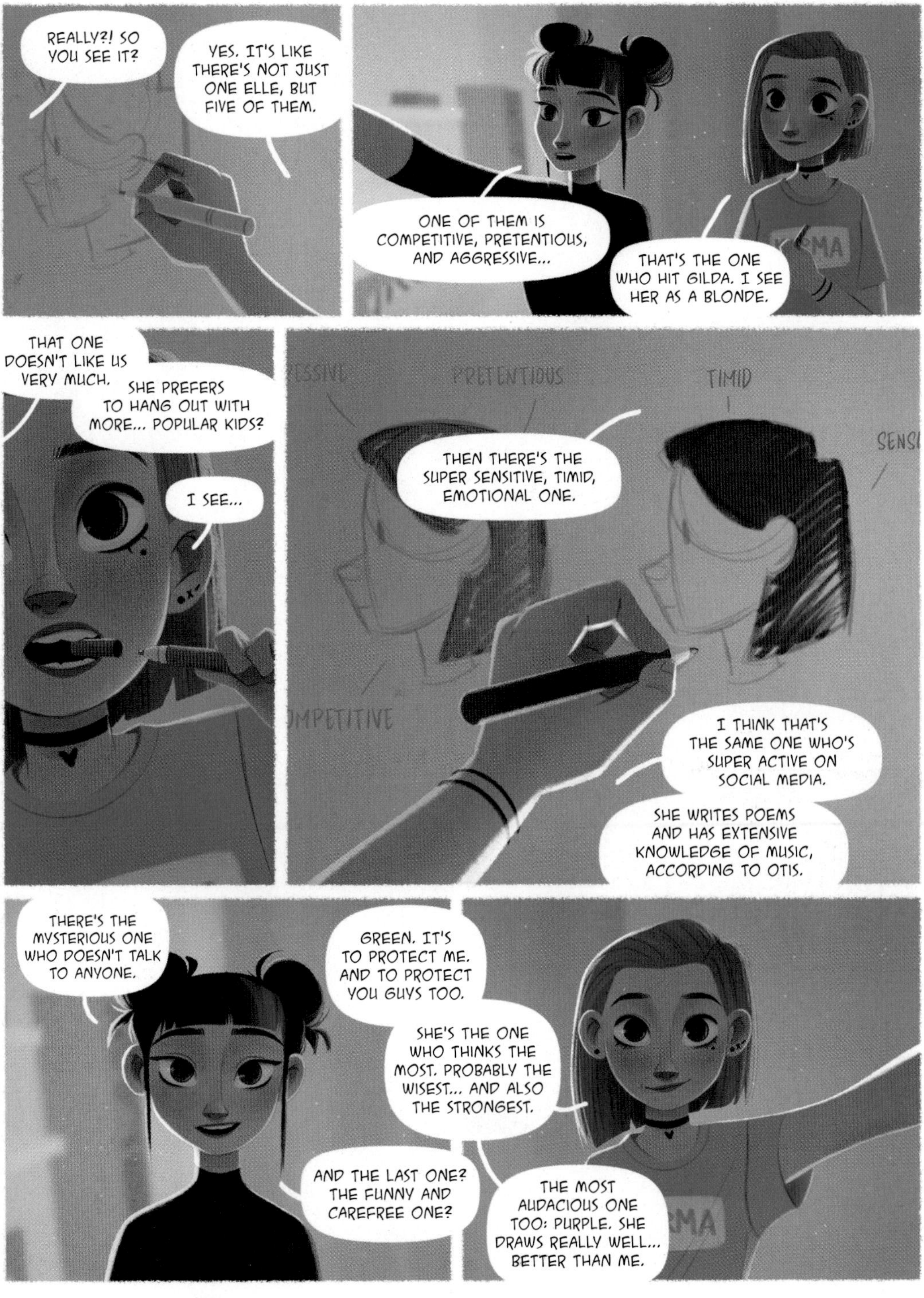

REALLY?! SO YOU SEE IT?
YES. IT'S LIKE THERE'S NOT JUST ONE ELLE, BUT FIVE OF THEM.
ONE OF THEM IS COMPETITIVE, PRETENTIOUS, AND AGGRESSIVE...
THAT'S THE ONE WHO HIT GILDA. I SEE HER AS A BLONDE.
THAT ONE DOESN'T LIKE US VERY MUCH.
SHE PREFERS TO HANG OUT WITH MORE... POPULAR KIDS?
I SEE...
PRETENTIOUS
TIMID
THEN THERE'S THE SUPER SENSITIVE, TIMID, EMOTIONAL ONE.
I THINK THAT'S THE SAME ONE WHO'S SUPER ACTIVE ON SOCIAL MEDIA.
SHE WRITES POEMS AND HAS EXTENSIVE KNOWLEDGE OF MUSIC, ACCORDING TO OTIS.
THERE'S THE MYSTERIOUS ONE WHO DOESN'T TALK TO ANYONE.
GREEN. IT'S TO PROTECT ME. AND TO PROTECT YOU GUYS TOO.
SHE'S THE ONE WHO THINKS THE MOST. PROBABLY THE WISEST... AND ALSO THE STRONGEST.
AND THE LAST ONE? THE FUNNY AND CAREFREE ONE?
THE MOST AUDACIOUS ONE TOO: PURPLE. SHE DRAWS REALLY WELL... BETTER THAN ME.

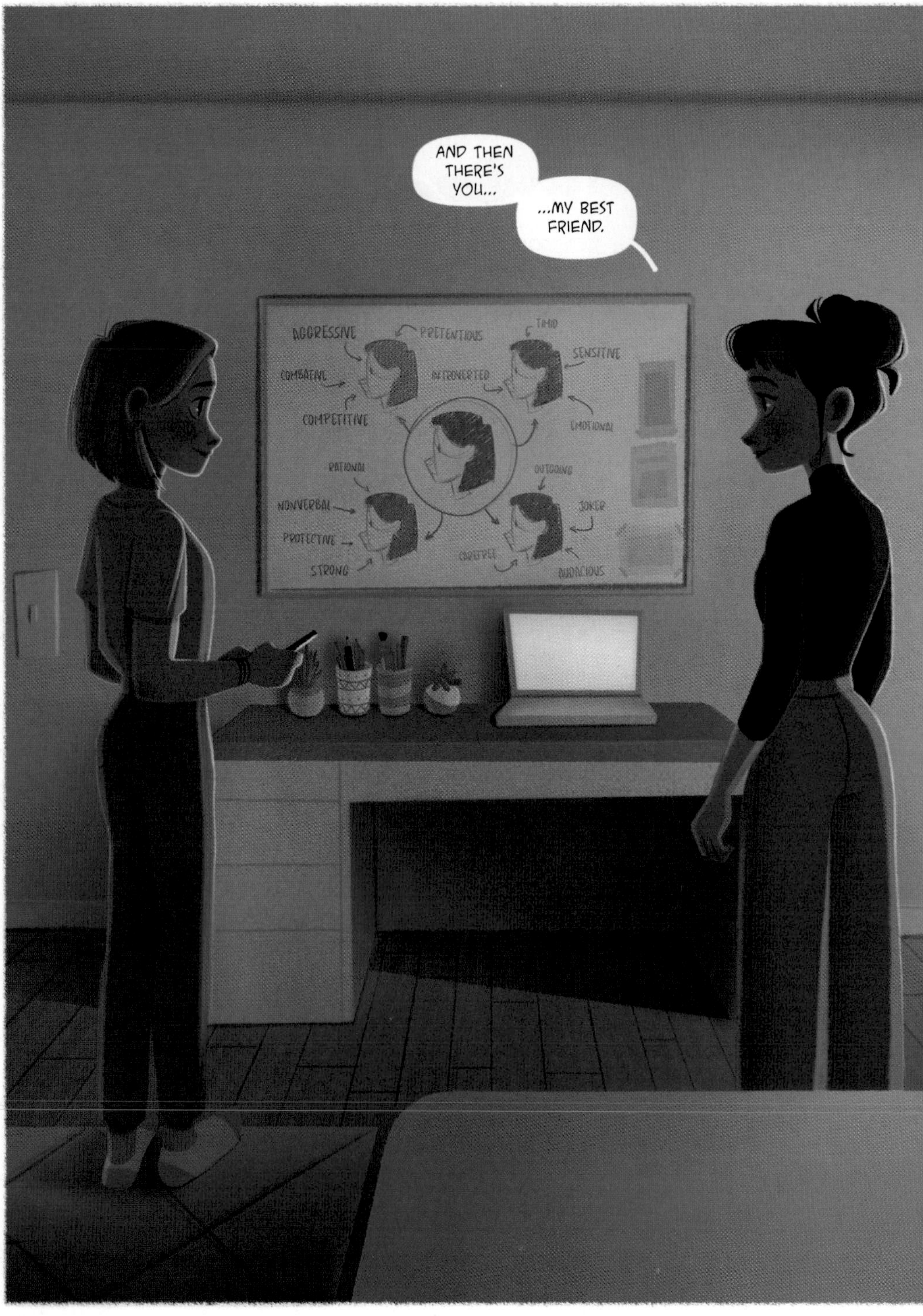
AND THEN THERE'S YOU...
...MY BEST FRIEND.
AGGRESSIVE
PRETENTIOUS
COMBATIVE
COMPETITIVE
TIMID
SENSITIVE
INTROVERTED
EMOTIONAL
RATIONAL
NONVERBAL
PROTECTIVE
STRONG
OUTGOING
JOKER
CAREFREE
AUDACIOUS

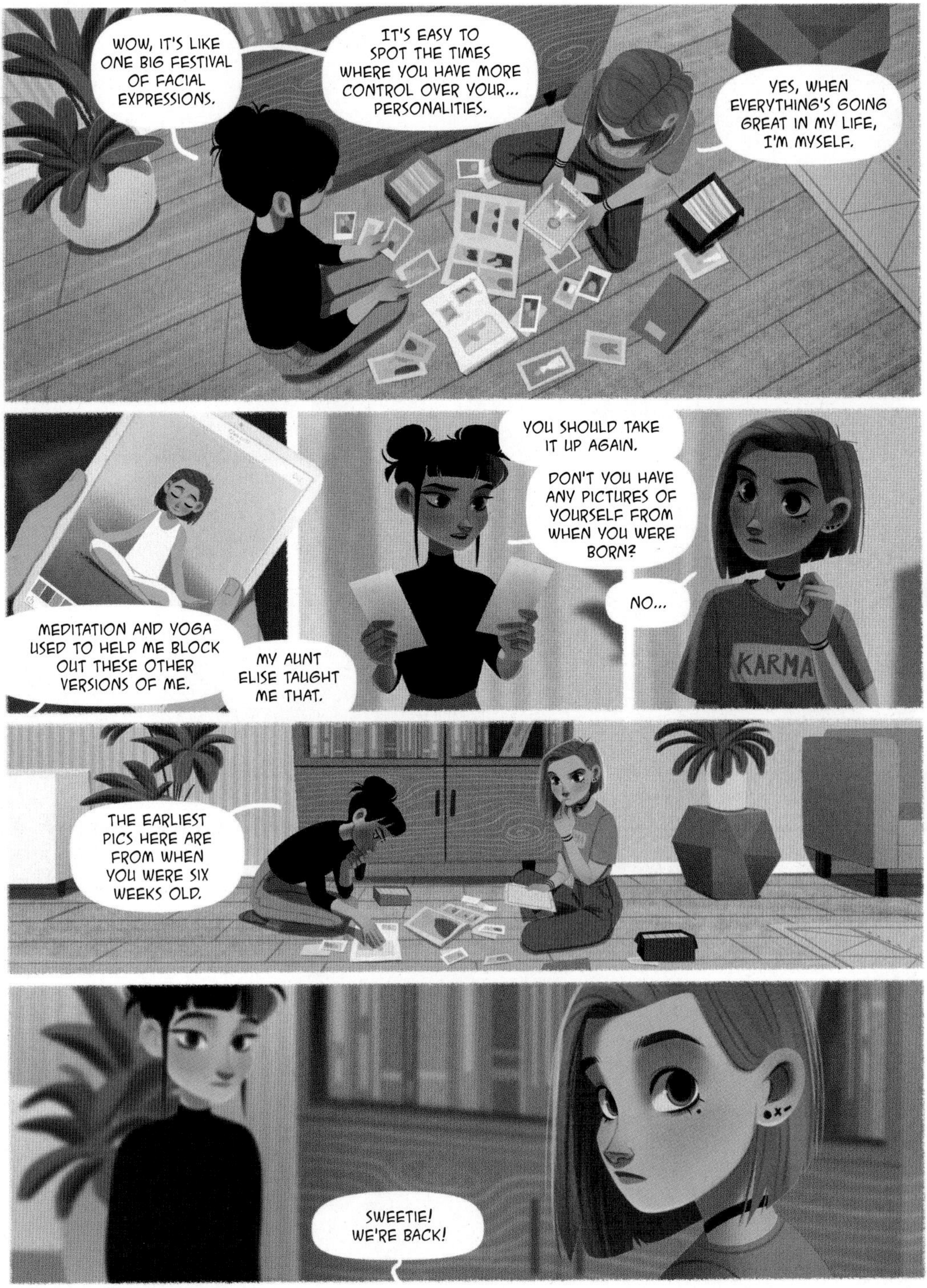

WOW, IT'S LIKE ONE BIG FESTIVAL OF FACIAL EXPRESSIONS.
IT'S EASY TO SPOT THE TIMES WHERE YOU HAVE MORE CONTROL OVER YOUR... PERSONALITIES.
YES, WHEN EVERYTHING'S GOING GREAT IN MY LIFE, I'M MYSELF.
MEDITATION AND YOGA USED TO HELP ME BLOCK OUT THESE OTHER VERSIONS OF ME.
MY AUNT ELISE TAUGHT ME THAT.
YOU SHOULD TAKE IT UP AGAIN.
DON'T YOU HAVE ANY PICTURES OF YOURSELF FROM WHEN YOU WERE BORN?
NO...
KARMA
THE EARLIEST PICS HERE ARE FROM WHEN YOU WERE SIX WEEKS OLD.
SWEETIE! WE'RE BACK!

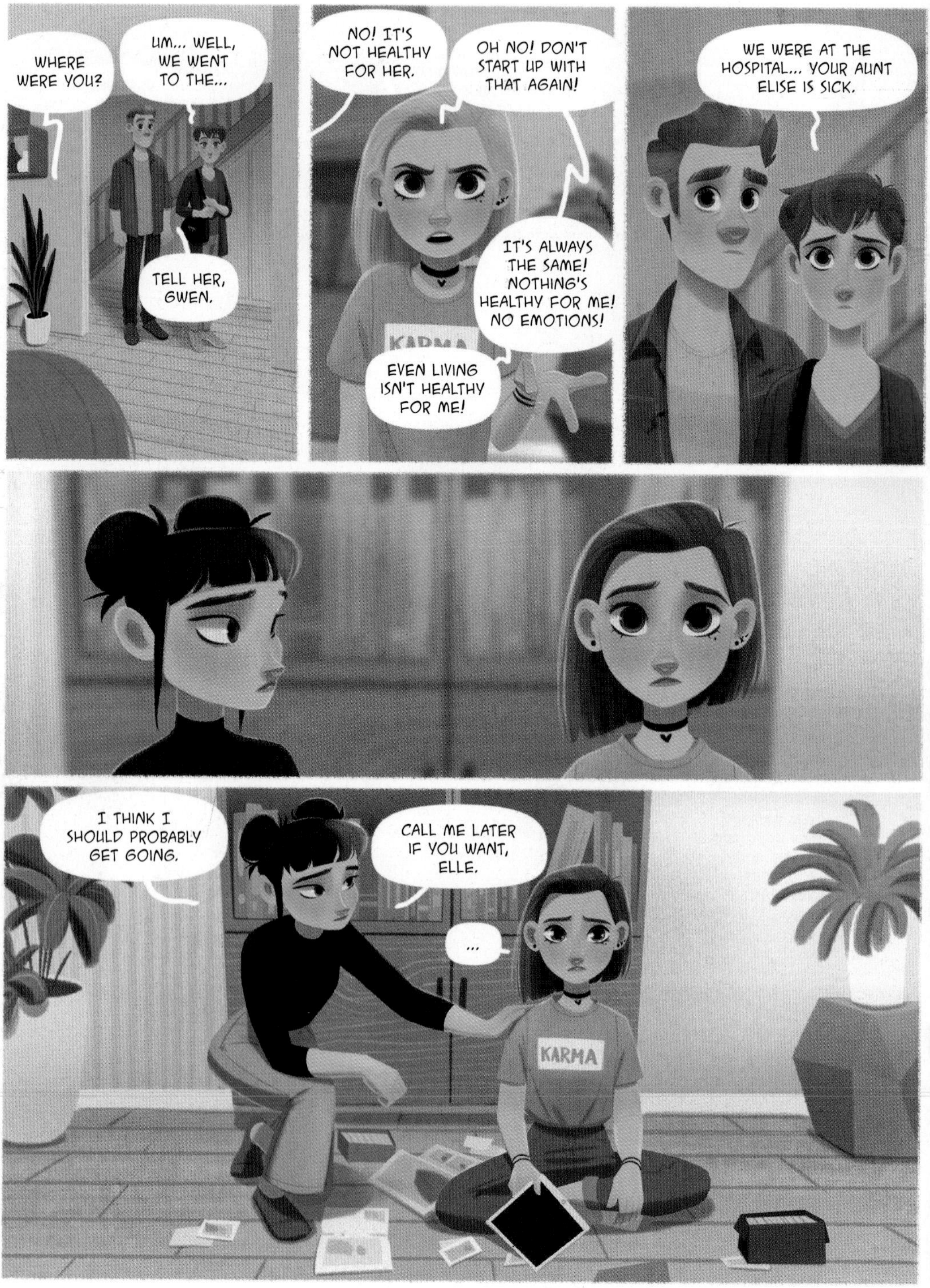
WHERE WERE YOU?
UM... WELL, WE WENT TO THE...
TELL HER, GWEN.
NO! IT'S NOT HEALTHY FOR HER.
OH NO! DON'T START UP WITH THAT AGAIN!
IT'S ALWAYS THE SAME! NOTHING'S HEALTHY FOR ME! NO EMOTIONS!
EVEN LIVING ISN'T HEALTHY FOR ME!
KARMA
WE WERE AT THE HOSPITAL... YOUR AUNT ELISE IS SICK.
I THINK I SHOULD PROBABLY GET GOING.
CALL ME LATER IF YOU WANT, ELLE.
...
KARMA

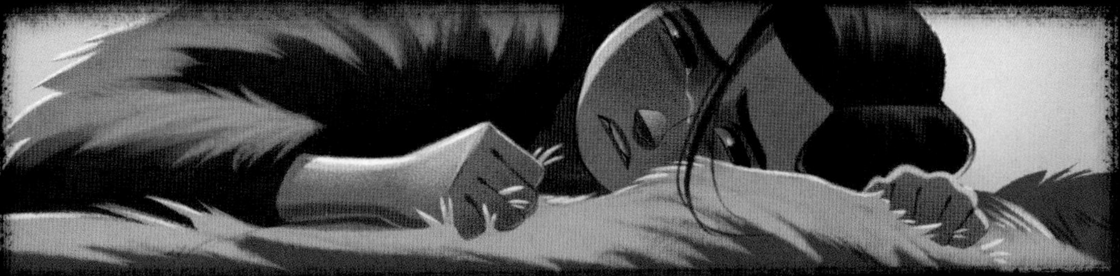

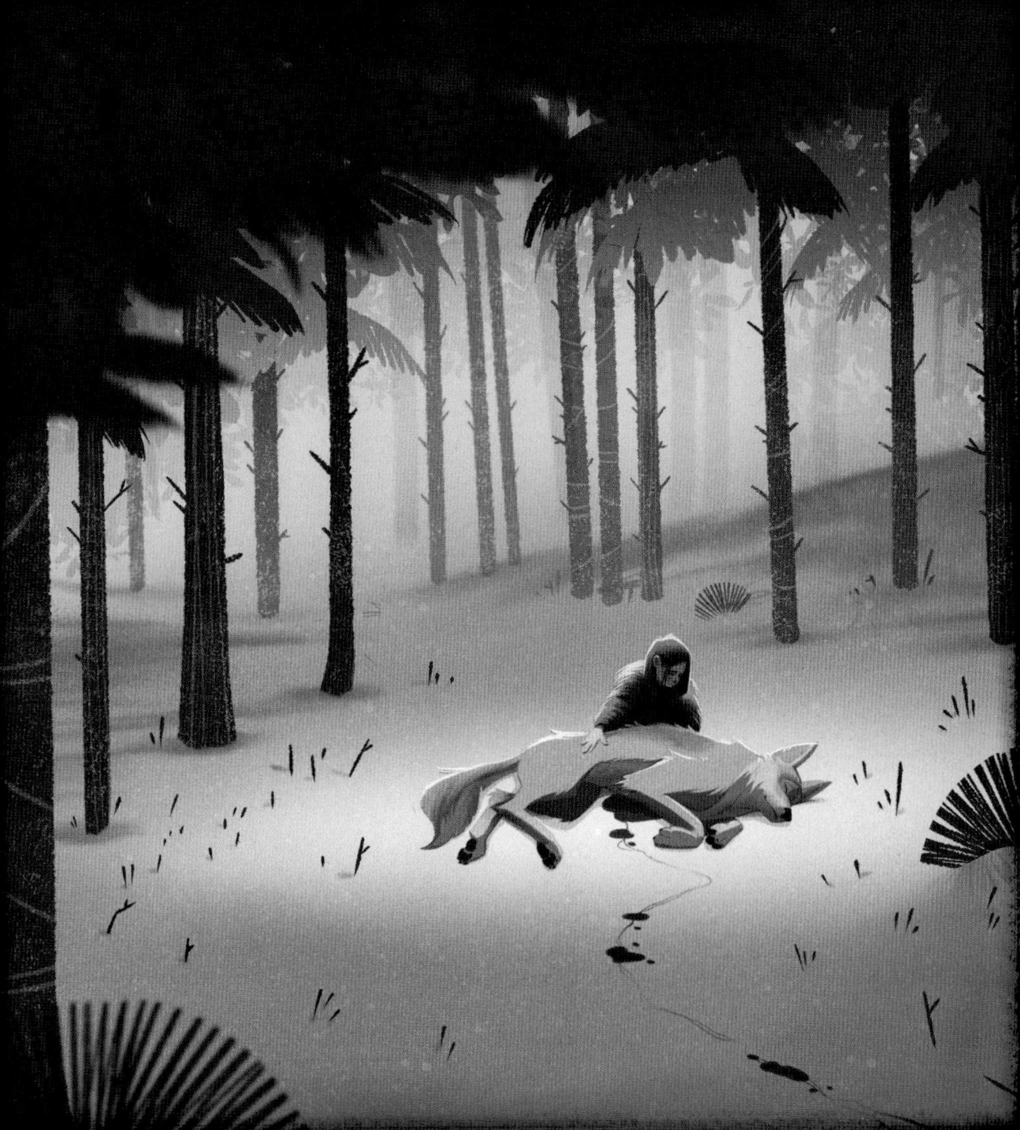

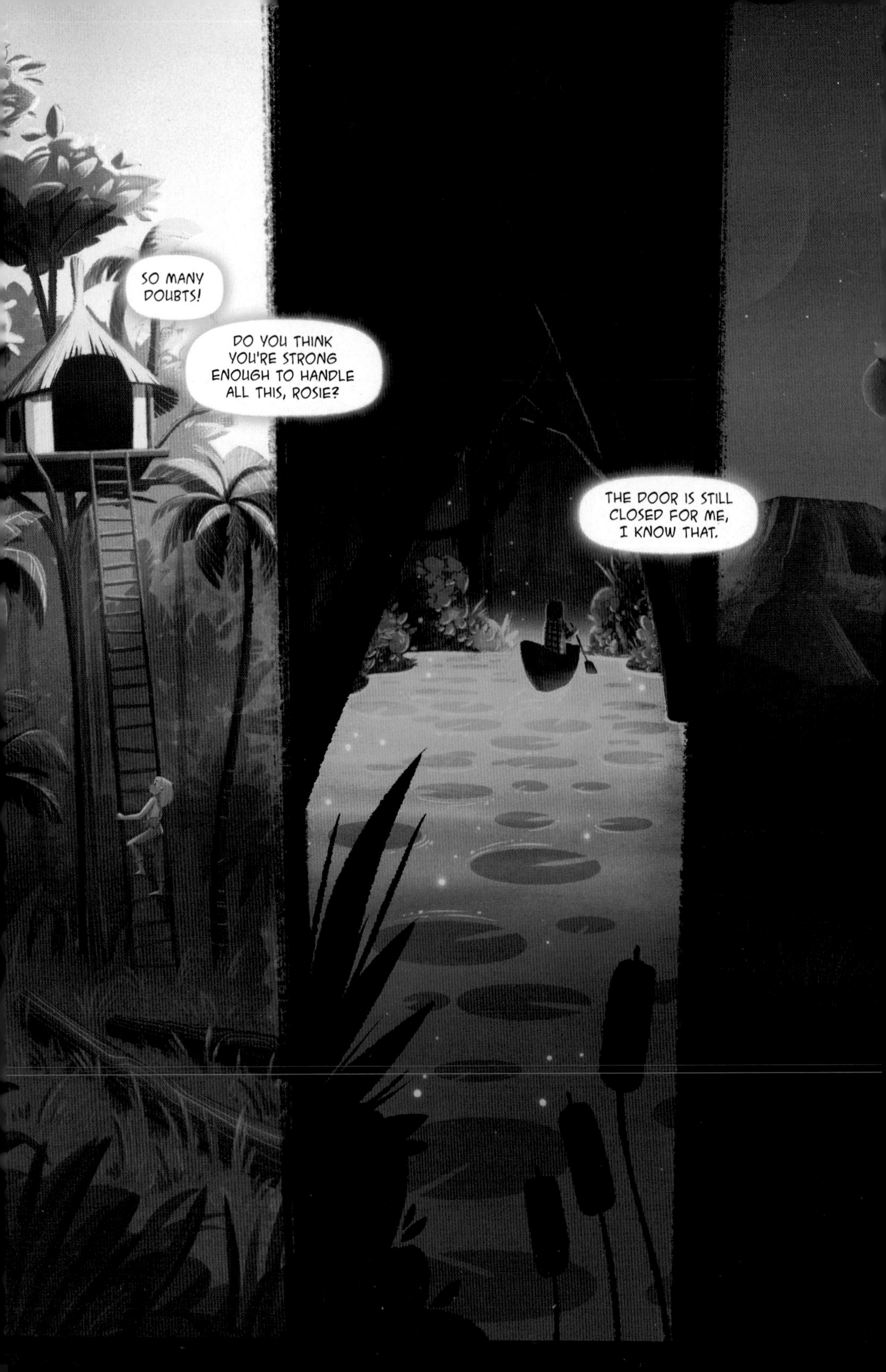
SO MANY DOUBTS!
DO YOU THINK YOU'RE STRONG ENOUGH TO HANDLE ALL THIS, ROSIE?
THE DOOR IS STILL CLOSED FOR ME, I KNOW THAT.

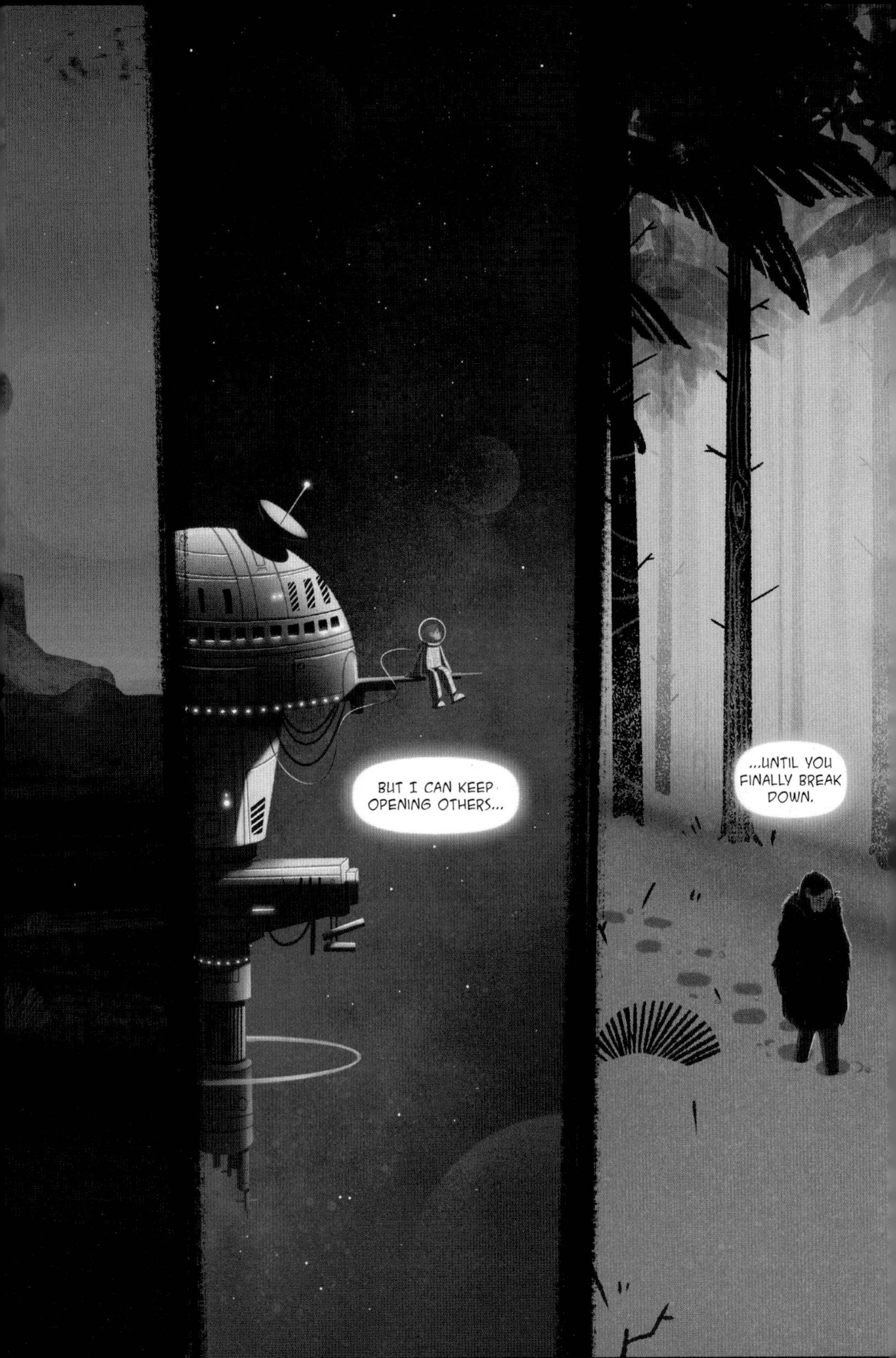
BUT I CAN KEEP OPENING OTHERS...
...UNTIL YOU FINALLY BREAK DOWN.

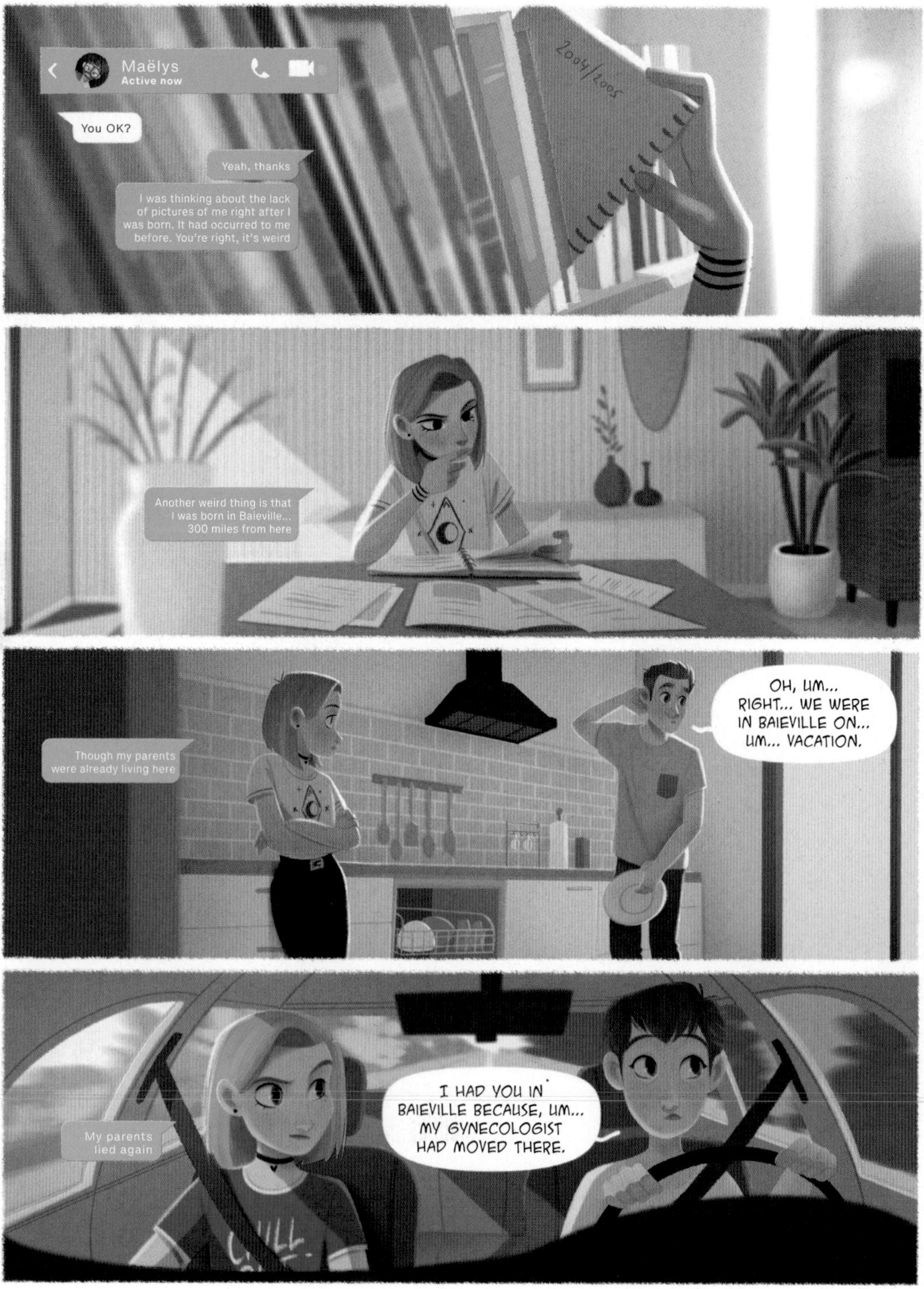

Maëlys
Active now
You OK?
Yeah, thanks
I was thinking about the lack of pictures of me right after I was born. It had occurred to me before. You're right, it's weird
2004/2005
Another weird thing is that I was born in Baieville... 300 miles from here
Though my parents were already living here
OH, UM... RIGHT... WE WERE IN BAIEVILLE ON... UM... VACATION.
My parents lied again
I HAD YOU IN BAIEVILLE BECAUSE, UM... MY GYNECOLOGIST HAD MOVED THERE.

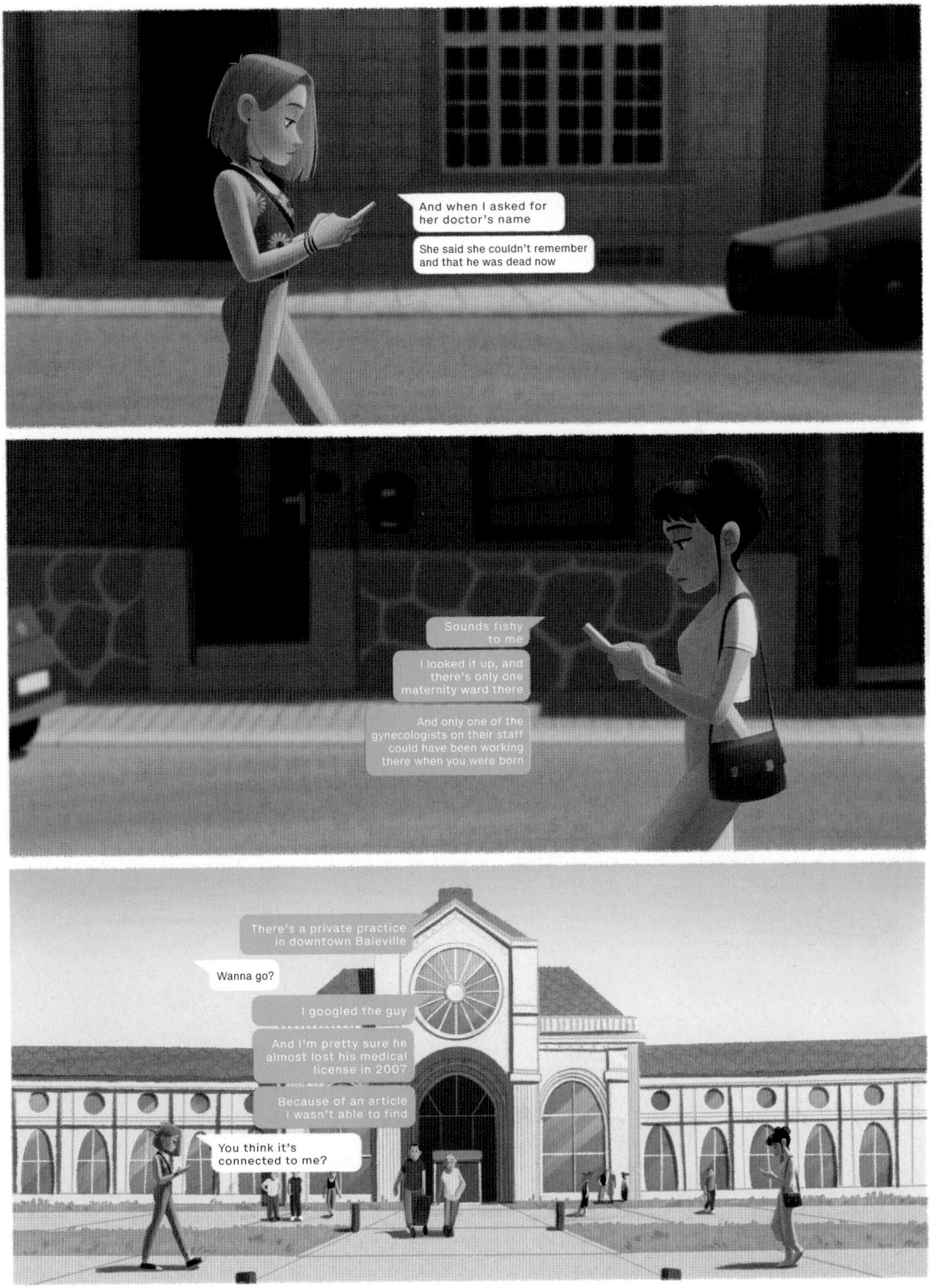
And when I asked for her doctor's name
She said she couldn't remember and that he was dead now
Sounds fishy to me
I looked it up, and there's only one maternity ward there
And only one of the gynecologists on their staff could have been working there when you were born
There's a private practice in downtown Baieville
Wanna go?
I googled the guy
And I'm pretty sure he almost lost his medical license in 2007
Because of an article I wasn't able to find
You think it's connected to me?

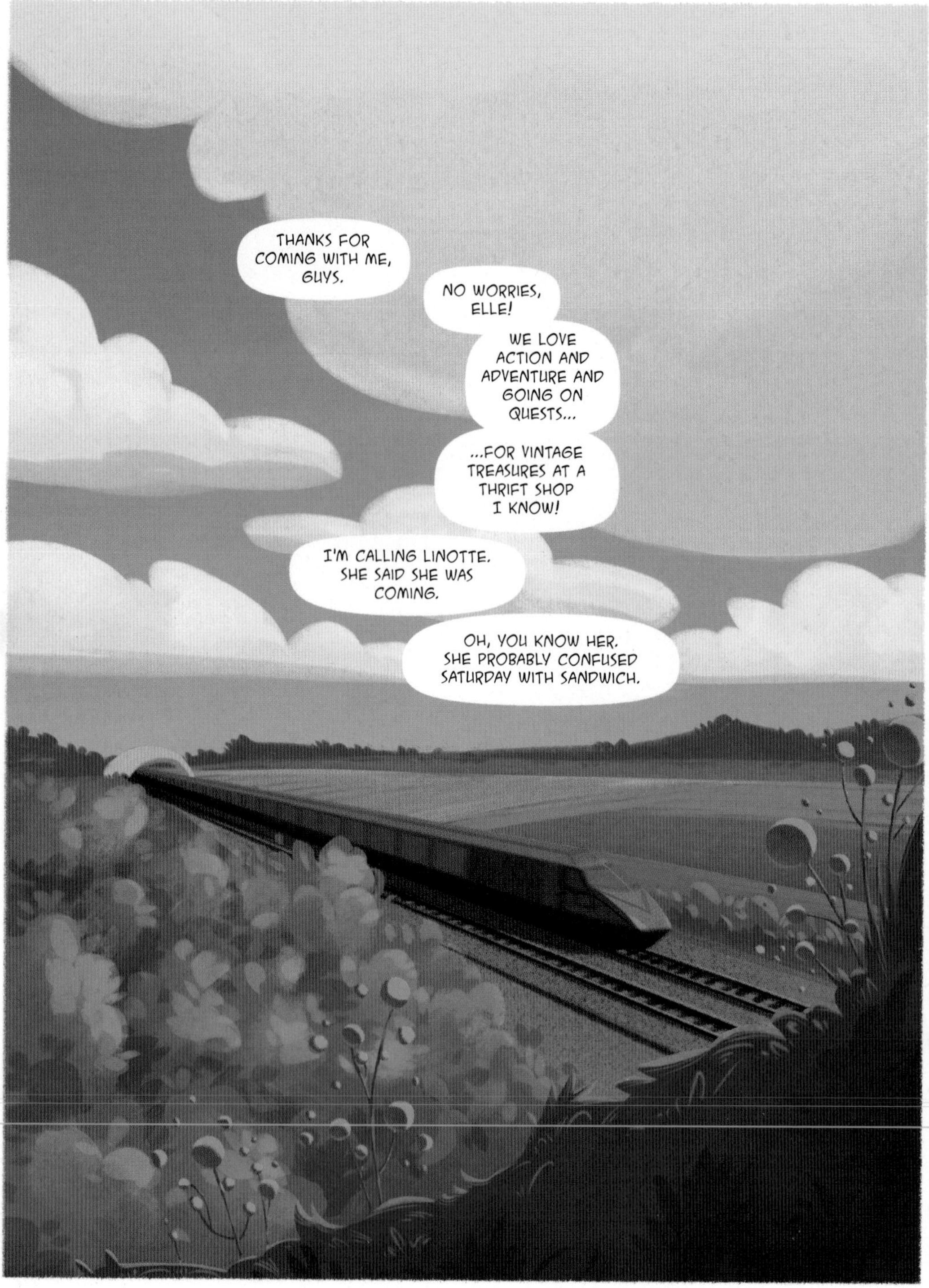
THANKS FOR COMING WITH ME, GUYS.
NO WORRIES, ELLE!
WE LOVE ACTION AND ADVENTURE AND GOING ON QUESTS...
...FOR VINTAGE TREASURES AT A THRIFT SHOP I KNOW!
I'M CALLING LINOTTE. SHE SAID SHE WAS COMING.
OH, YOU KNOW HER. SHE PROBABLY CONFUSED SATURDAY WITH SANDWICH.

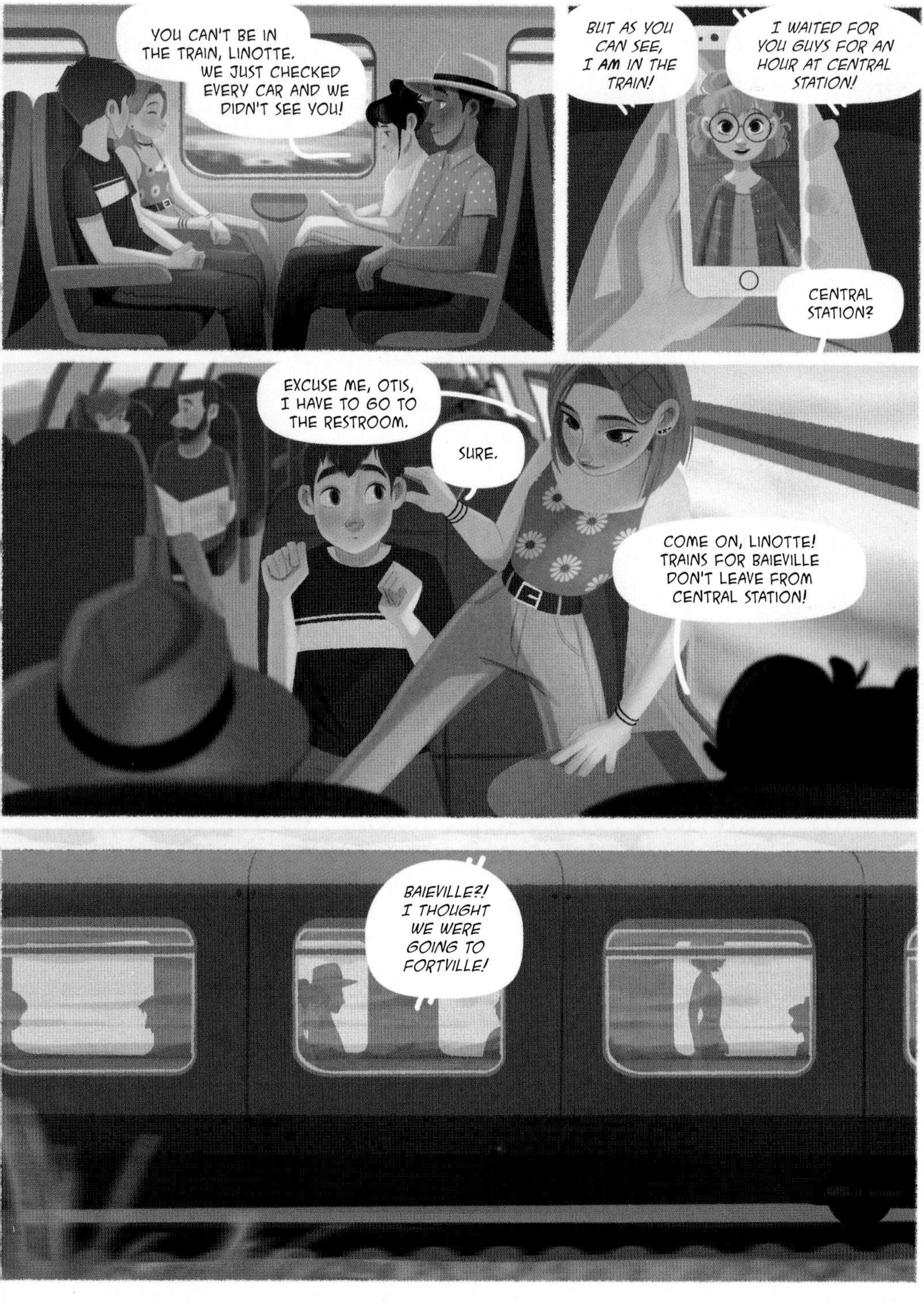
YOU CAN'T BE IN THE TRAIN, LINOTTE. WE JUST CHECKED EVERY CAR AND WE DIDN'T SEE YOU!
BUT AS YOU CAN SEE, I AM IN THE TRAIN!
I WAITED FOR YOU GUYS FOR AN HOUR AT CENTRAL STATION!
CENTRAL STATION?
EXCUSE ME, OTIS, I HAVE TO GO TO THE RESTROOM.
SURE.
COME ON, LINOTTE! TRAINS FOR BAIEVILLE DON'T LEAVE FROM CENTRAL STATION!
BAIEVILLE?! I THOUGHT WE WERE GOING TO FORTVILLE!

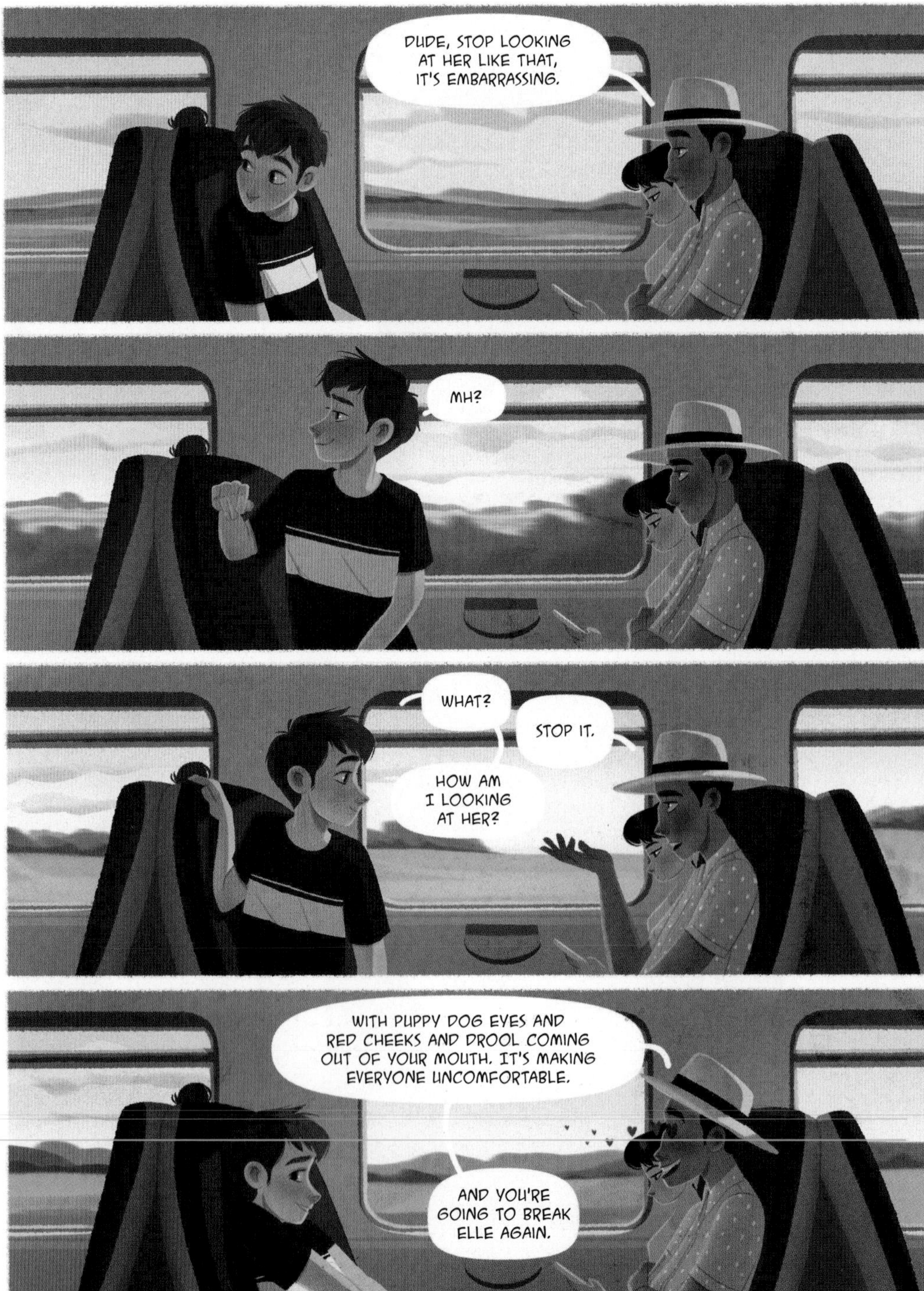
DUDE, STOP LOOKING AT HER LIKE THAT, IT'S EMBARRASSING.
MH?
WHAT?
STOP IT.
HOW AM I LOOKING AT HER?
WITH PUPPY DOG EYES AND RED CHEEKS AND DROOL COMING OUT OF YOUR MOUTH. IT'S MAKING EVERYONE UNCOMFORTABLE.
AND YOU'RE GOING TO BREAK ELLE AGAIN.

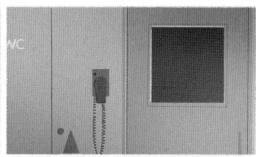

"BEEP" LADIES AND GENTLEMEN, THIS IS YOUR CONDUCTOR SPEAKING. WE ARE CURRENTLY LOOKING FOR A HOOLIGAN WEARING A BLUE AND WHITE T-SHIRT.

HE IS WANTED FOR A VICIOUS MANDOLIN ATTACK, WHERE HE SERENADED ONLOOKERS WITH COVER SONGS BEFORE UPLOADING THE VIDEO...

...FOR HIS SEVEN FOLLOWERS. IF YOU SEE HIM, PLEASE...

...ALERT US AT ONCE.

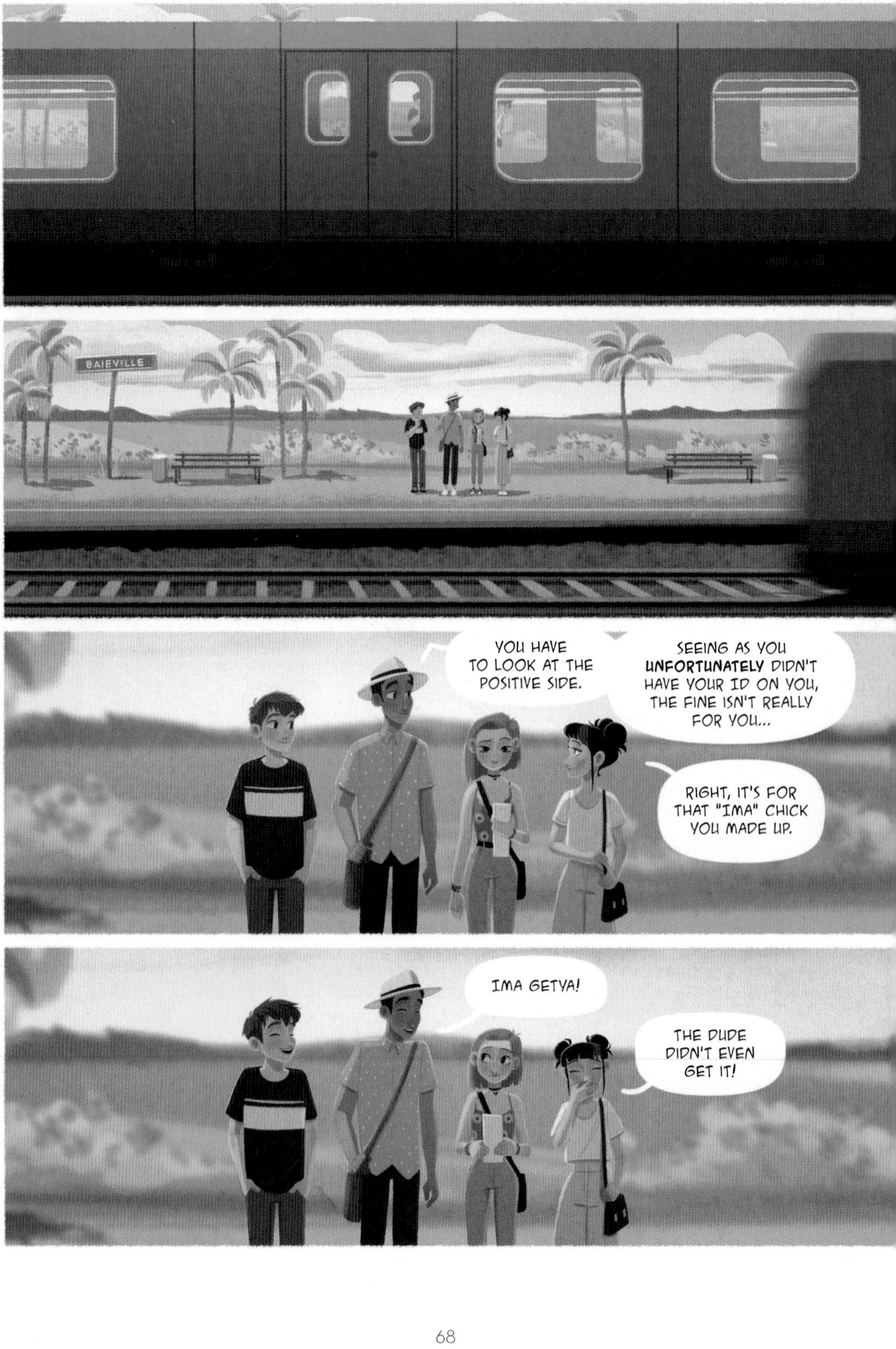
BAIEVILLE
YOU HAVE TO LOOK AT THE POSITIVE SIDE.
SEEING AS YOU **UNFORTUNATELY** DIDN'T HAVE YOUR ID ON YOU, THE FINE ISN'T REALLY FOR YOU...
RIGHT, IT'S FOR THAT "IMA" CHICK YOU MADE UP.
IMA GETYA!
THE DUDE DIDN'T EVEN GET IT!

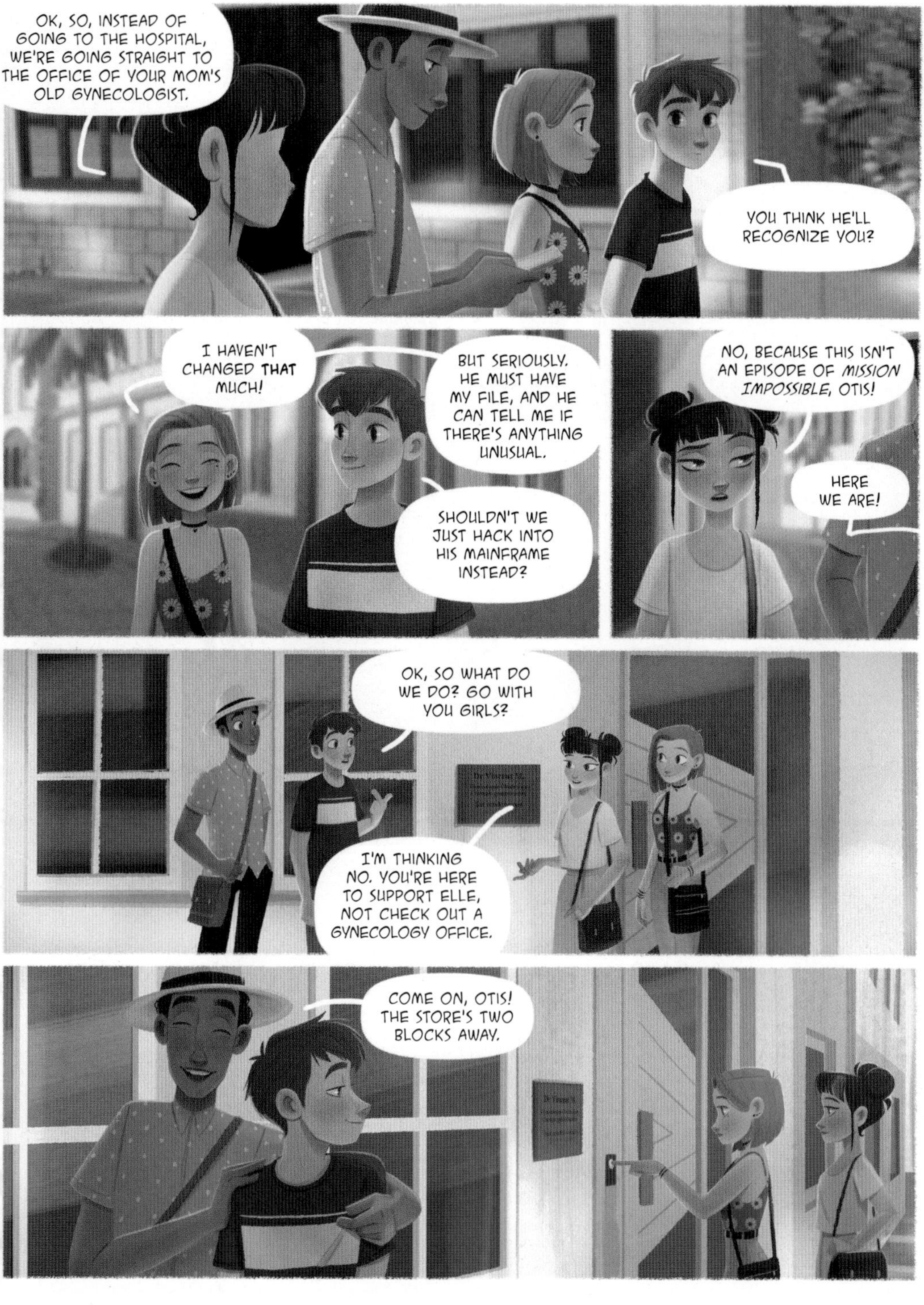
OK, SO, INSTEAD OF GOING TO THE HOSPITAL, WE'RE GOING STRAIGHT TO THE OFFICE OF YOUR MOM'S OLD GYNECOLOGIST.
YOU THINK HE'LL RECOGNIZE YOU?
I HAVEN'T CHANGED **THAT** MUCH!
BUT SERIOUSLY. HE MUST HAVE MY FILE, AND HE CAN TELL ME IF THERE'S ANYTHING UNUSUAL.
SHOULDN'T WE JUST HACK INTO HIS MAINFRAME INSTEAD?
NO, BECAUSE THIS ISN'T AN EPISODE OF *MISSION IMPOSSIBLE*, OTIS!
HERE WE ARE!
OK, SO WHAT DO WE DO? GO WITH YOU GIRLS?
I'M THINKING NO. YOU'RE HERE TO SUPPORT ELLE, NOT CHECK OUT A GYNECOLOGY OFFICE.
COME ON, OTIS! THE STORE'S TWO BLOCKS AWAY.

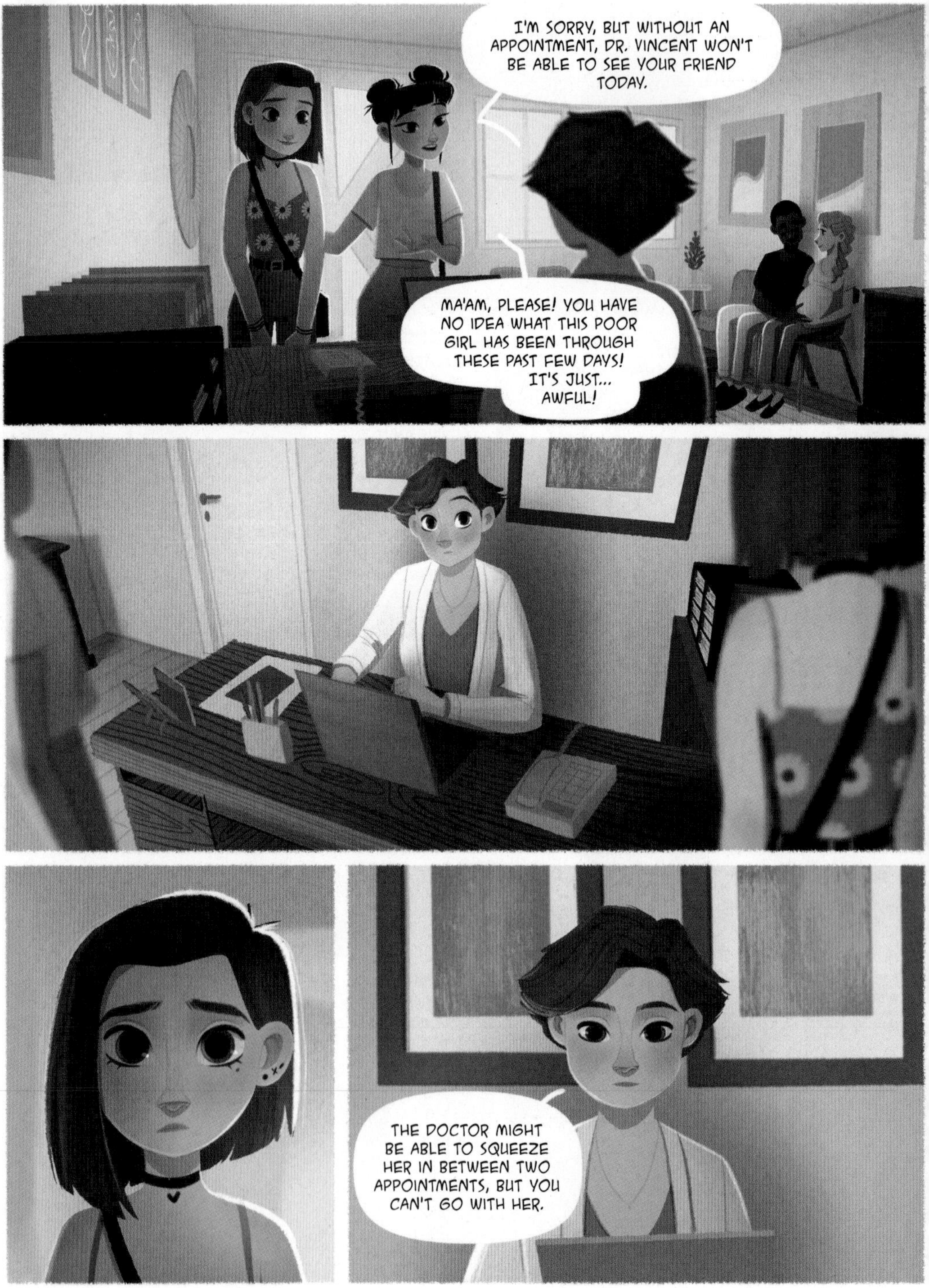
I'M SORRY, BUT WITHOUT AN APPOINTMENT, DR. VINCENT WON'T BE ABLE TO SEE YOUR FRIEND TODAY.
MA'AM, PLEASE! YOU HAVE NO IDEA WHAT THIS POOR GIRL HAS BEEN THROUGH THESE PAST FEW DAYS! IT'S JUST... AWFUL!
THE DOCTOR MIGHT BE ABLE TO SQUEEZE HER IN BETWEEN TWO APPOINTMENTS, BUT YOU CAN'T GO WITH HER.

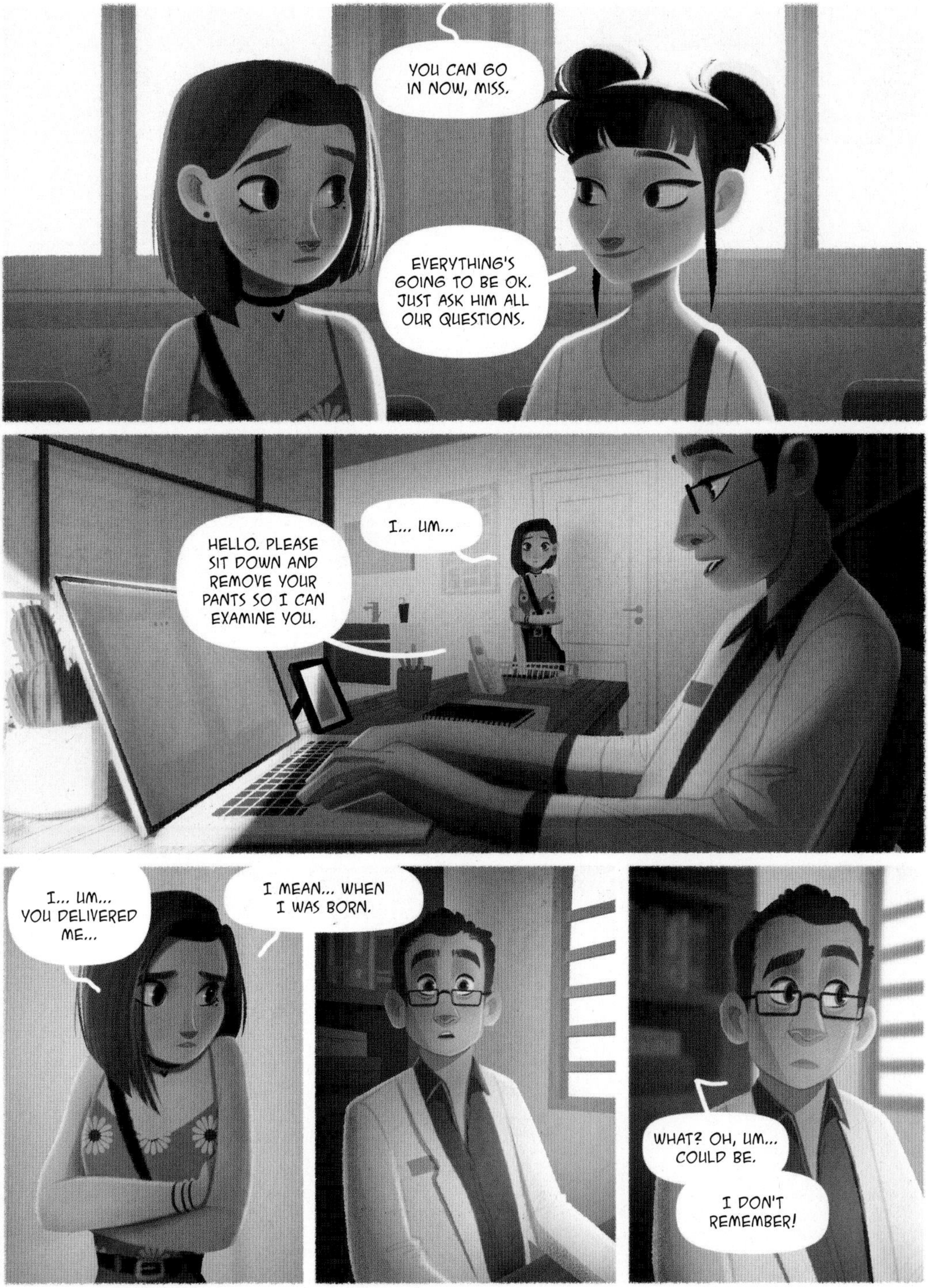
YOU CAN GO IN NOW, MISS.
EVERYTHING'S GOING TO BE OK. JUST ASK HIM ALL OUR QUESTIONS.
HELLO. PLEASE SIT DOWN AND REMOVE YOUR PANTS SO I CAN EXAMINE YOU.
I... UM...
I... UM... YOU DELIVERED ME...
I MEAN... WHEN I WAS BORN.
WHAT? OH, UM... COULD BE.
I DON'T REMEMBER!

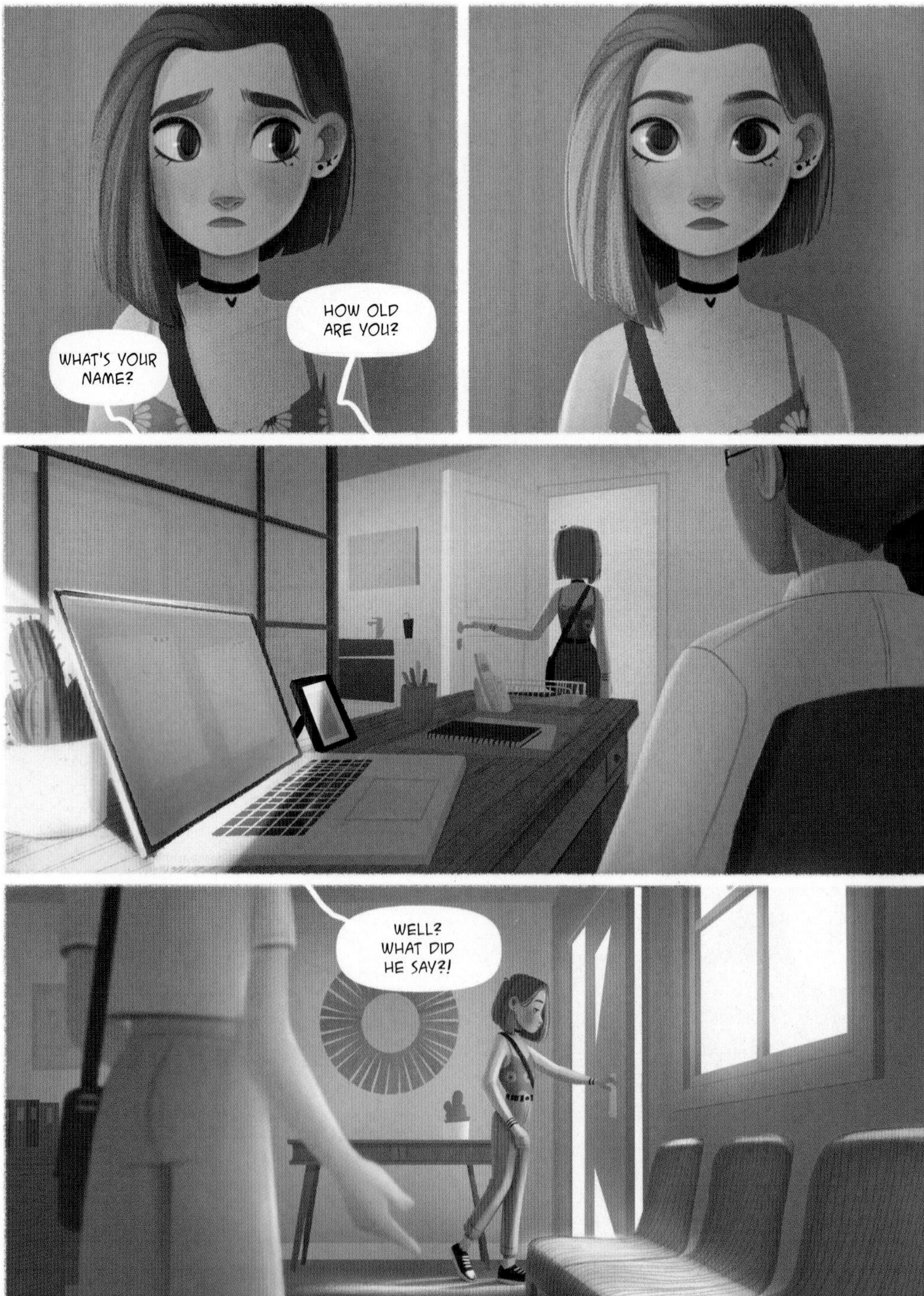
WHAT'S YOUR NAME?
HOW OLD ARE YOU?
WELL? WHAT DID HE SAY?!

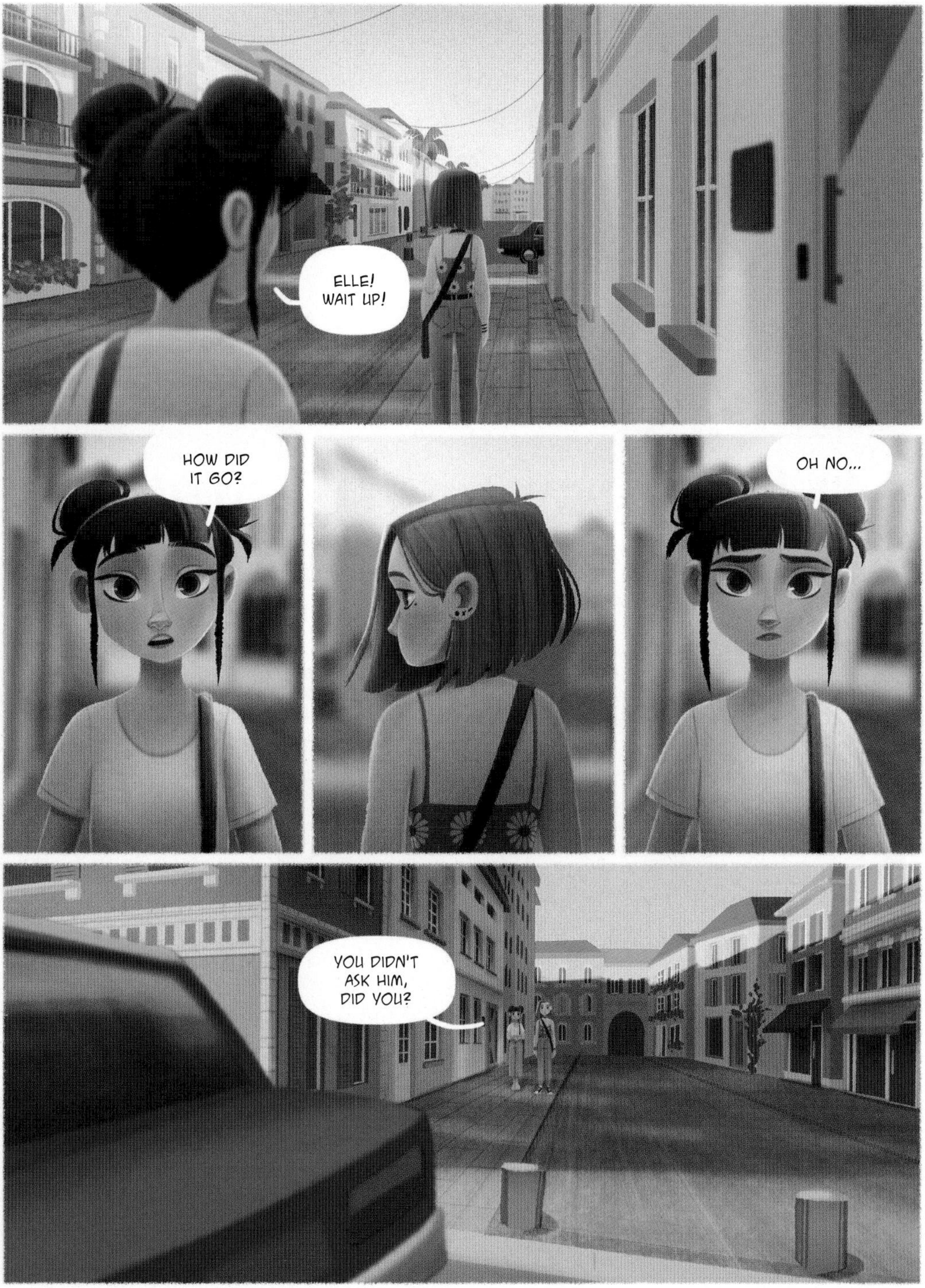
ELLE! WAIT UP!
HOW DID IT GO?
OH NO...
YOU DIDN'T ASK HIM, DID YOU?

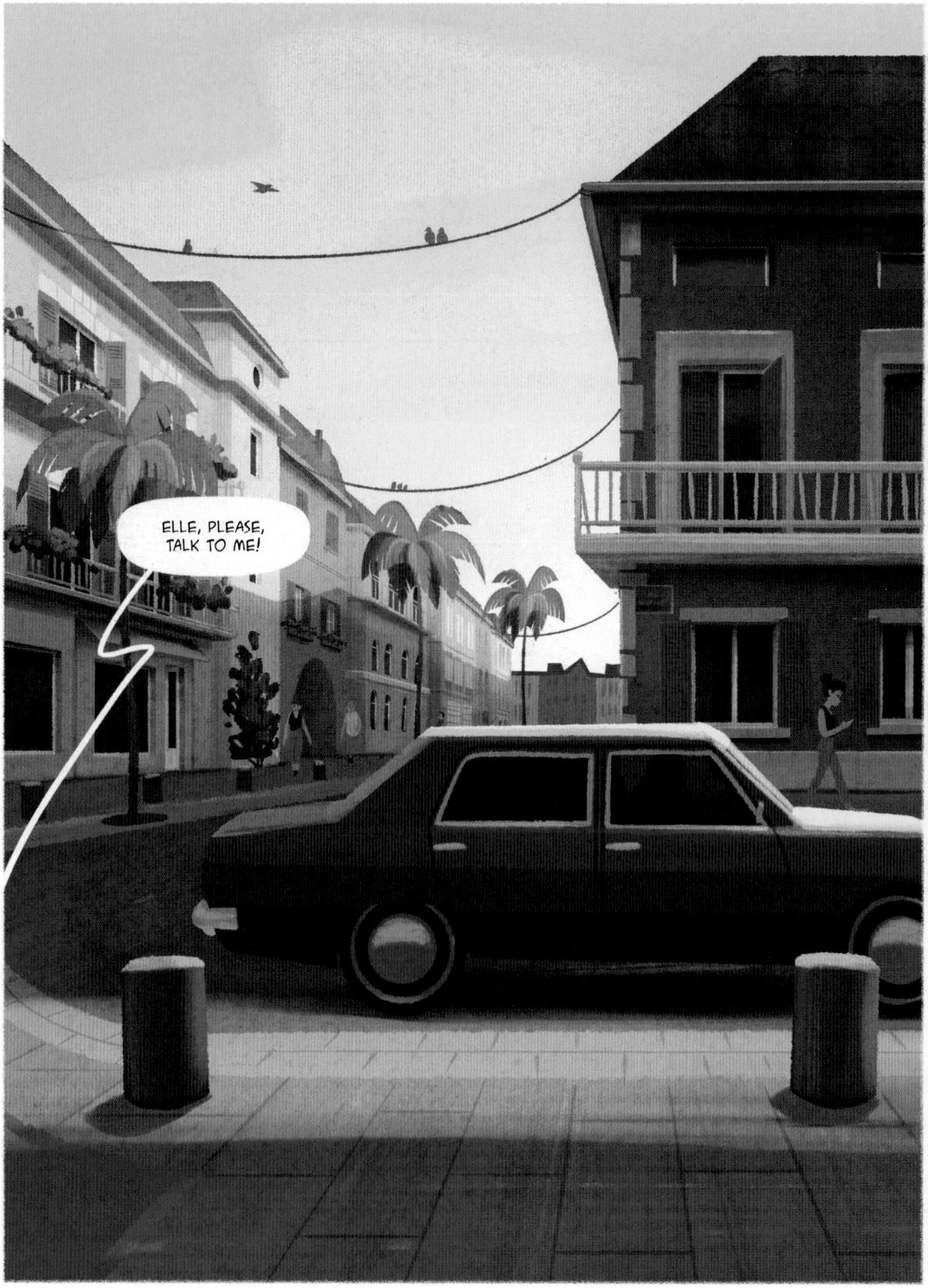
ELLE, PLEASE, TALK TO ME!

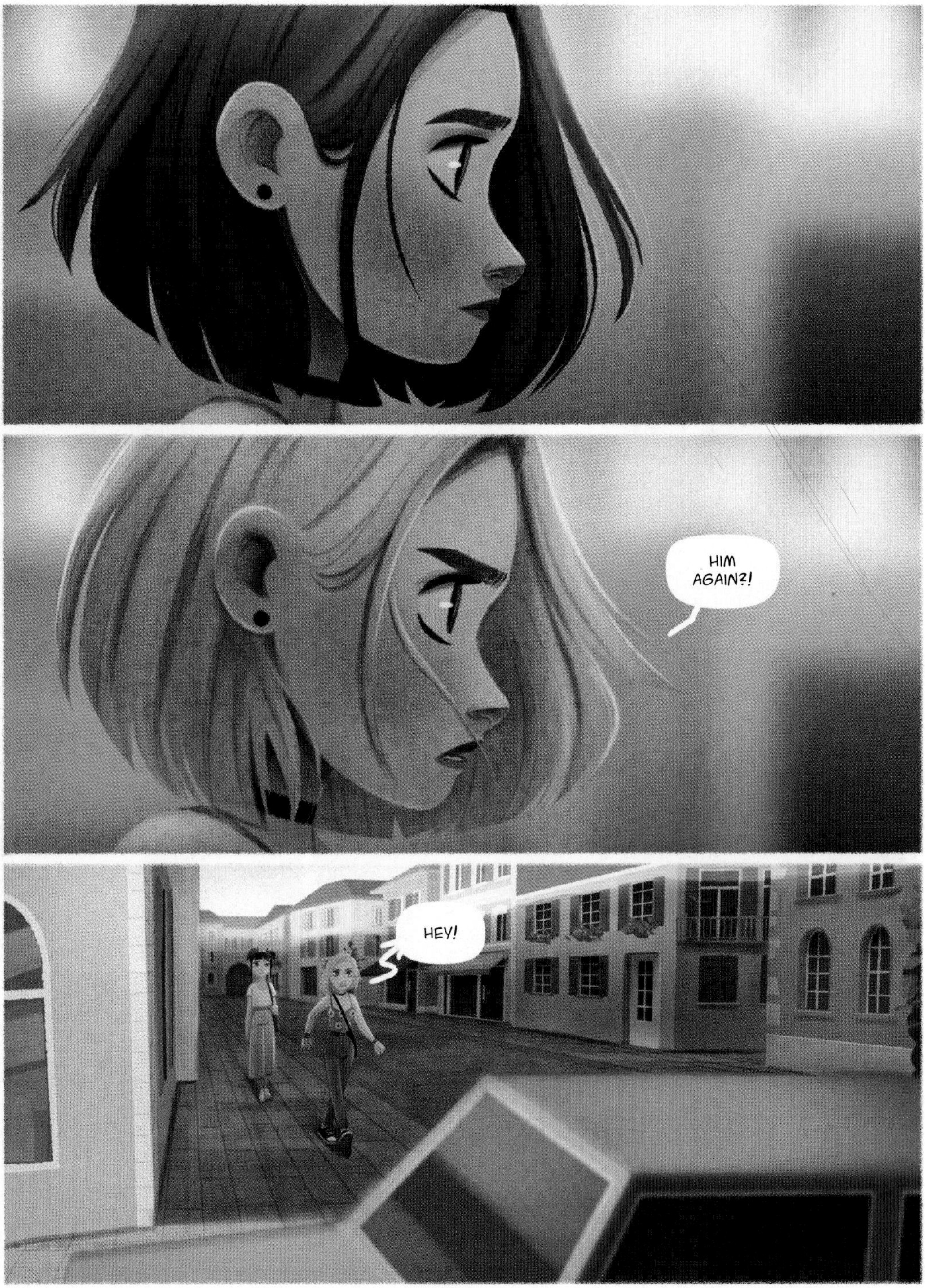
HIM AGAIN?!
HEY!

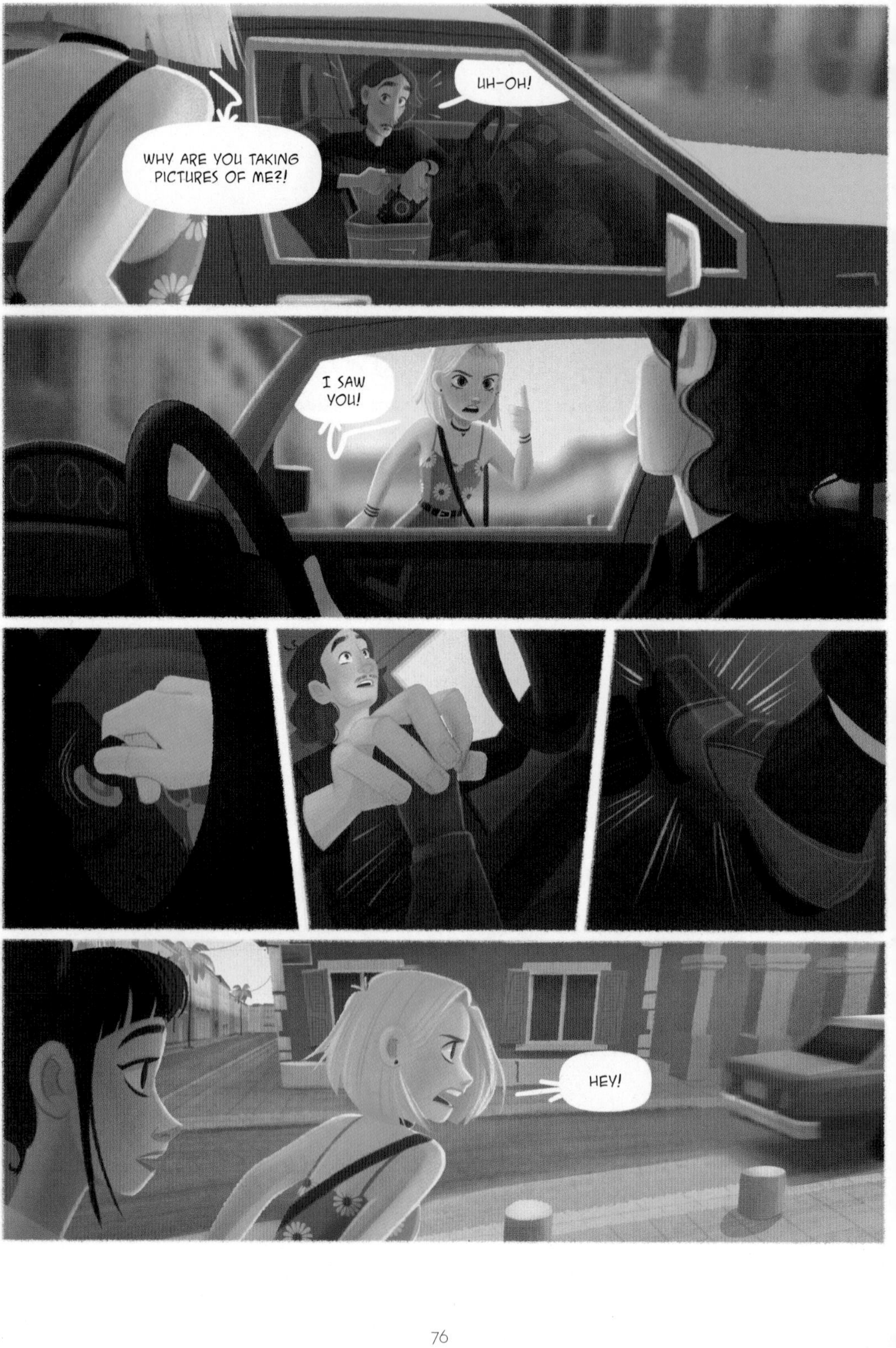
UH-OH!
WHY ARE YOU TAKING PICTURES OF ME?!
I SAW YOU!
HEY!

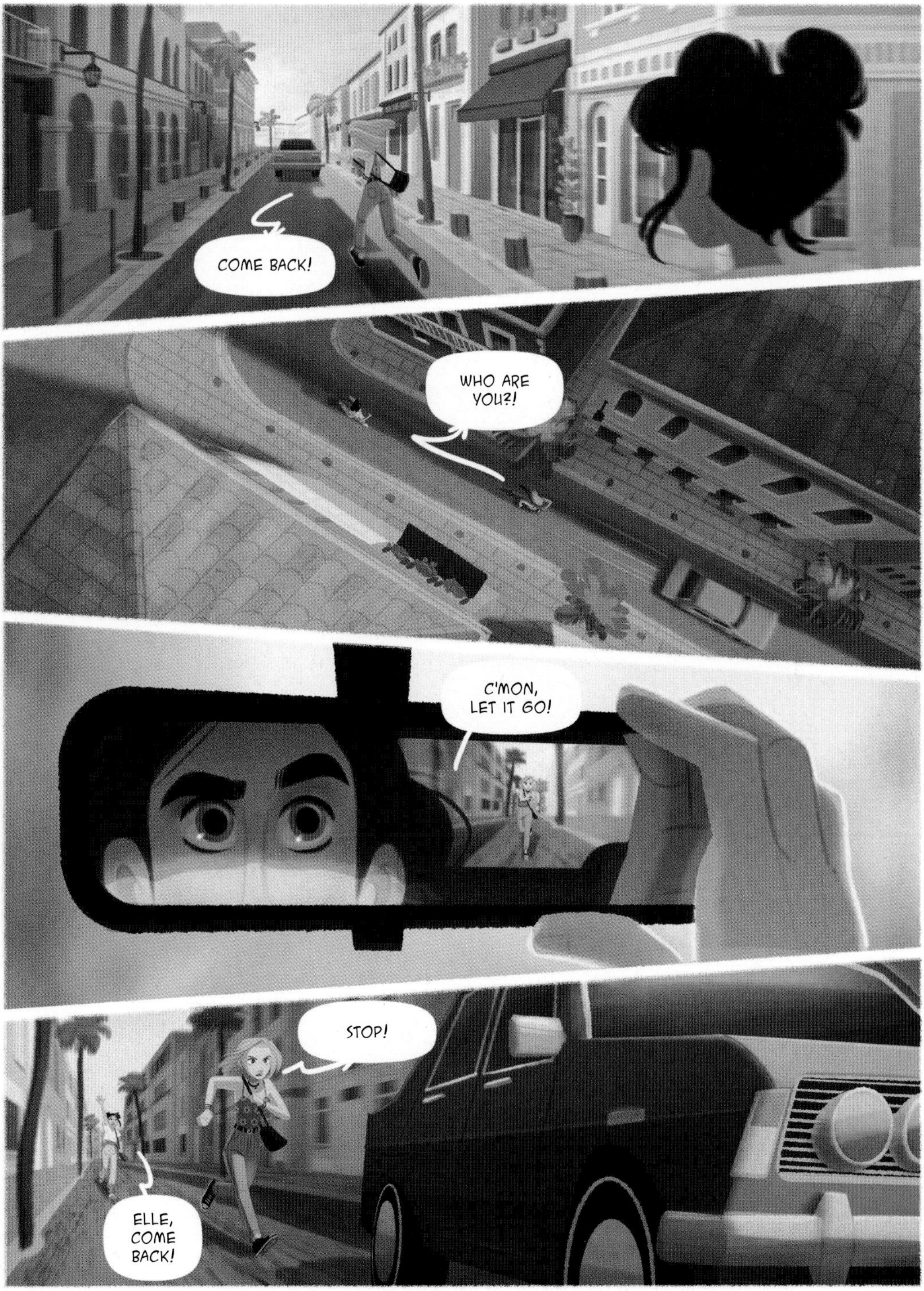
COME BACK!
WHO ARE YOU?!
C'MON, LET IT GO!
STOP!
ELLE, COME BACK!

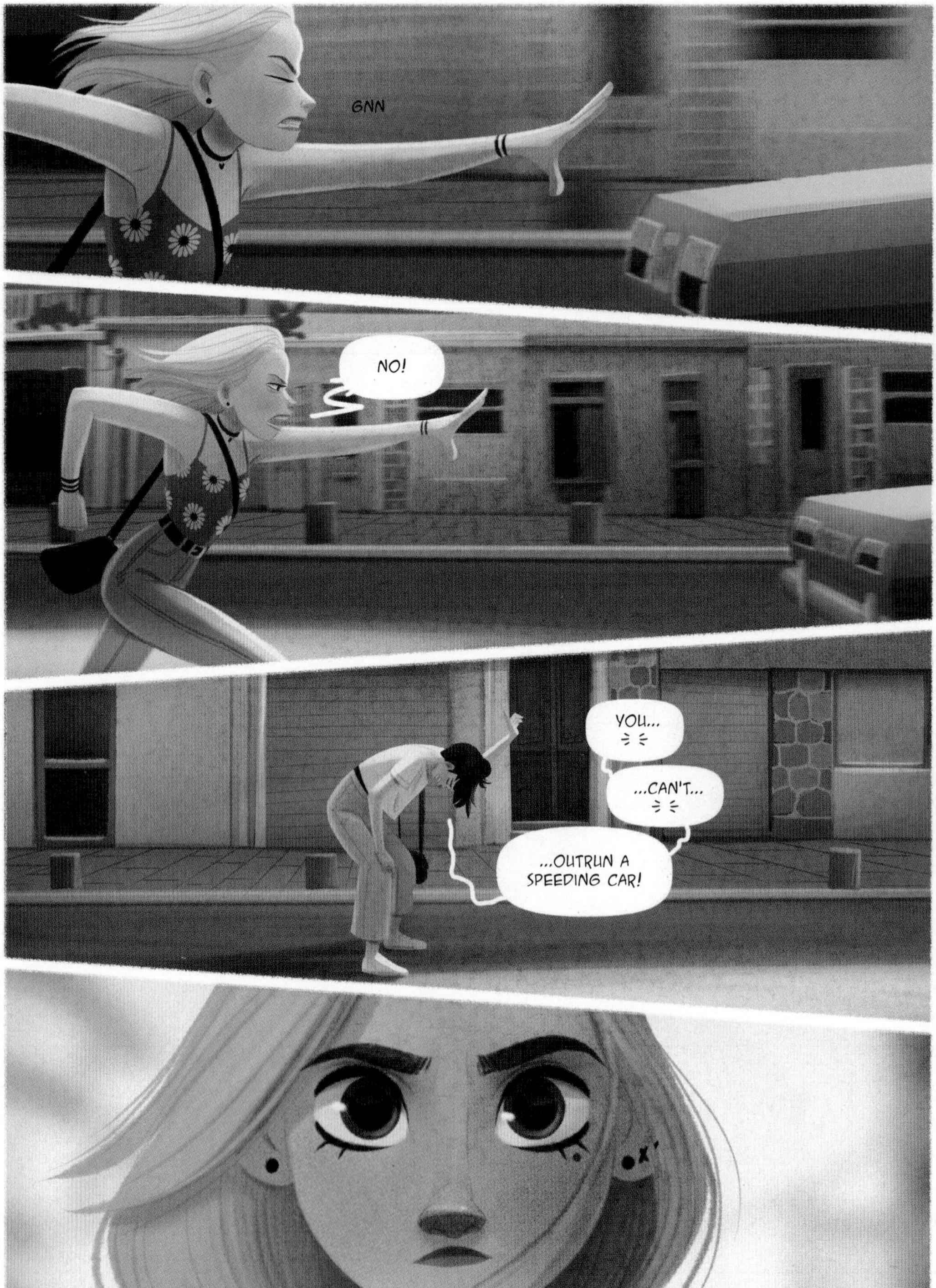
GNN
NO!
YOU...
...CAN'T...
...OUTRUN A SPEEDING CAR!

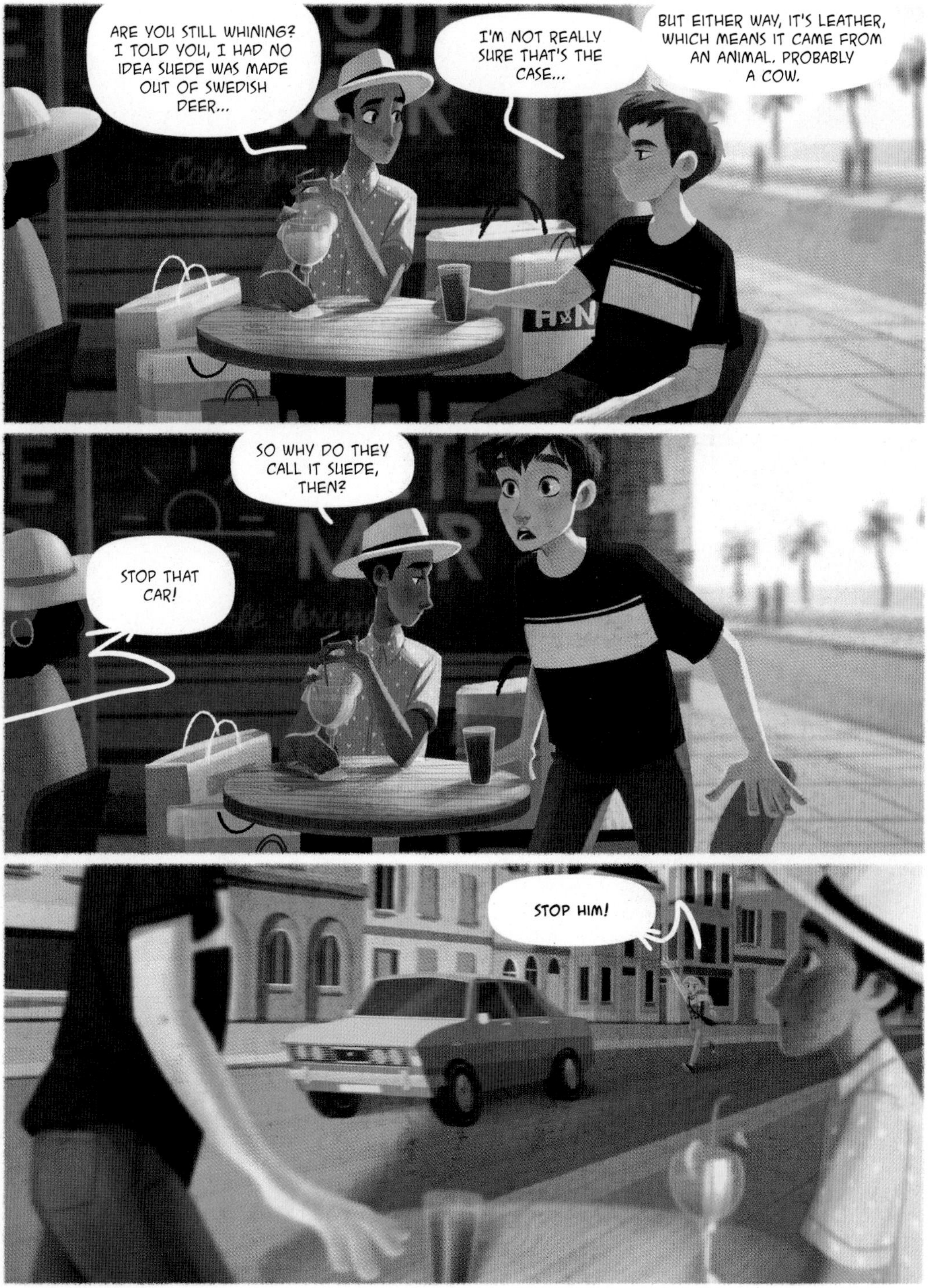
ARE YOU STILL WHINING? I TOLD YOU, I HAD NO IDEA SUEDE WAS MADE OUT OF SWEDISH DEER...
I'M NOT REALLY SURE THAT'S THE CASE...
BUT EITHER WAY, IT'S LEATHER, WHICH MEANS IT CAME FROM AN ANIMAL. PROBABLY A COW.
SO WHY DO THEY CALL IT SUEDE, THEN?
STOP THAT CAR!
STOP HIM!

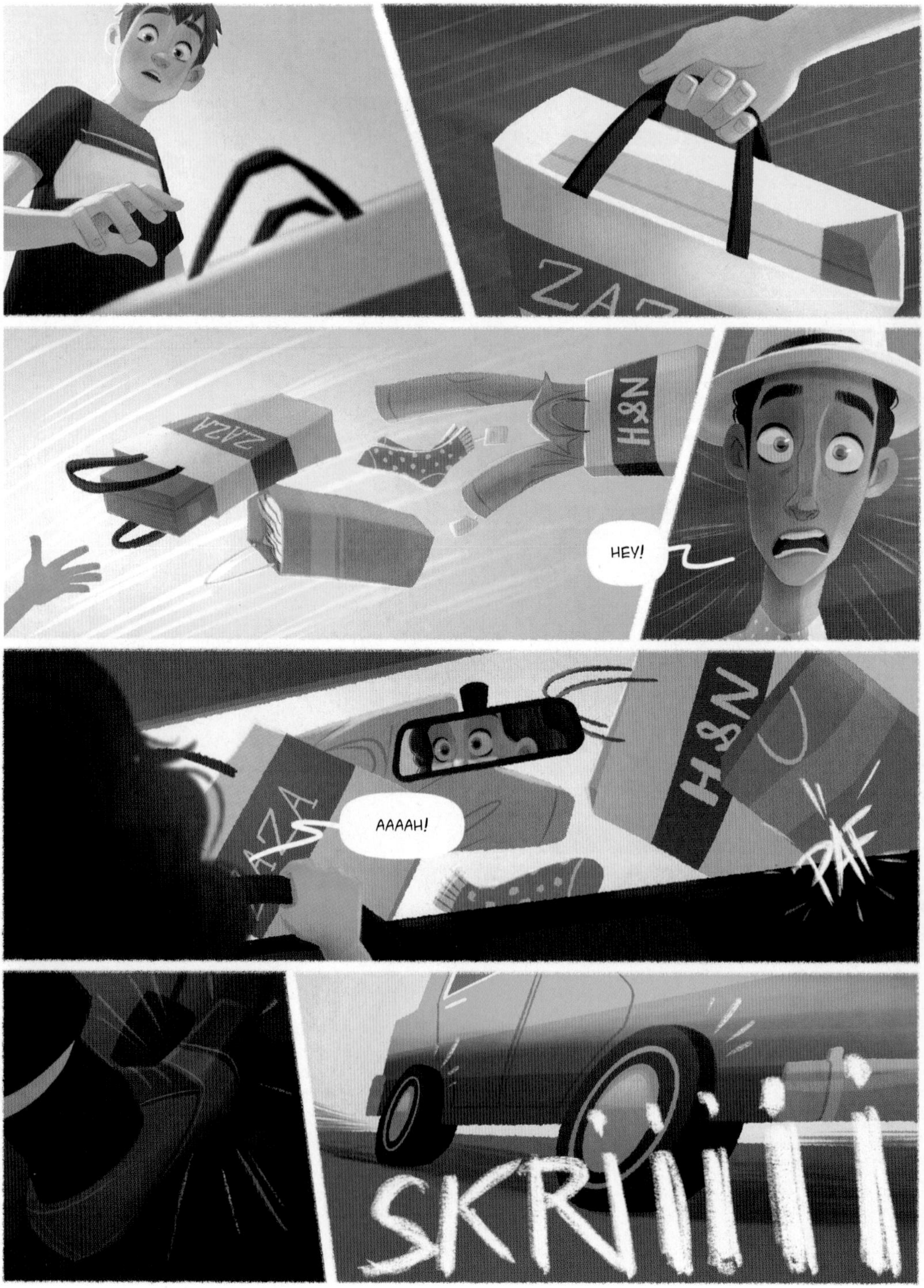
HEY!
AAAAH!
PAF
SKRIIIII

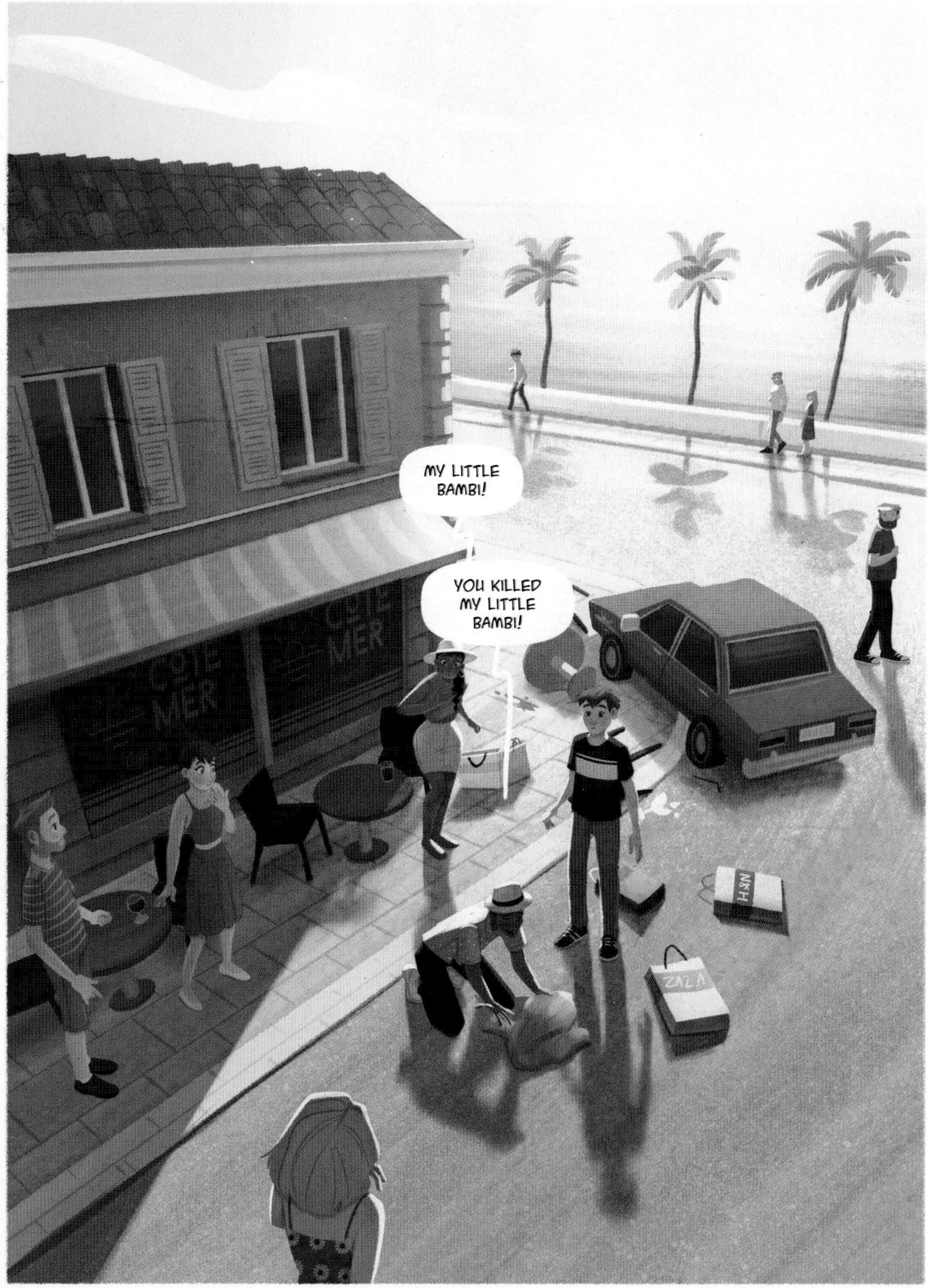
MY LITTLE BAMBI!
YOU KILLED MY LITTLE BAMBI!
CÔTE MER
ZAZA

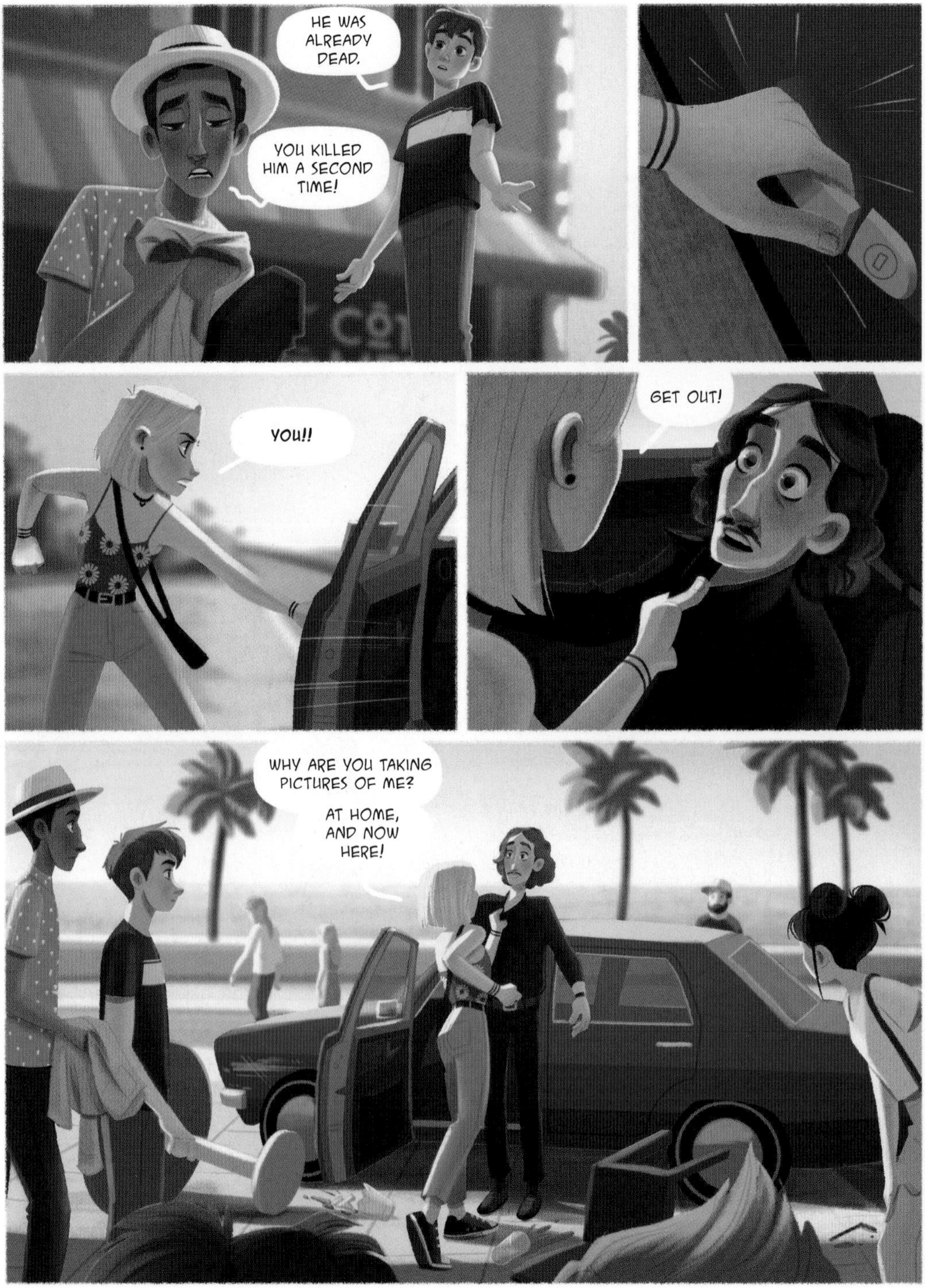
HE WAS ALREADY DEAD.
YOU KILLED HIM A SECOND TIME!
YOU!!
GET OUT!
WHY ARE YOU TAKING PICTURES OF ME?
AT HOME, AND NOW HERE!

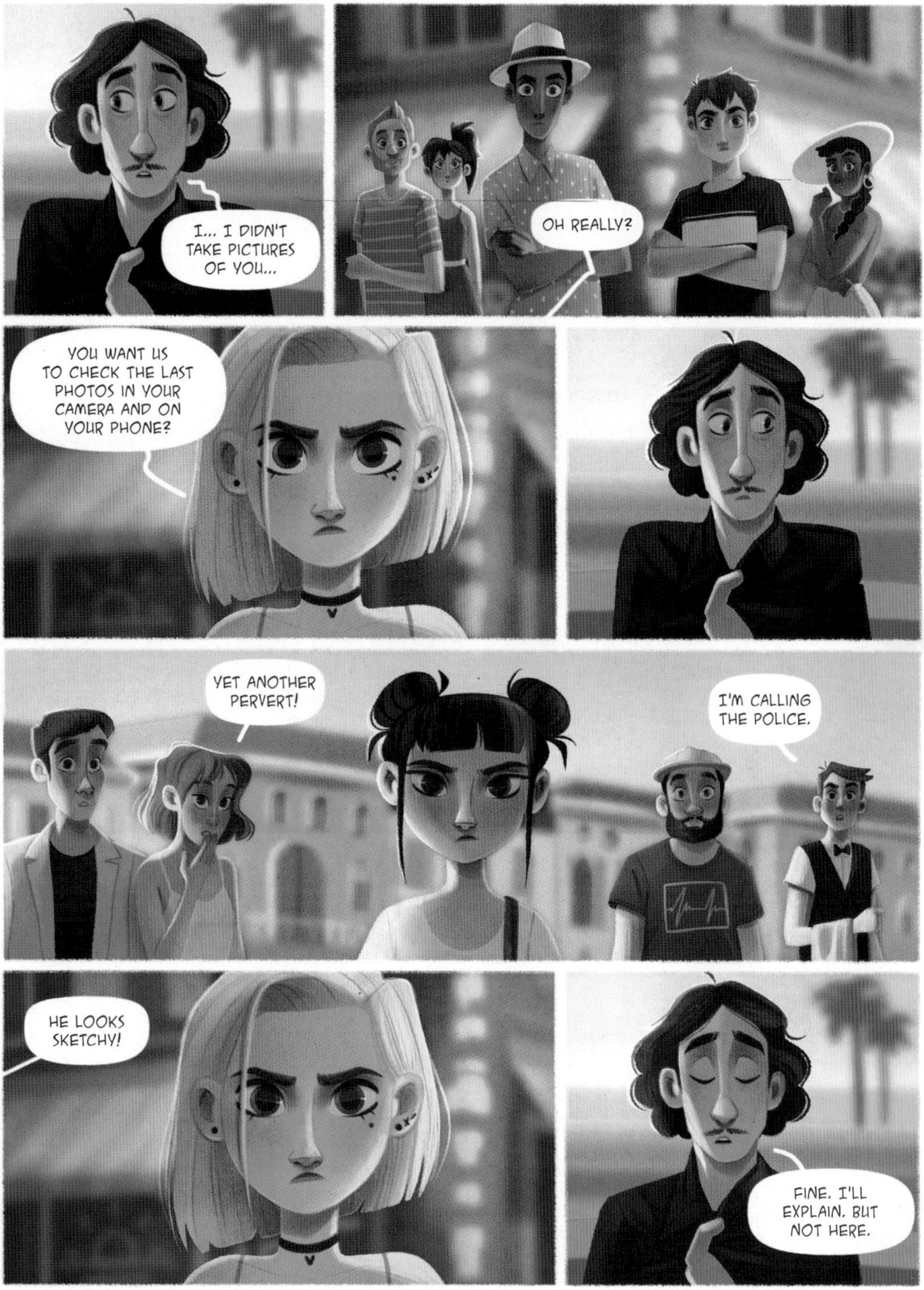
I... I DIDN'T TAKE PICTURES OF YOU...
OH REALLY?
YOU WANT US TO CHECK THE LAST PHOTOS IN YOUR CAMERA AND ON YOUR PHONE?
YET ANOTHER PERVERT!
I'M CALLING THE POLICE.
HE LOOKS SKETCHY!
FINE. I'LL EXPLAIN. BUT NOT HERE.

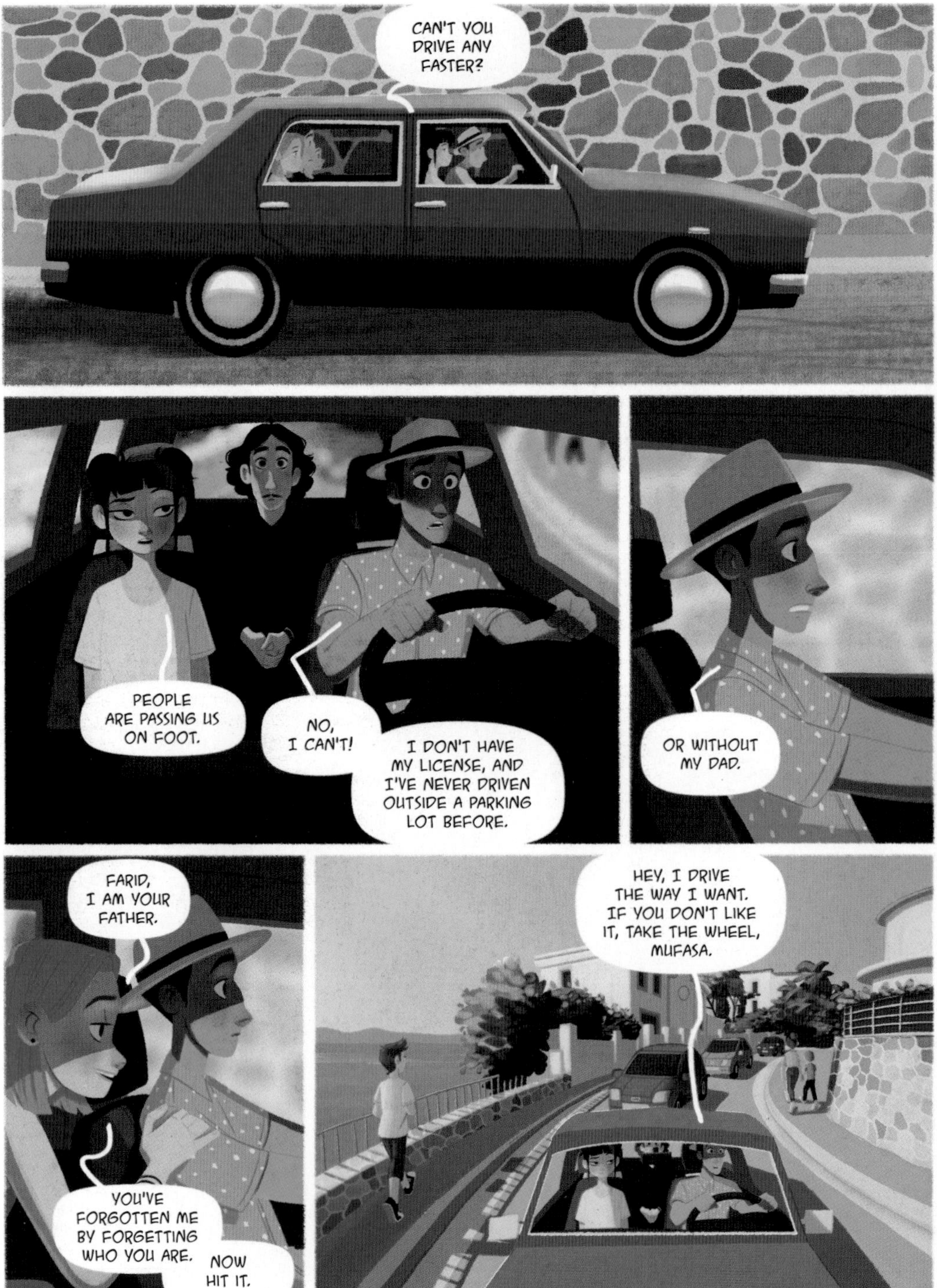
CAN'T YOU DRIVE ANY FASTER?
PEOPLE ARE PASSING US ON FOOT.
NO, I CAN'T!
I DON'T HAVE MY LICENSE, AND I'VE NEVER DRIVEN OUTSIDE A PARKING LOT BEFORE.
OR WITHOUT MY DAD.
FARID, I AM YOUR FATHER.
YOU'VE FORGOTTEN ME BY FORGETTING WHO YOU ARE.
NOW HIT IT.
HEY, I DRIVE THE WAY I WANT. IF YOU DON'T LIKE IT, TAKE THE WHEEL, MUFASA.

YOU, IN THE BACK, MR. PEEPING TOM PERVERT, START TALKING.

I'M NOT UNDER ANY CONTRACTUAL OBLIGATION TO KEEP QUIET. I'LL GET PAID NO MATTER WHAT I SAY, SO...

MY NAME IS NATHAN ZELJA. I'M A PRIVATE DETECTIVE, AND YES, I TOOK PICTURES OF YOU...

...AT YOUR MOTHER'S REQUEST.

WHAT?!

SO MUCH FOR TRUST!

SHE GOES TO VISIT MY AUNT IN THE HOSPITAL AND HAS ME FOLLOWED TO MAKE SURE I DON'T GET INTO ANY TROUBLE?!

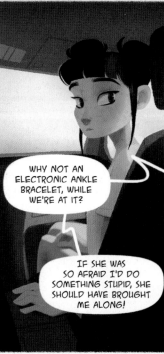

WHY NOT AN ELECTRONIC ANKLE BRACELET, WHILE WE'RE AT IT?

IF SHE WAS SO AFRAID I'D DO SOMETHING STUPID, SHE SHOULD HAVE BROUGHT ME ALONG!

NO, I DON'T THINK WE'RE TALKING ABOUT THE SAME PERSON.

I'M TALKING ABOUT...

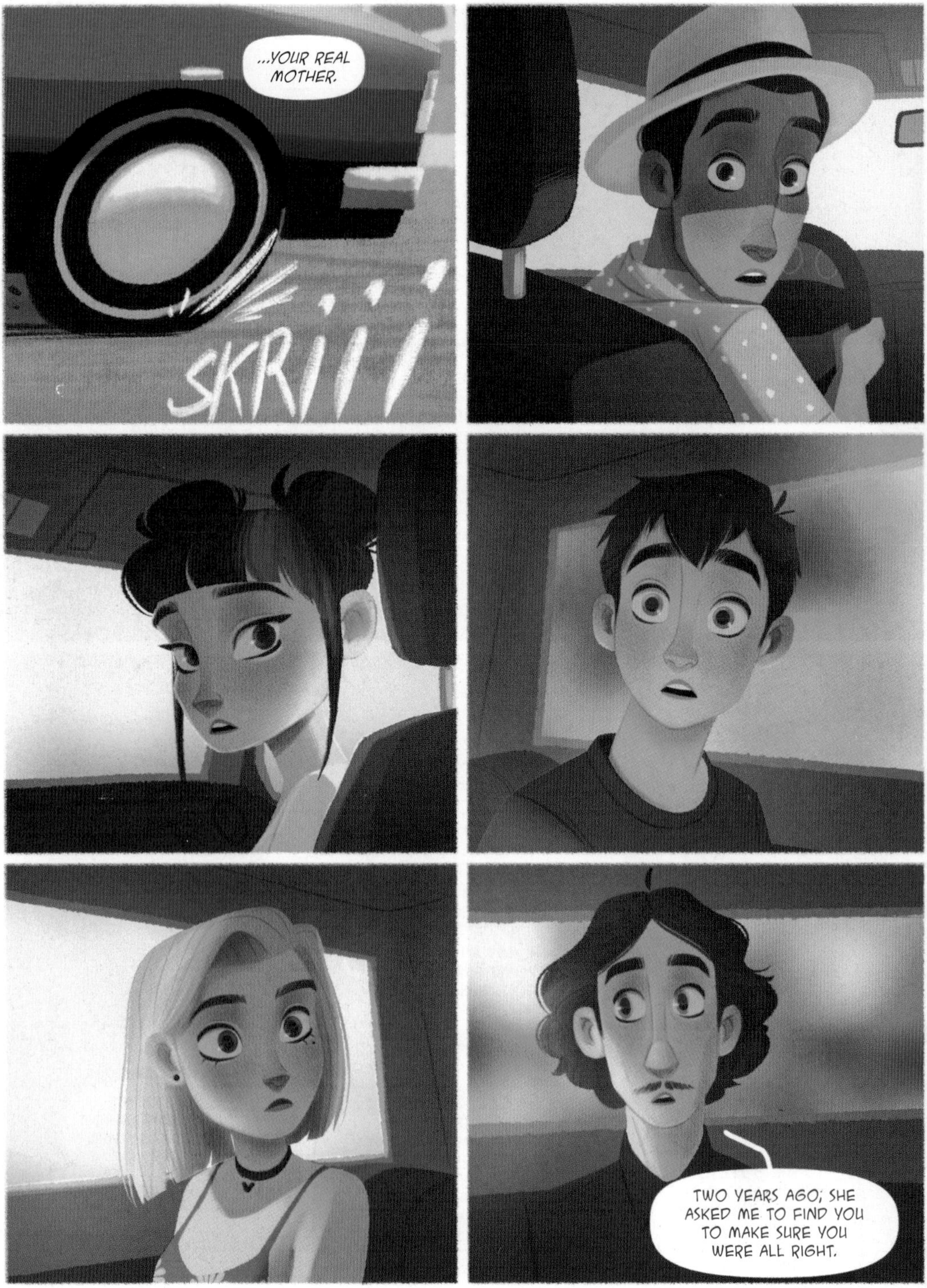
...YOUR REAL MOTHER.
SKRIII
TWO YEARS AGO; SHE ASKED ME TO FIND YOU TO MAKE SURE YOU WERE ALL RIGHT.

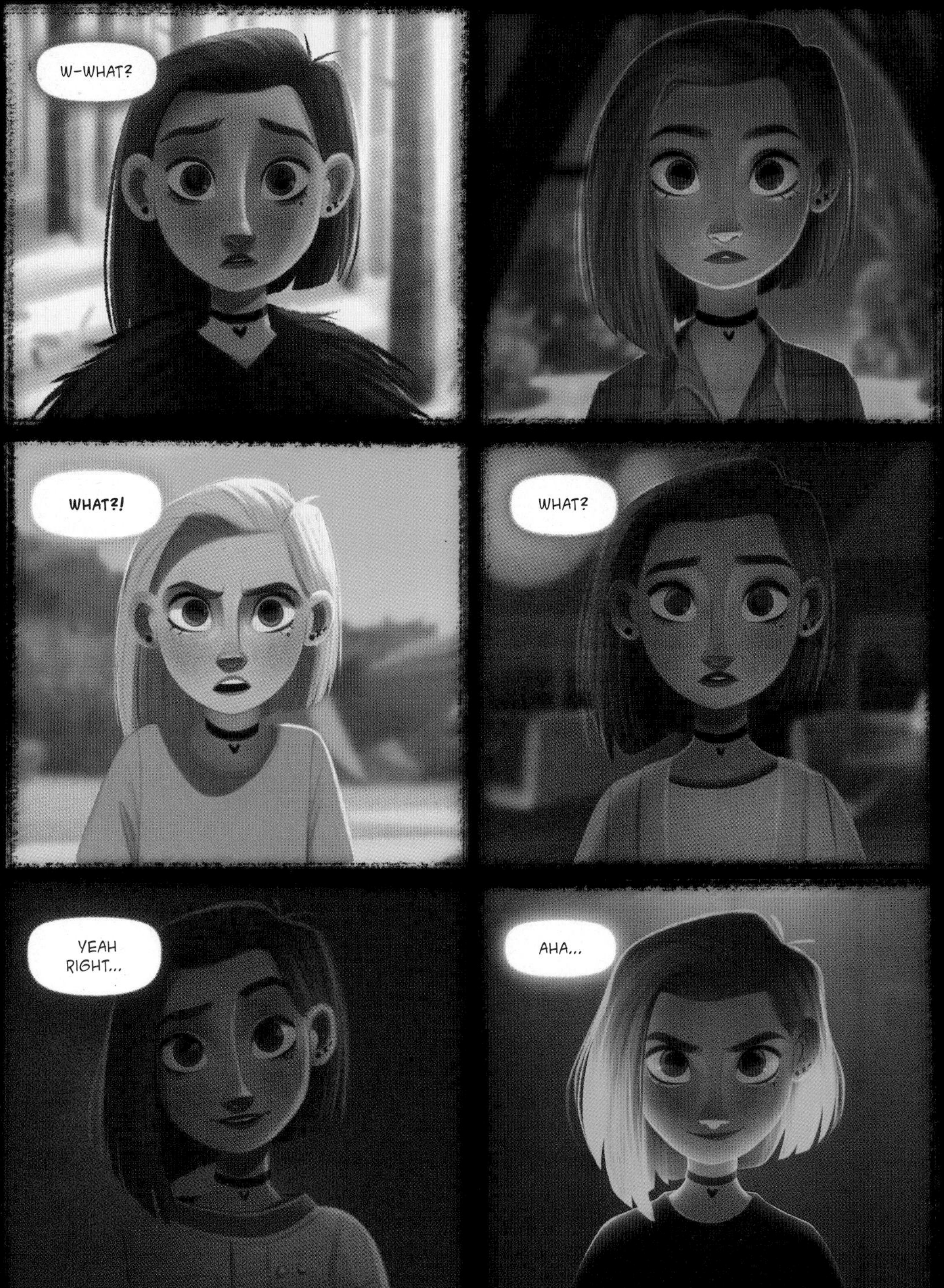
W-WHAT?
WHAT?!
WHAT?
YEAH RIGHT...
AHA...

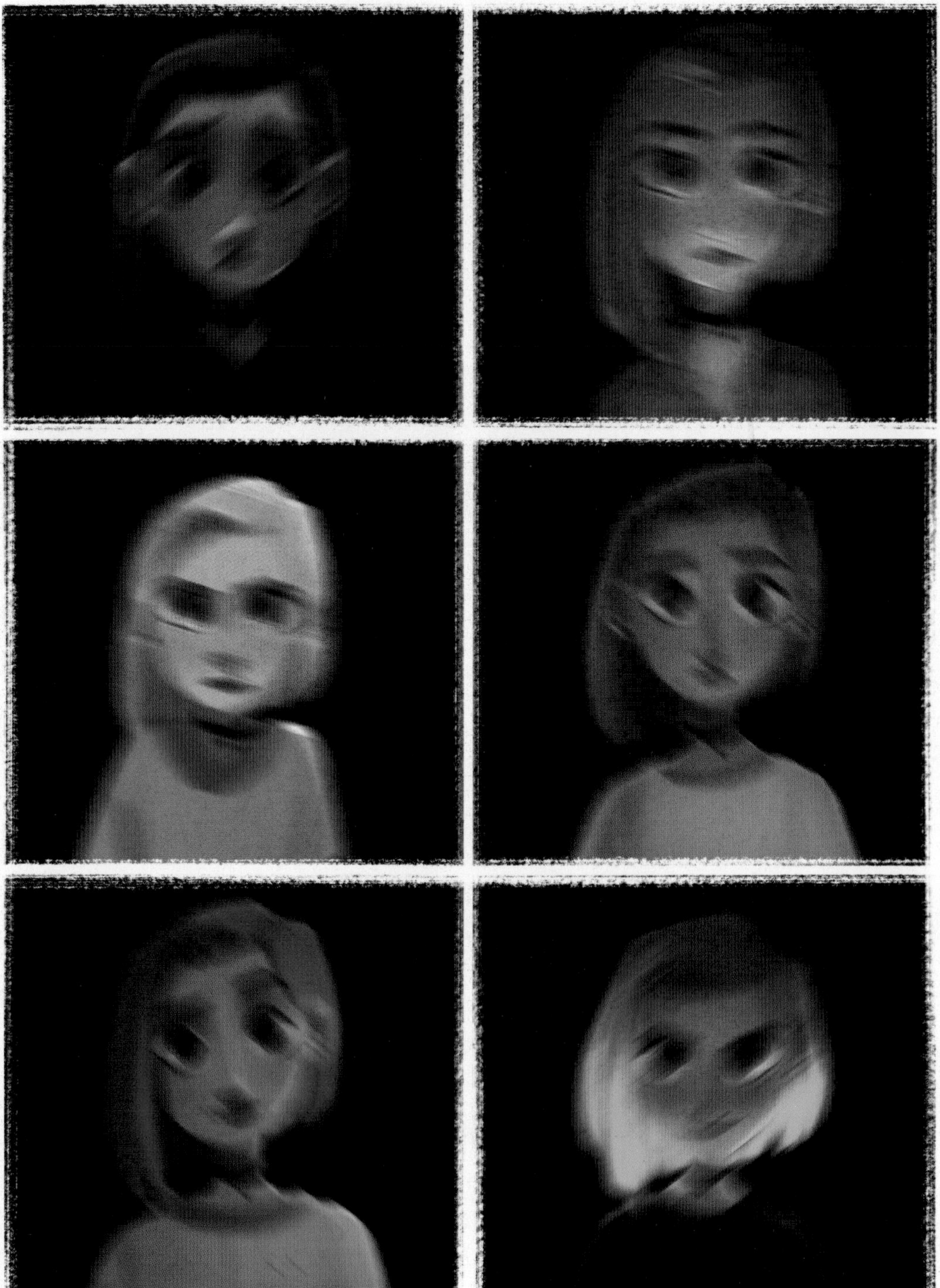

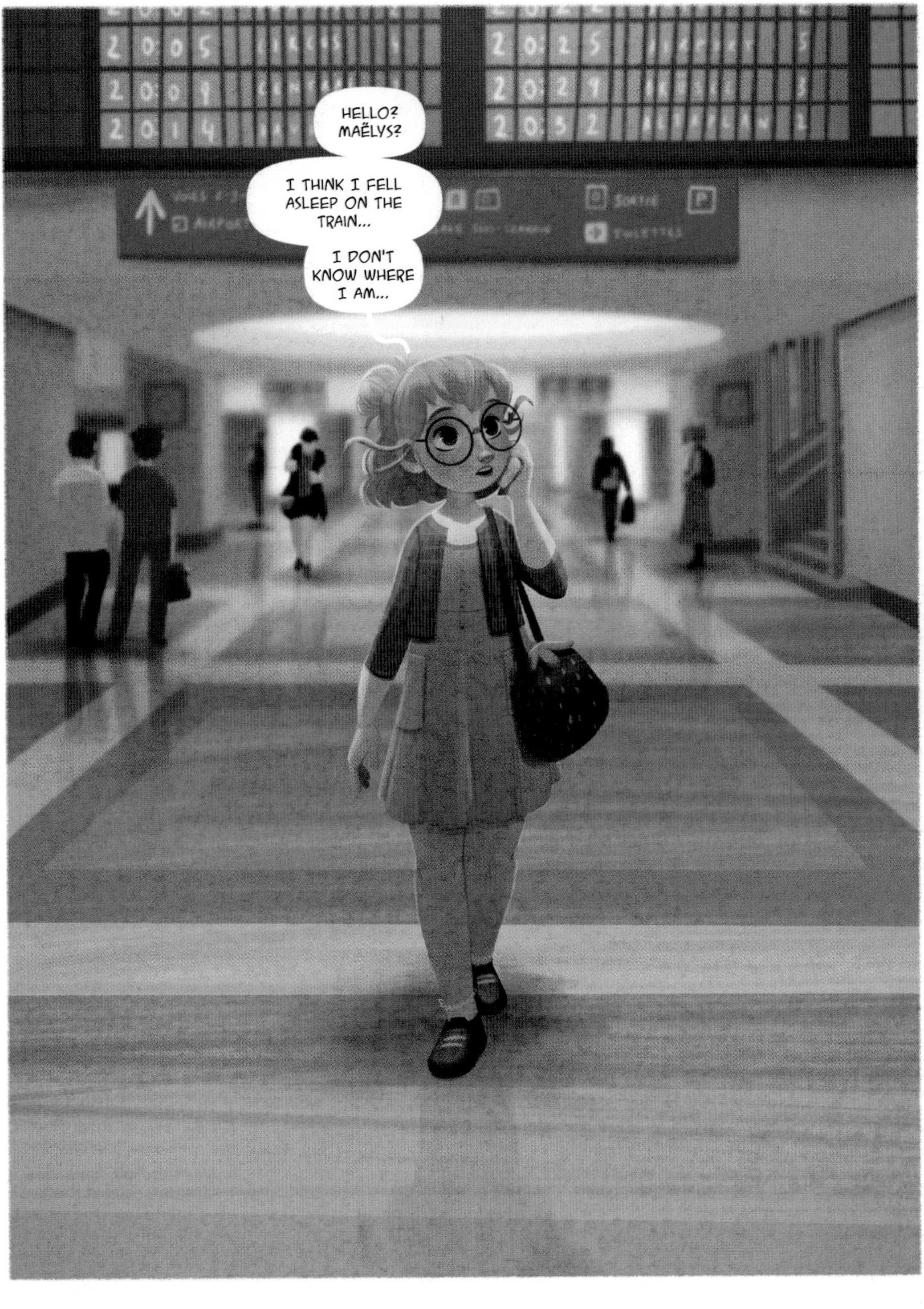
HELLO? MAËLYS?
I THINK I FELL ASLEEP ON THE TRAIN...
I DON'T KNOW WHERE I AM...

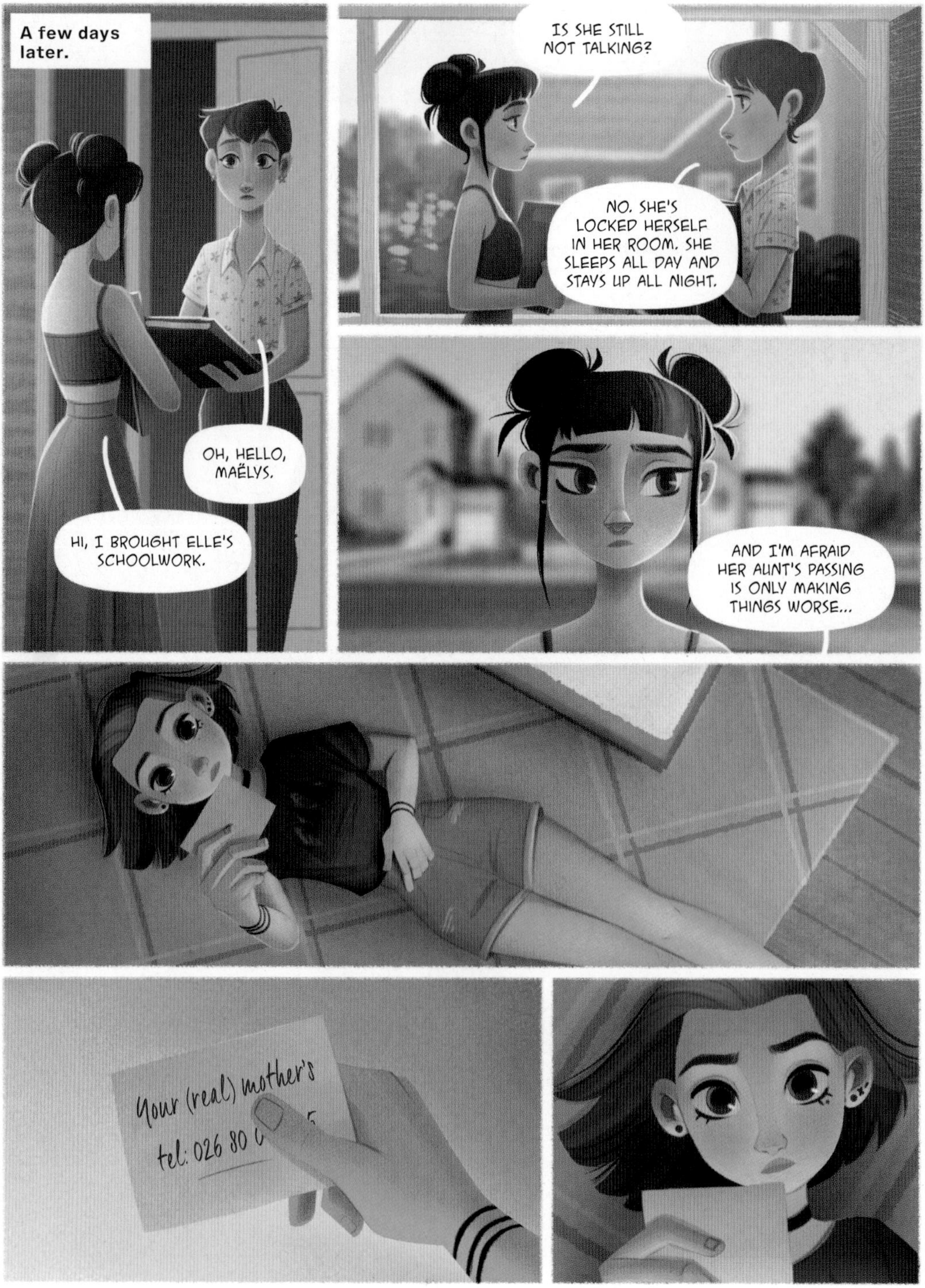
A few days later.
HI, I BROUGHT ELLE'S SCHOOLWORK.
OH, HELLO, MAËLYS.
IS SHE STILL NOT TALKING?
NO. SHE'S LOCKED HERSELF IN HER ROOM. SHE SLEEPS ALL DAY AND STAYS UP ALL NIGHT.
AND I'M AFRAID HER AUNT'S PASSING IS ONLY MAKING THINGS WORSE...
Your (real) mother's
tel: 026 80

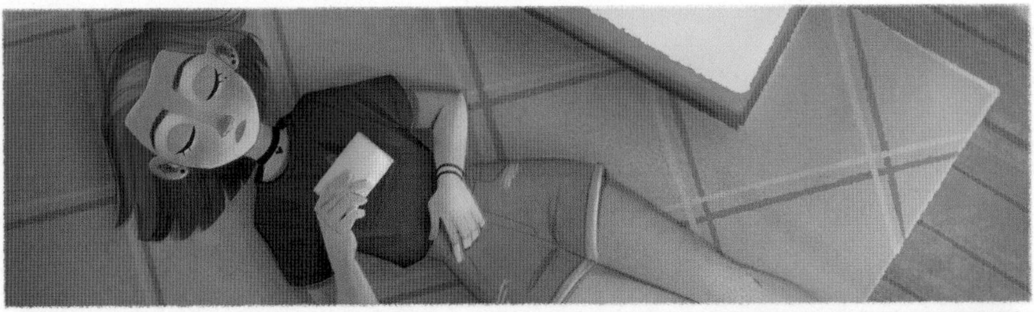

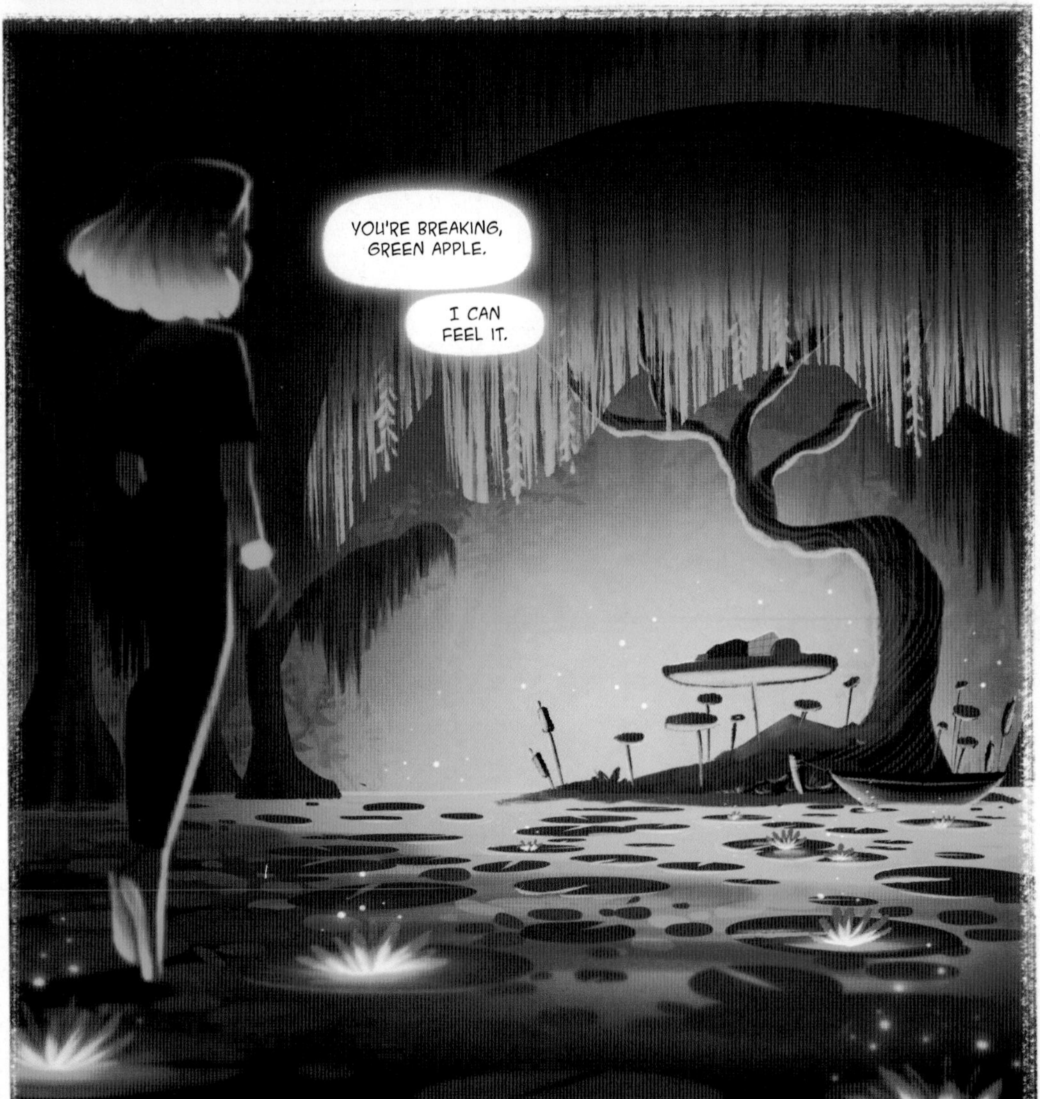
YOU'RE BREAKING,
GREEN APPLE.
I CAN
FEEL IT.

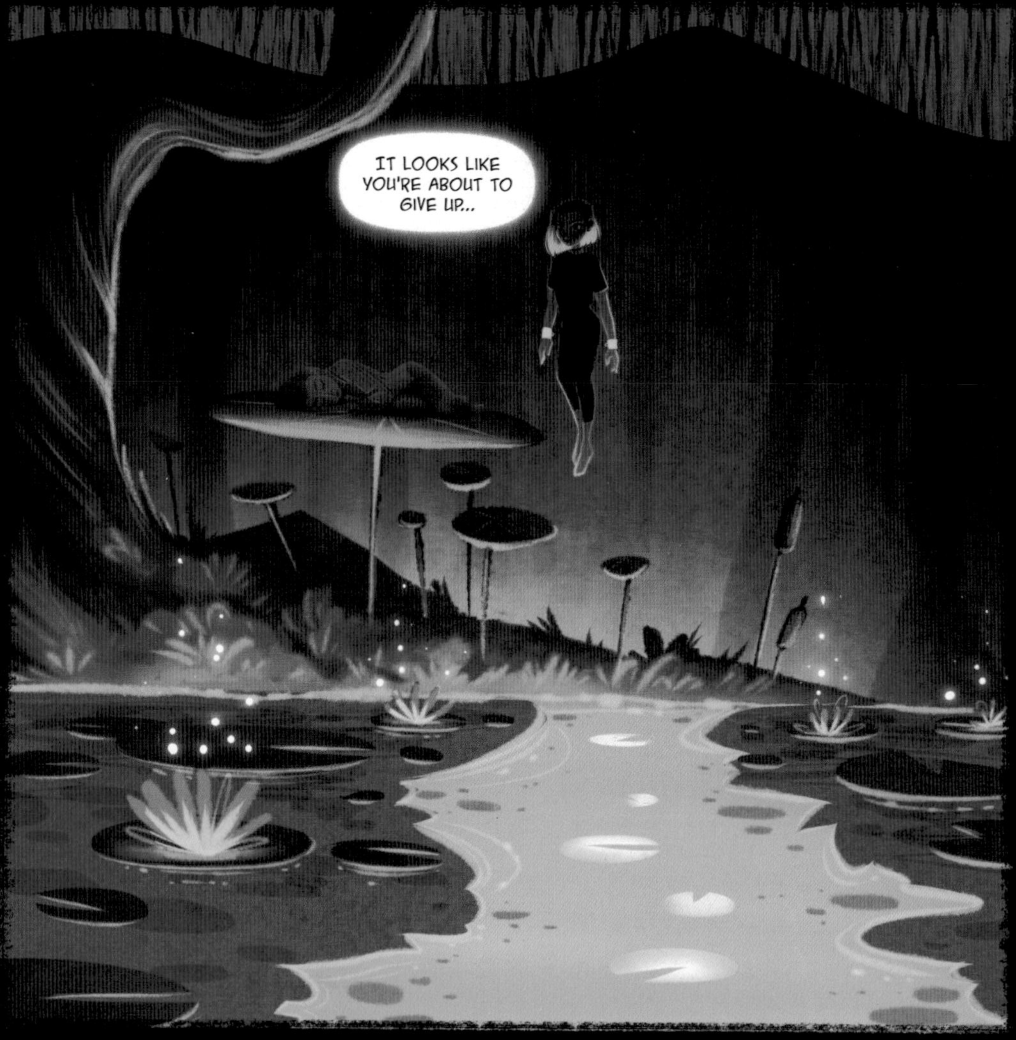
IT LOOKS LIKE YOU'RE ABOUT TO GIVE UP...

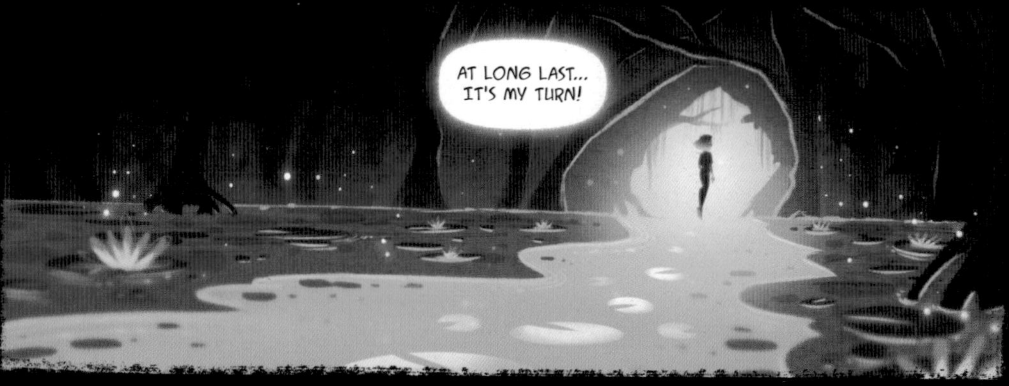
AT LONG LAST... IT'S MY TURN!

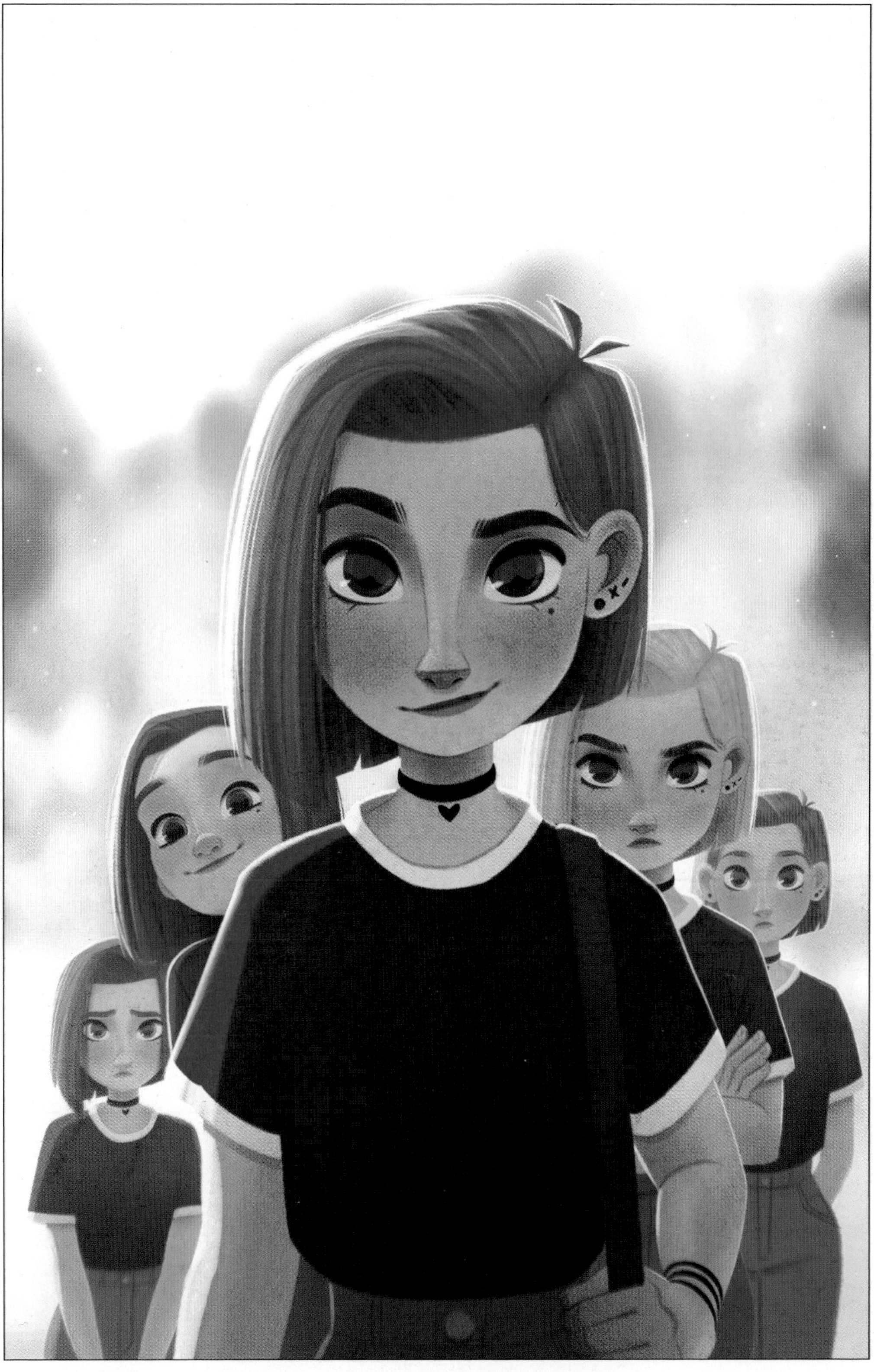

ISSUE #1 MAIN COVER BY **AVELINE STOKART**

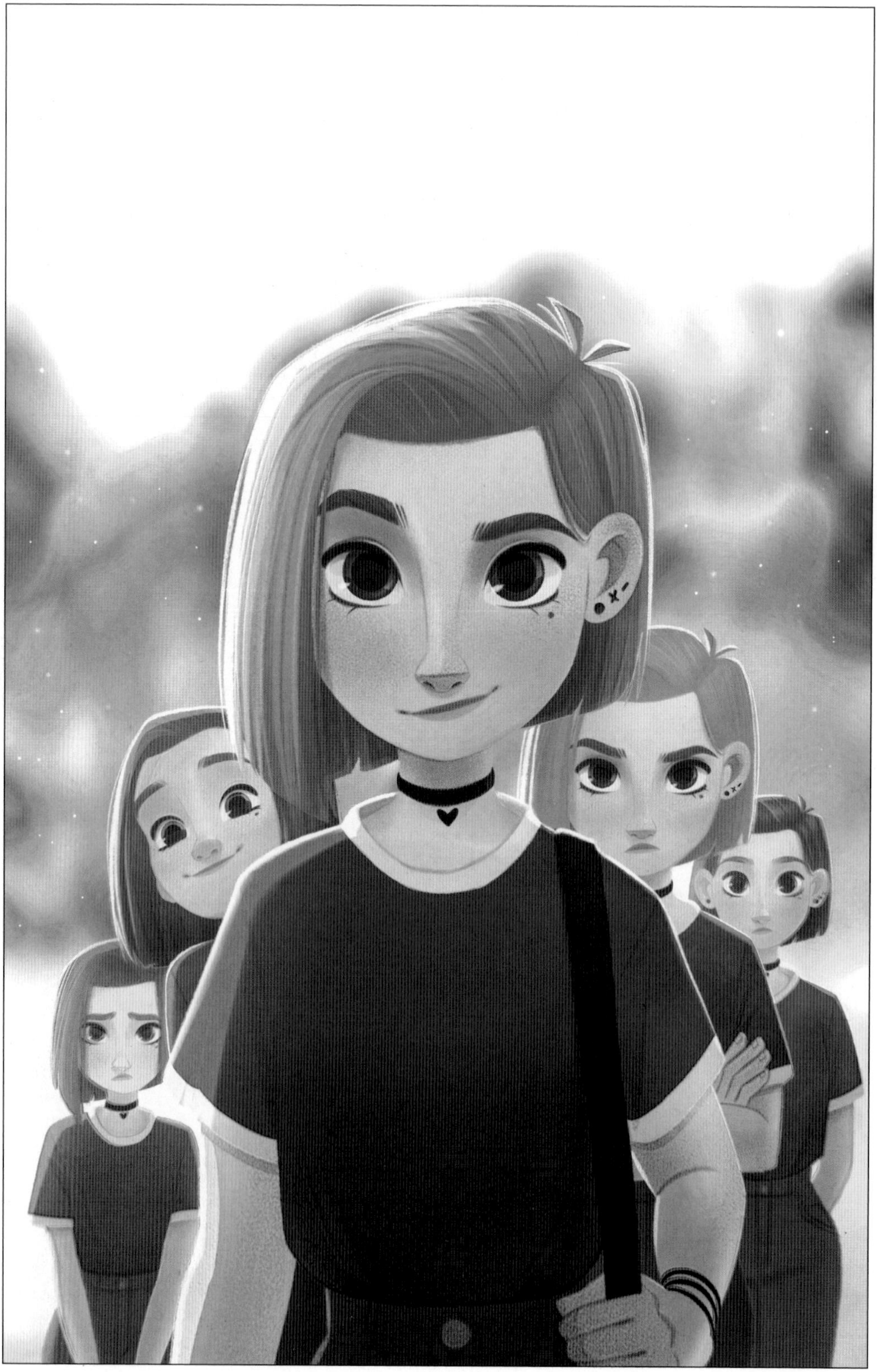

ISSUE #1 B&W VARIANT COVER BY **AVELINE STOKART**

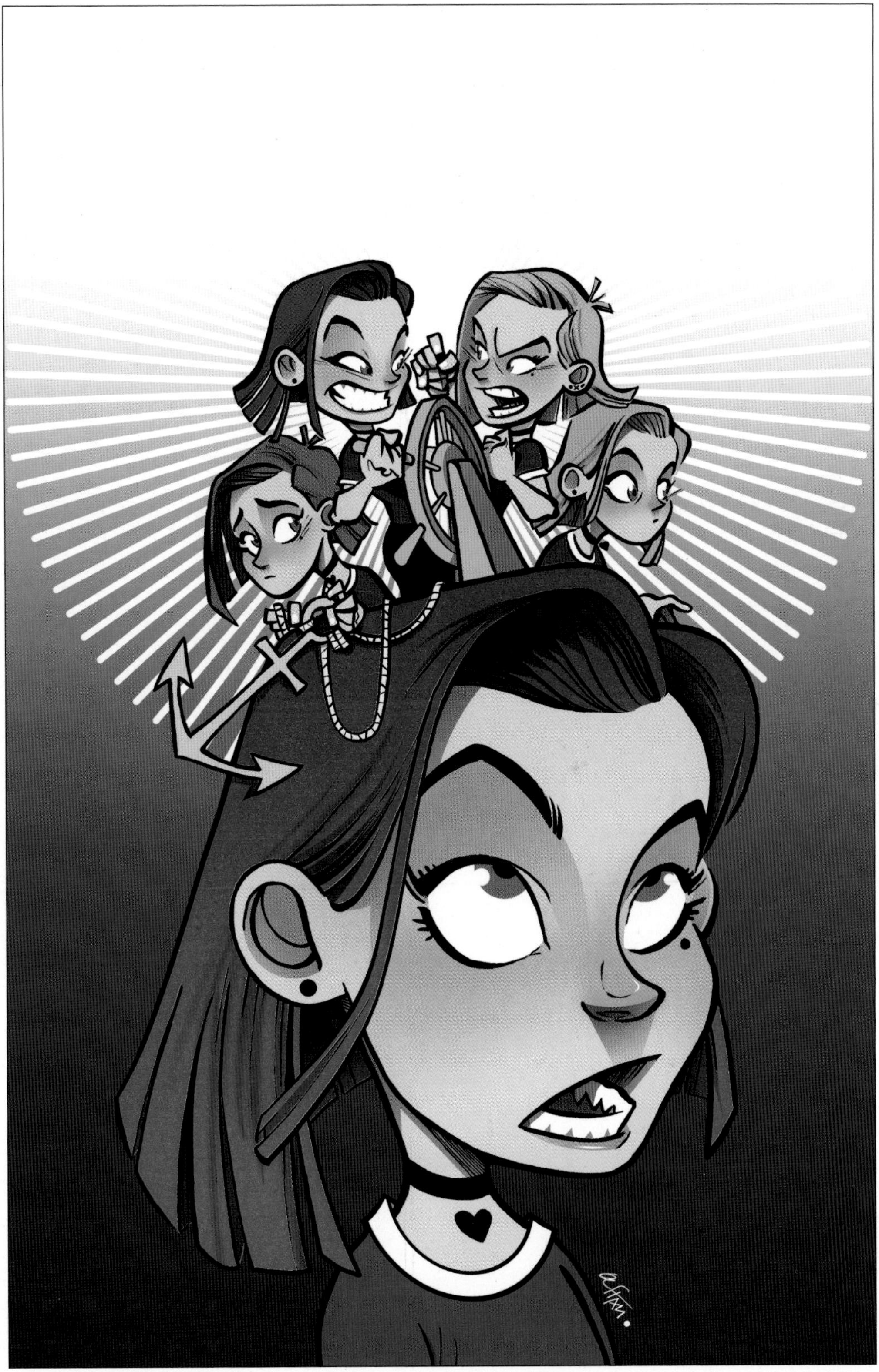

ISSUE #1 VARIANT COVER BY **GUSTAVO DUARTE**

Aveline
STOKART

Elle(s)

Kid
TOUSSAINT

ABLAZE
1

ISSUE #1 BLANK VARIANT COVER

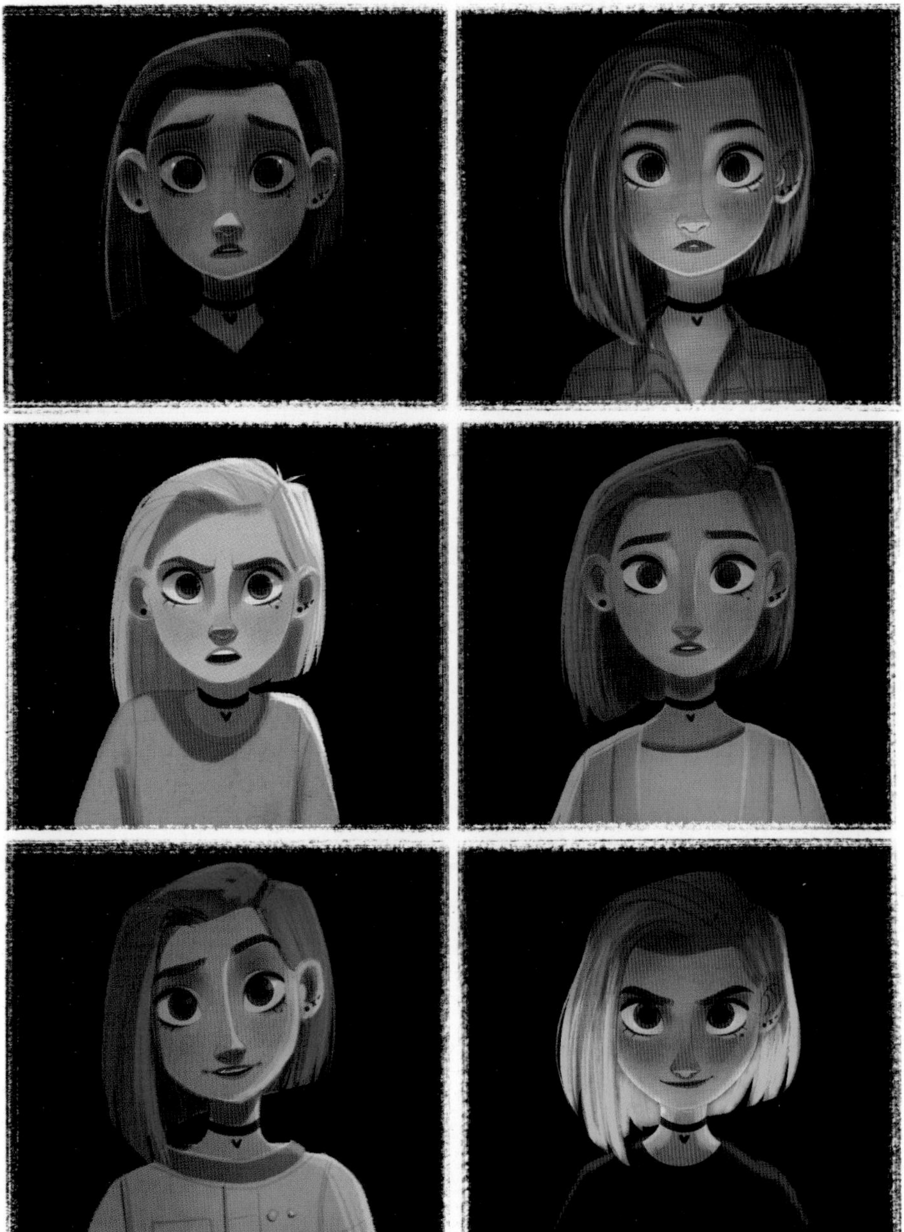

ISSUE #2 MAIN COVER BY **AVELINE STOKART**

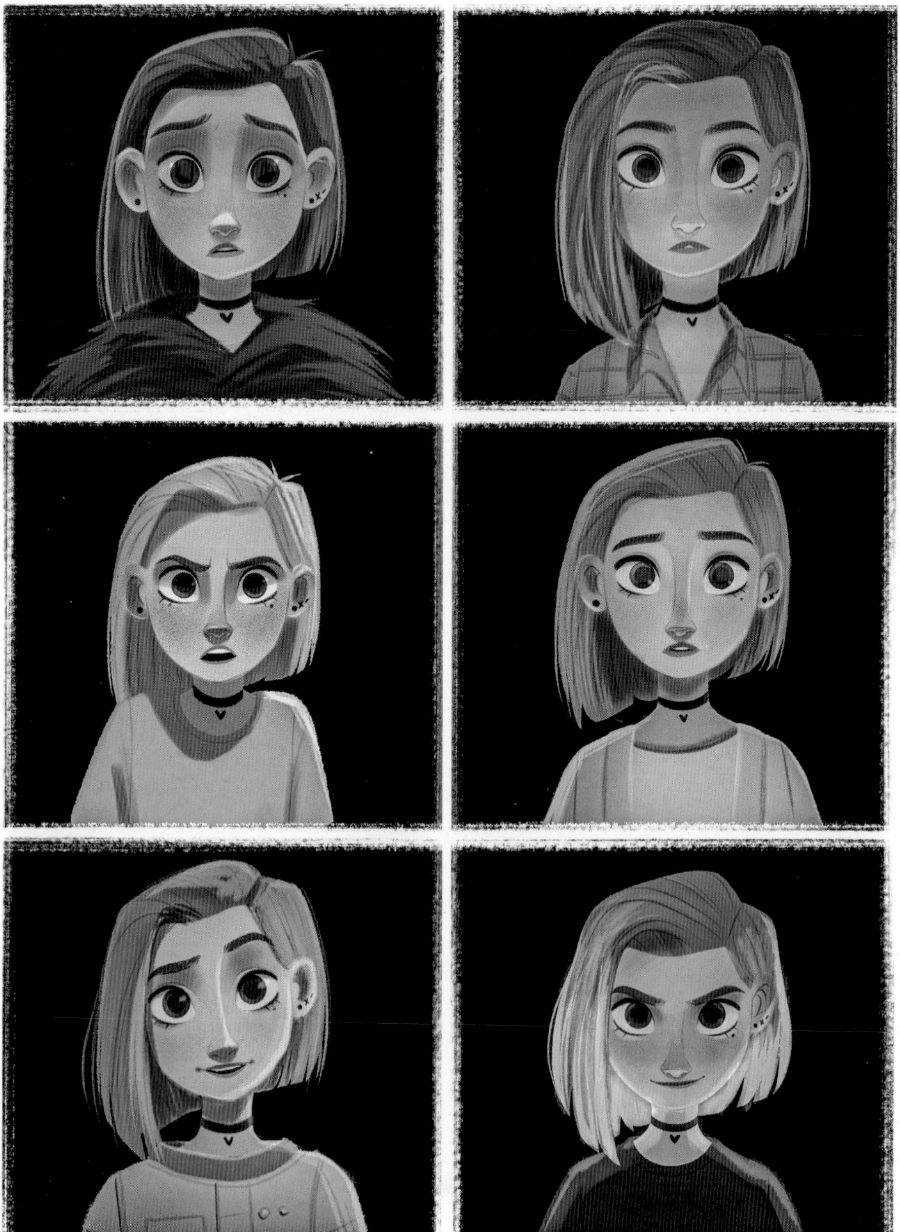

ISSUE #2 B&W VARIANT COVER BY **AVELINE STOKART**

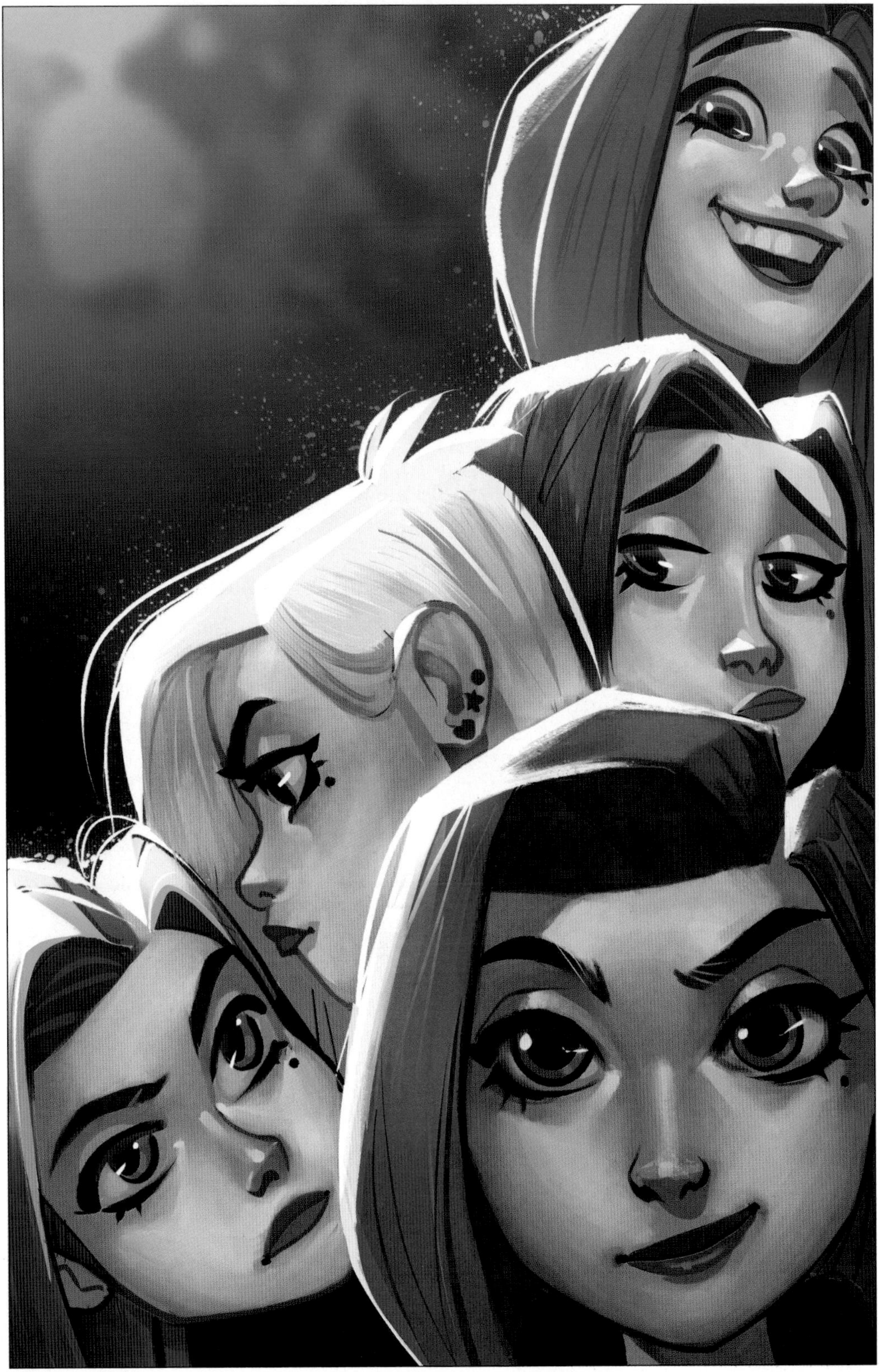

ISSUE #2 VARIANT COVER BY **MEL MILTON**

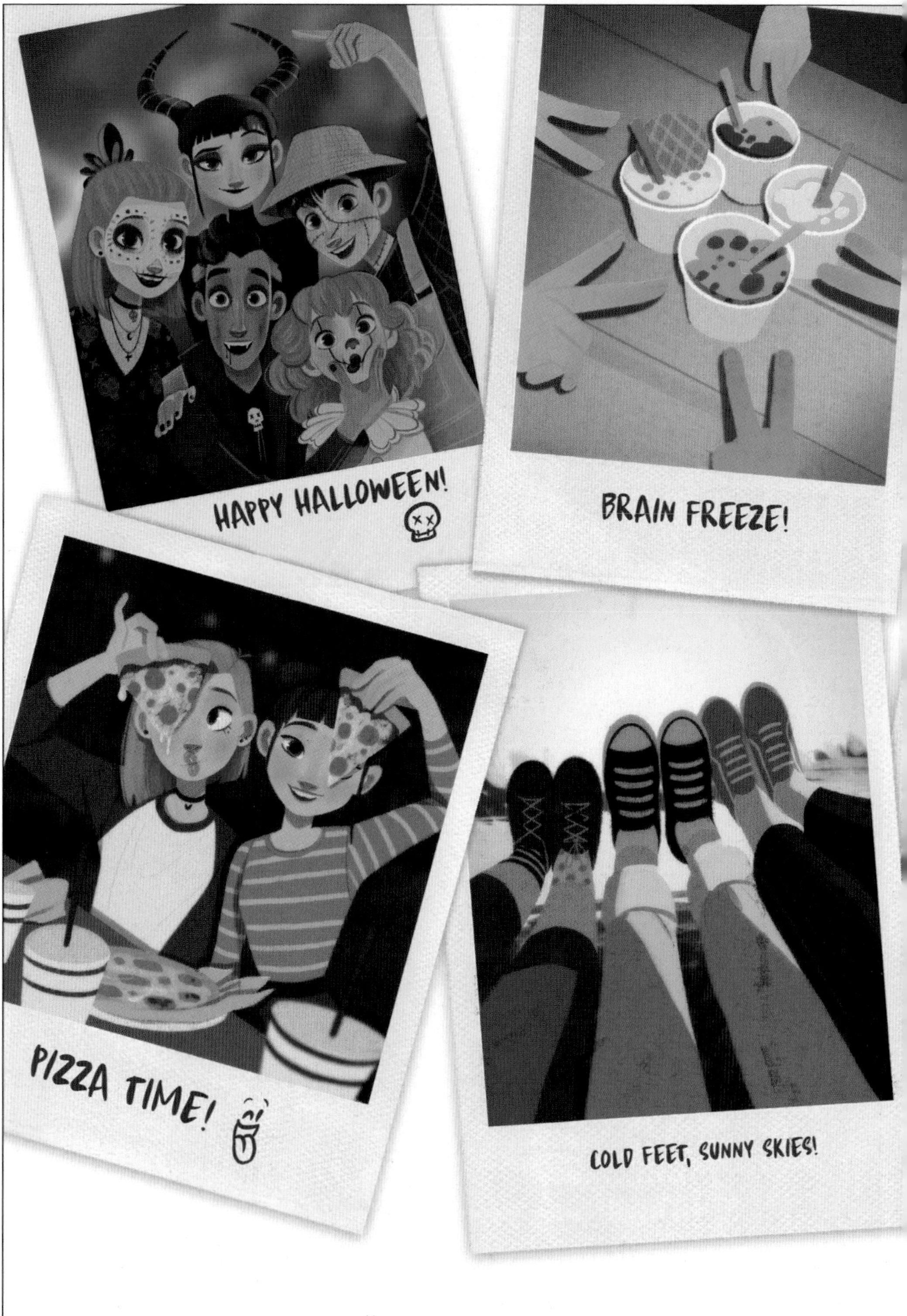
HAPPY HALLOWEEN!
BRAIN FREEZE!
PIZZA TIME!
COLD FEET, SUNNY SKIES!

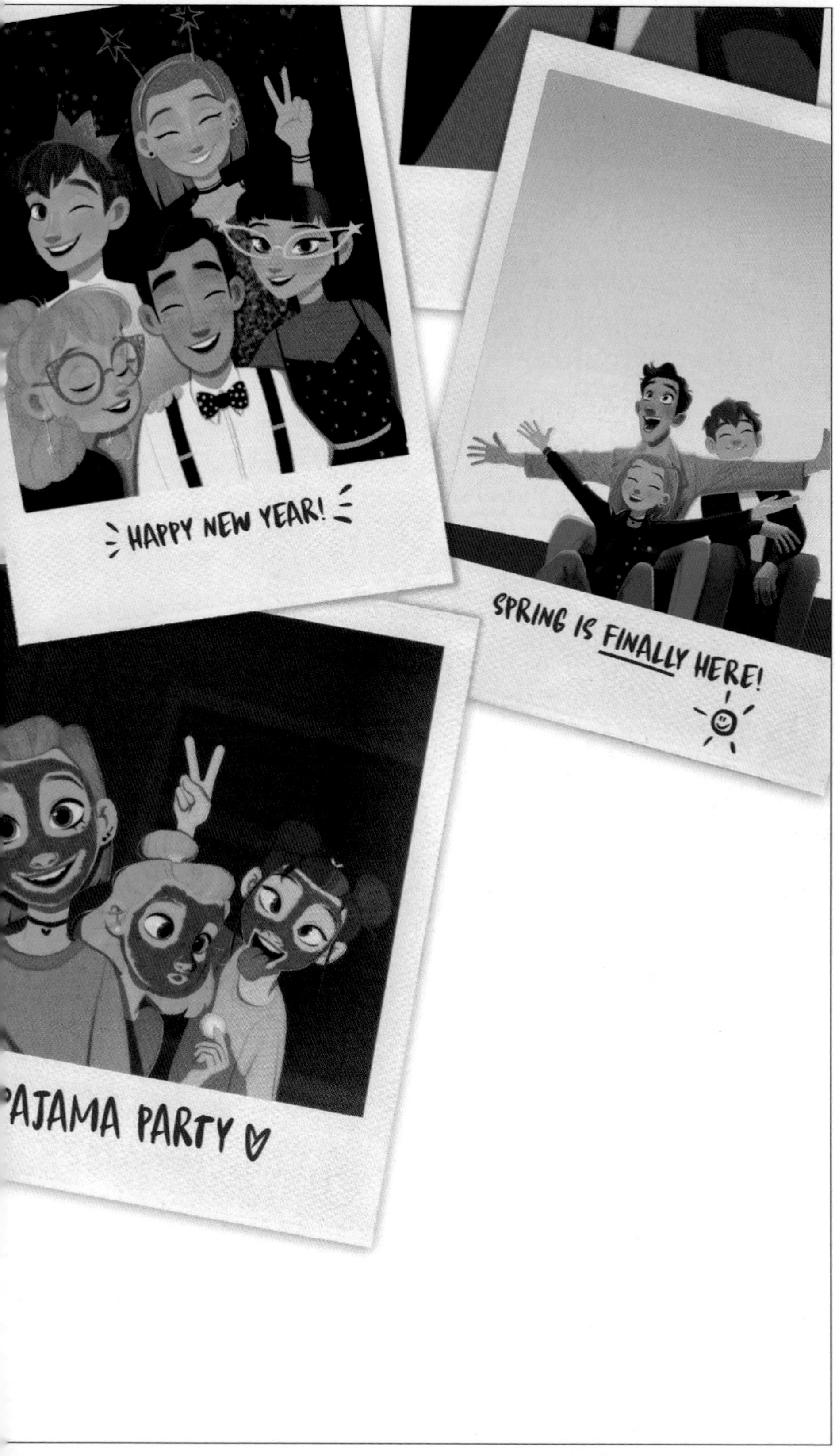
HAPPY NEW YEAR!
SPRING IS FINALLY HERE!
AJAMA PARTY

ISSUE #3 MAIN COVER BY **AVELINE STOKART**

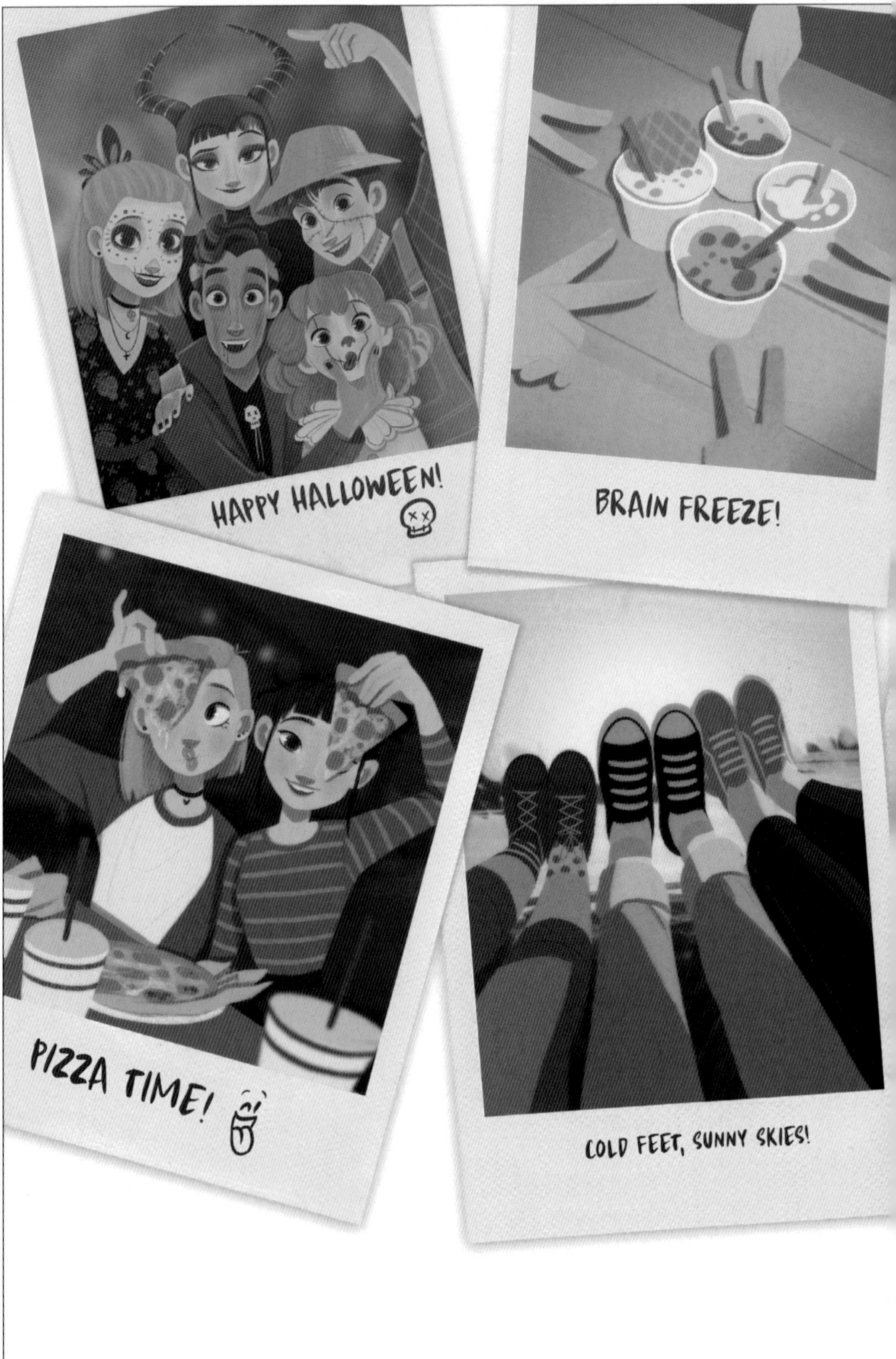
HAPPY HALLOWEEN!
BRAIN FREEZE!
PIZZA TIME!
COLD FEET, SUNNY SKIES!

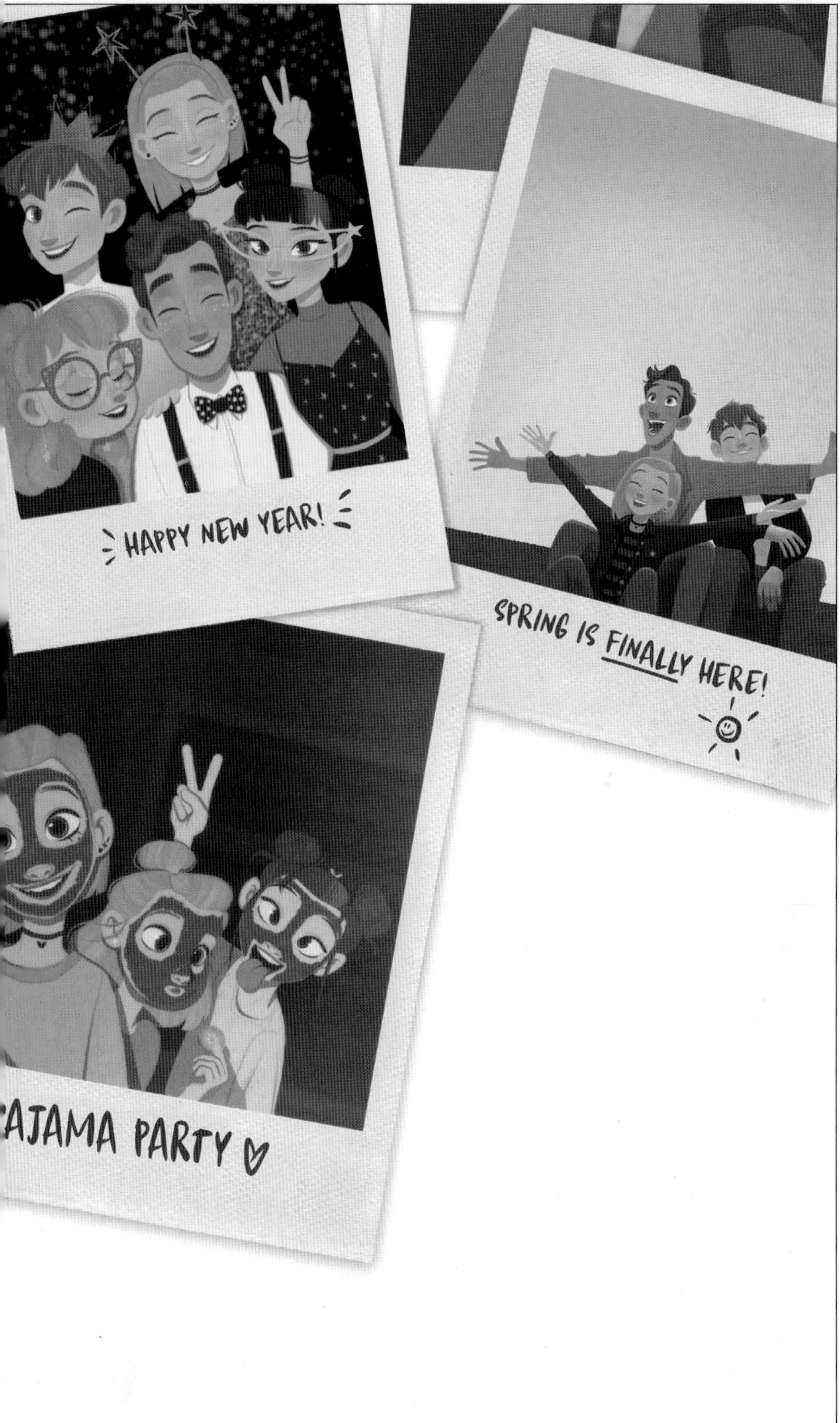
HAPPY NEW YEAR!
SPRING IS FINALLY HERE!
AJAMA PARTY

ISSUE #3 B&W VARIANT COVER BY **AVELINE STOKART**

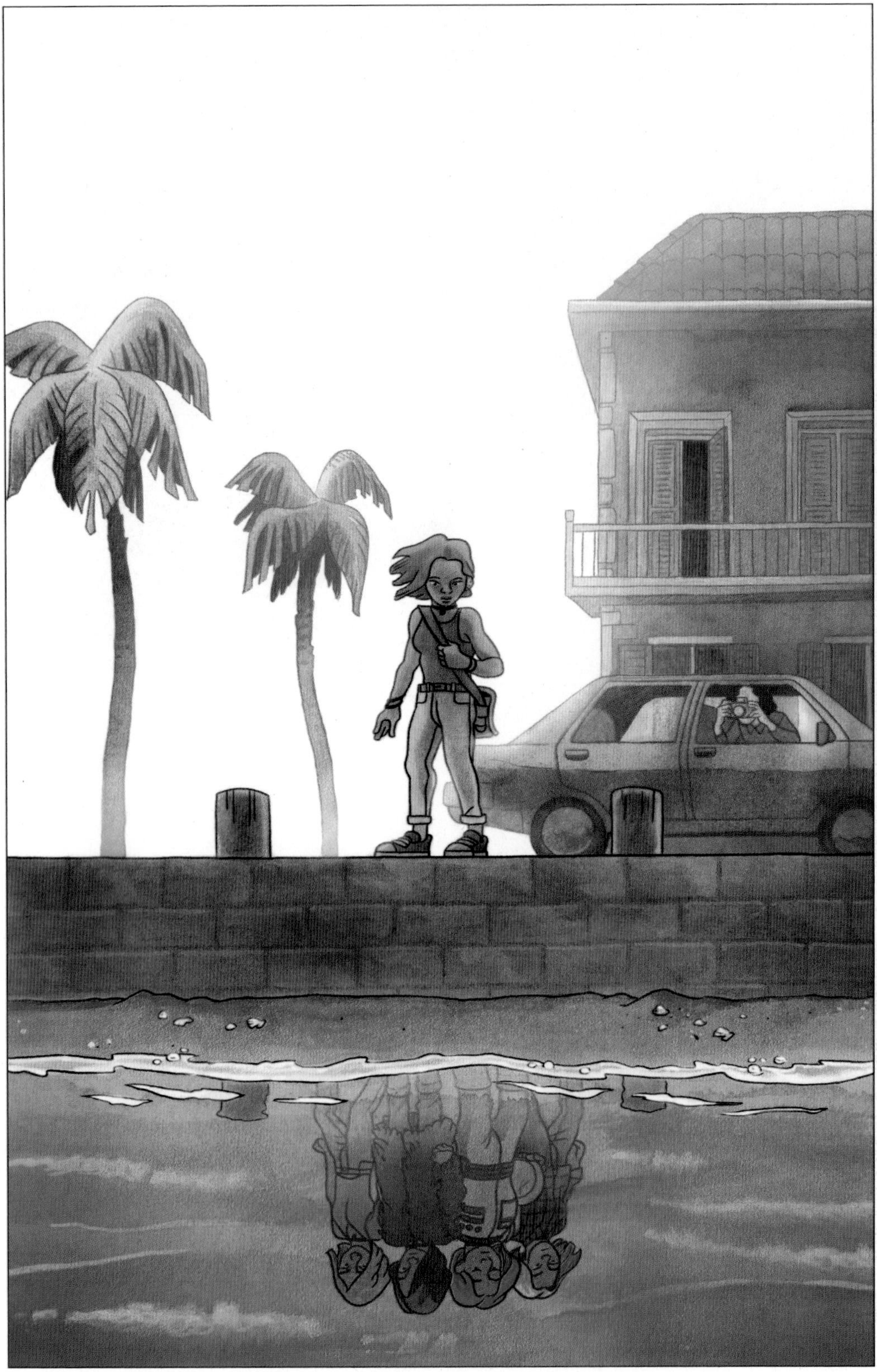

ISSUE #3 VARIANT COVER BY **JUL MAROH**

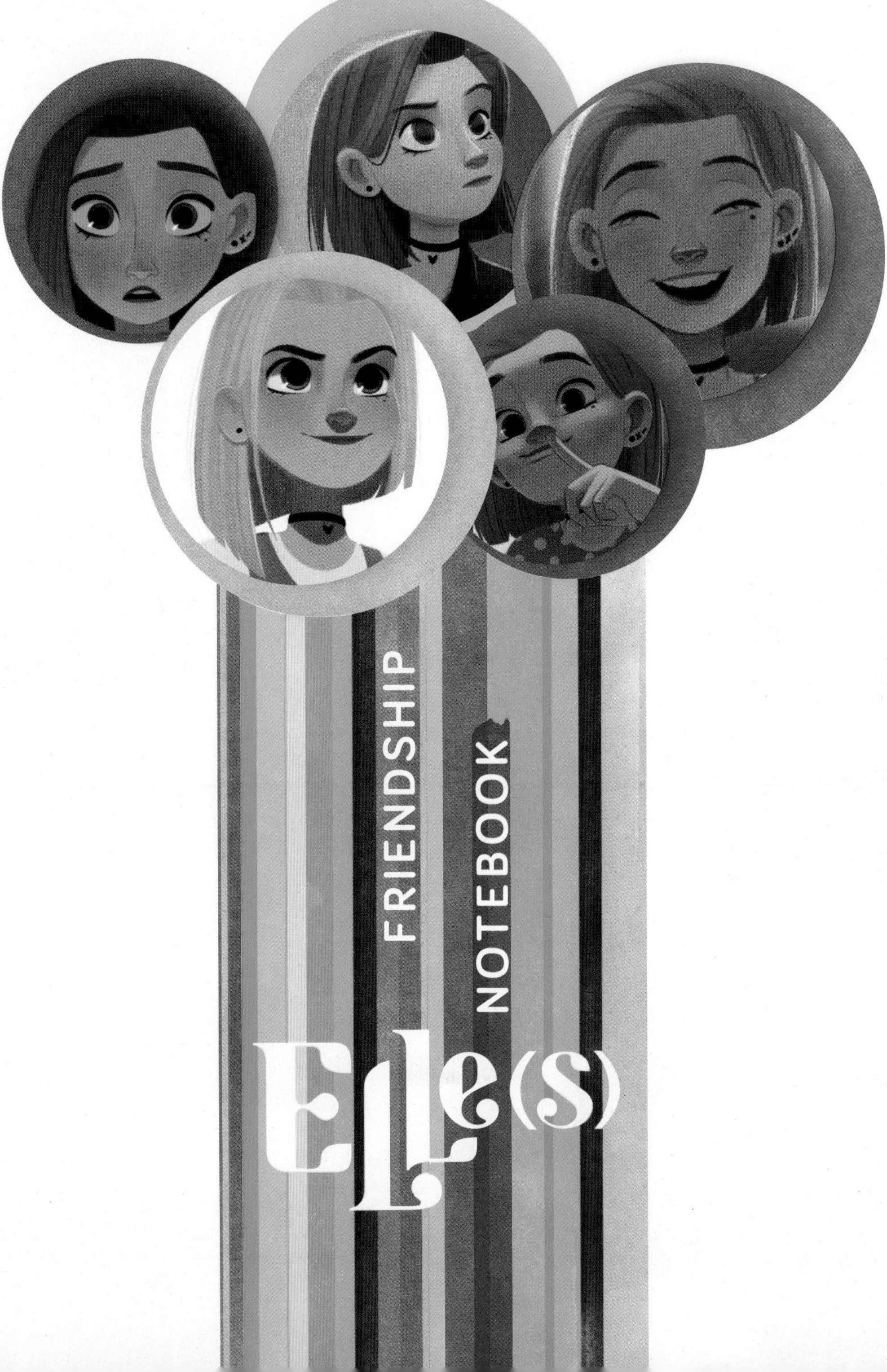
FRIENDSHIP
NOTEBOOK
Elle(s)

Love

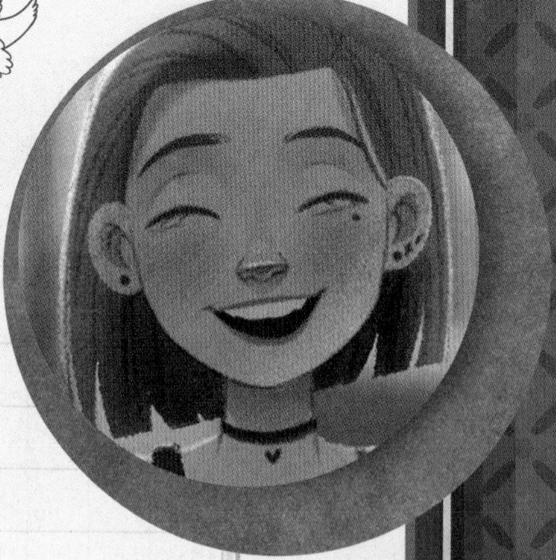

Name: *Elle*

Favorite Drink: *Water is life.*

Best friend: *Maëlys*

In the future, I will be... *A yoga teacher?*

What I would take to a desert island:

All of my friends to throw a huge party.

Clothes:

T-shirt and jeans

Anything else?:

Will there be pizza?

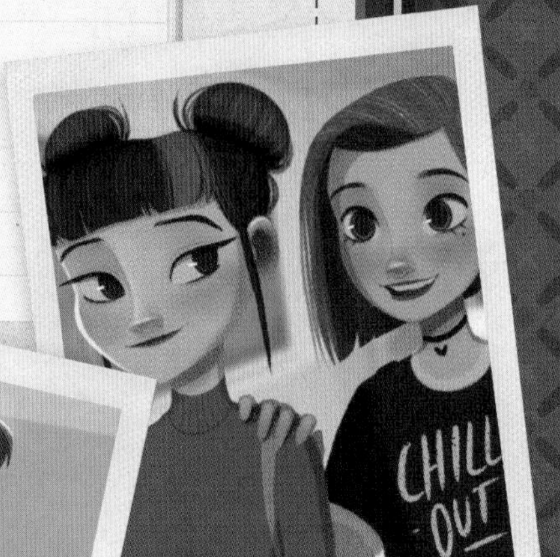
CHILL OUT

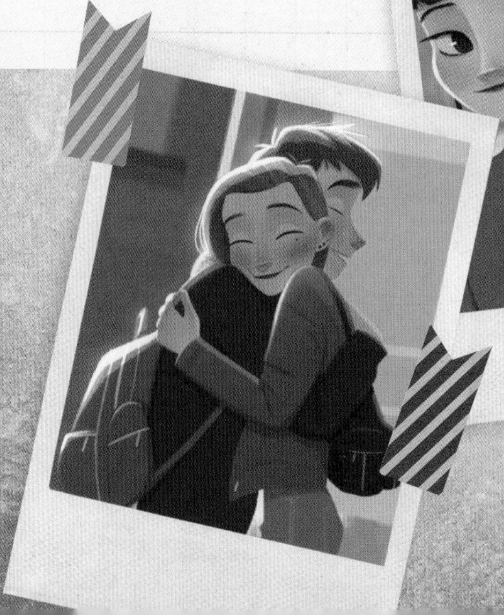

LOL

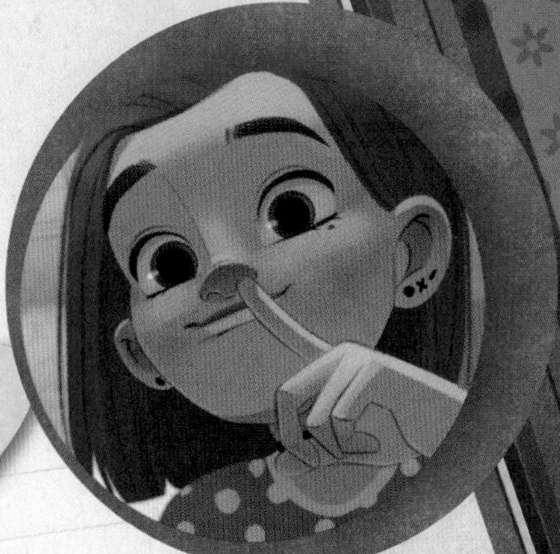

Name: *Yes*

Favorite Drink: *The catfish or the little goldfish.*

Best friend: *"Poooooongo, funny bear! He's my friend! He can be yours, too ..."*

In the future, I will be... *Running after the bus; I'm late.*

What I would take to a desert island: *Another desert island, so she never feels alone.*

Clothes: *Often*

Anything else?: *I wrote all of this under duress and torture.*

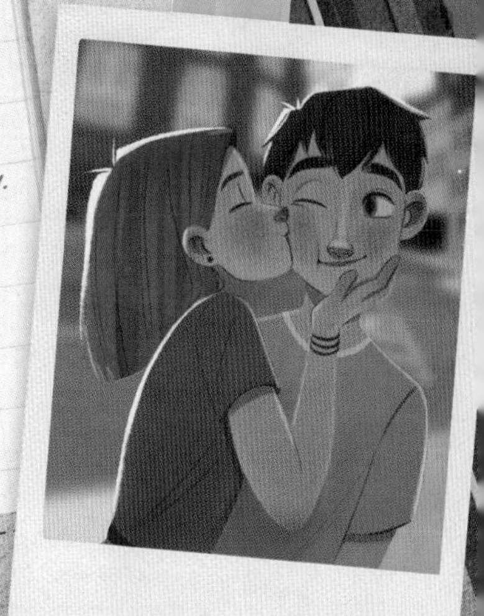

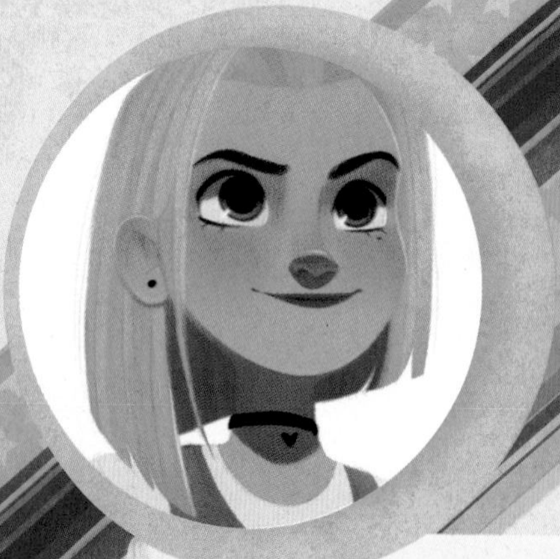

VICTORY

Name: *L*

Favorite Drink: *Coffee*

Best friend: *Pfff... Is this really useful? Maybe Clea.*

In the future, I will be... *A CEO.*

What I would take to a desert island: *A boat to get me away from there.*

Clothes: *Sporty but stylish.*

Anything else?: *No. I have already wasted enough time on this dumb questionnaire.*

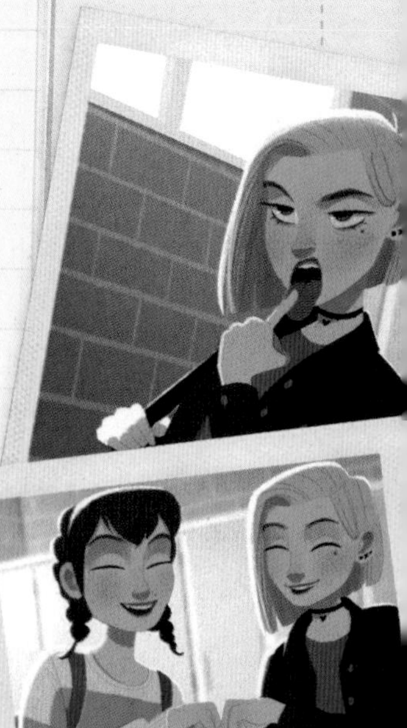

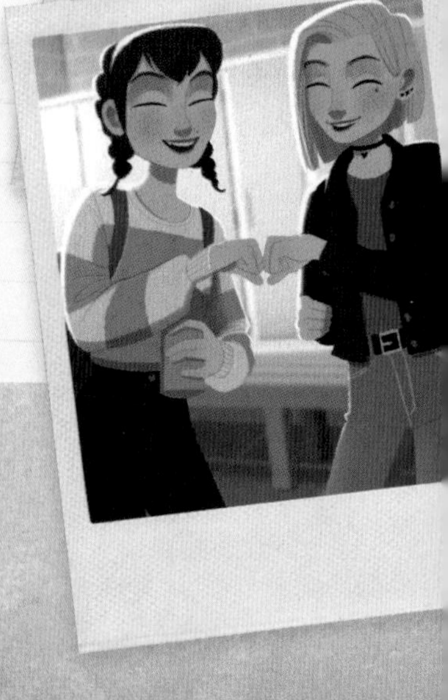

Silence

Name:

Favorite Drink:

Best friend:

In the future, I will be...

What I would take to a desert island:

Clothes:

Anything else?:

Name: *My name is a palindrome that can fly because it has two "wings."*

Favorite Drink: *Black and green tea blend with bergamot and cardamom*

Best friend: *Otis (on Instagram)*

In the future, I will be... *Someone else.*

What I would take to a desert island:
Books, books, and more books.

Clothes: *"Appearance is nothing, it is at the bottom of the heart that is the wound."—Euripides*

Anything else?: *I hope my answers aren't too bad. I would understand it if you tore out this page.*

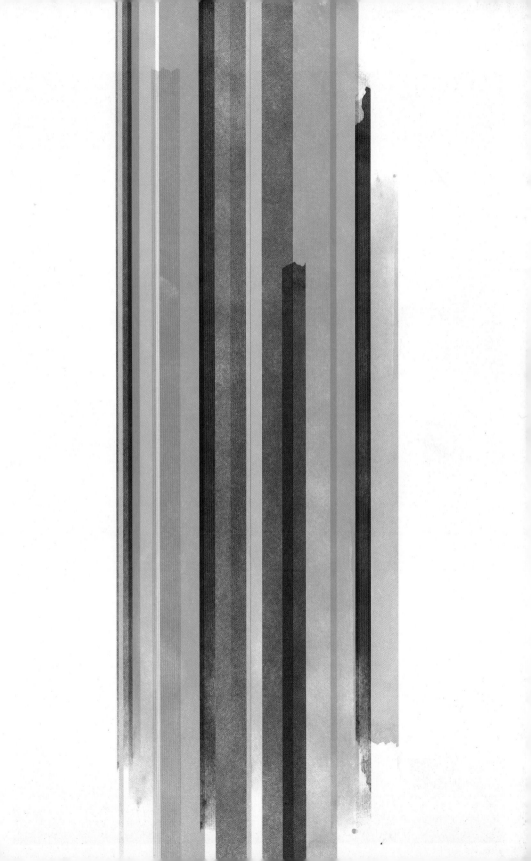

coming soon...

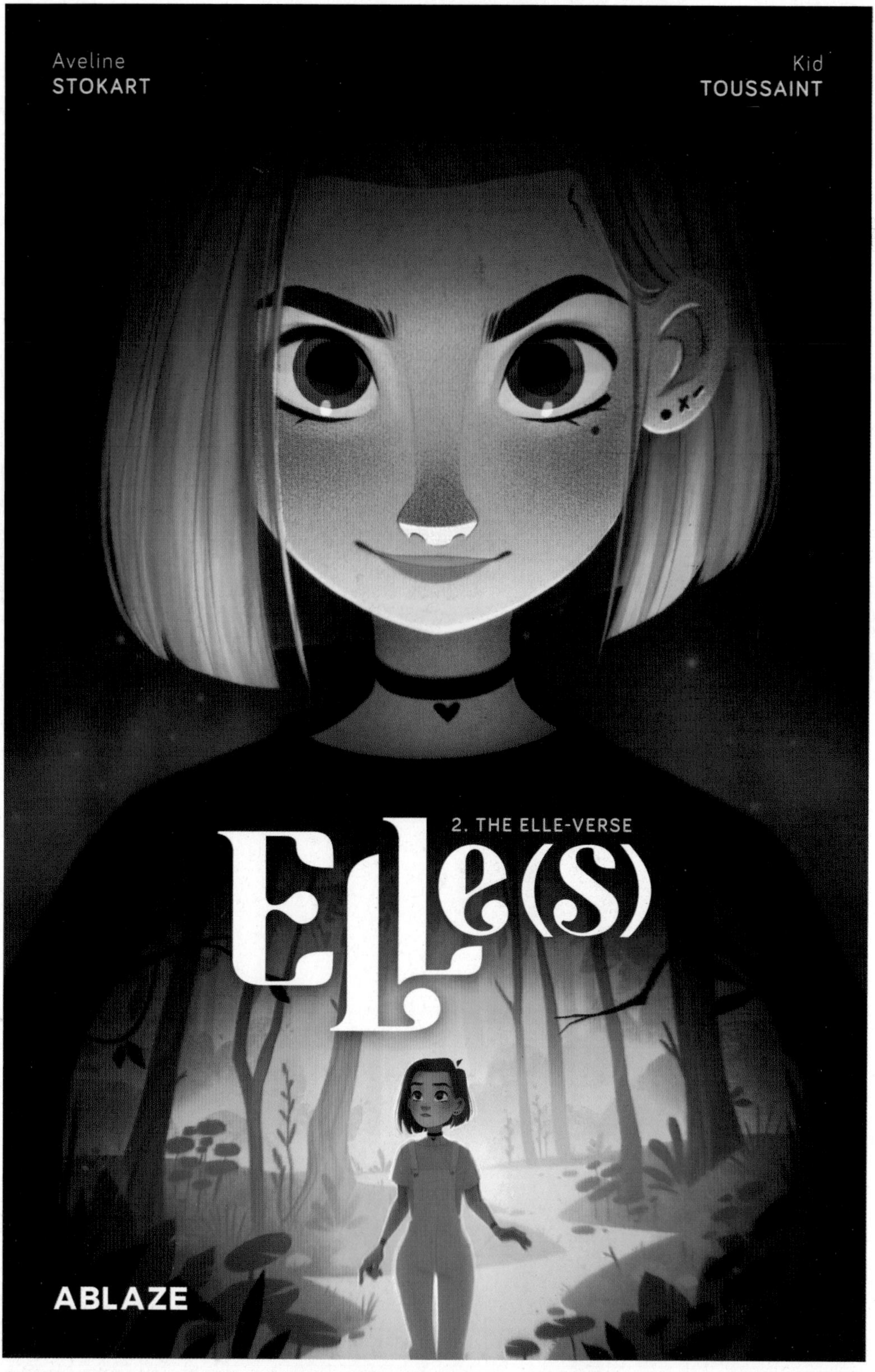

Aveline
STOKART
Kid
TOUSSAINT
2. THE ELLE-VERSE
Elle(s)
ABLAZE